THE SWORD AND THE ROSE

Borgo Press Books by VICTOR J. BANIS

THE SWORD AND THE ROSE

AN HISTORICAL NOVEL

V. J. BANIS

THE BORGO PRESS

MMXII

THE SWORD AND THE ROSE

FIRST BORGO PRESS EDITION

Published by Wildside Press LLC

www.wildsidebooks.com

DEDICATION

Special thanks to my editor, Rob Reginald,

And to my friend, Heather,

For their generous support and assistance.

CONTENTS

AUTHOR'S NOTE

This is a work of fiction. While I have used some actual persons and a few actual events, most of what is written here will not be confirmed by history books.

It is a fact that there was a Third Crusade, that King Richard I the Lionhearted of England did lead it and was accompanied by his queen, Berengaria, and her ladies. The other princes named here were also there, including Conrad of Montserrat, whose animosity toward Richard and the crusade—and whose treachery—are documented. Also factual is the resentment between Richard and Leopold of Austria, who later captured Richard on his way home and held him for considerable ransom. Entirely fictional are Lady Joan and her romance with Prince David.

As to Saladin, who was certainly real, the admiration between that sultan and Richard is documented. There have been many fictional accounts of meetings between these two, but there is no real evidence that they ever met, except on the battlefield. The idea of their meeting in disguise is not original with me, but has been used by other writers, especially Sir Walter Scott, to whom I am grateful for the inspiration.

This novel was written and first published in 1975; in 2010, I wrote a second gay or m/m version of it, which was published as *The Knight of the Hawk*, available as a Kindle e-book. This original version, however, is reissued here for the intended enjoyment of those less inclined to male on male action. I doubt that the two versions will be in conflict with one another, since they are intended for different audiences, and I mention the alternative version here only for the sake of clarity.

CHAPTER ONE

Streaming the ensign of the Christian cross
Against black pagans, Turks and Saracens....
—Richard II

"Joan, Joan! Stop that infernal humming and bring me some water."

Lady Joan put aside her embroidery and went to fetch some water from the leather skin by the door. It was only midmorning, and already the air in the royal tent was stifling. Modesty commanded that the tent flaps be securely closed so that not even a stray desert breeze could bring relief.

She carried the water back to the chair in which Queen Berengaria sat. "I am sorry, Royal Mistress, if my humming offended you," she said.

She herself might have taken offense at the way the young queen ordered her about as if she were a lady-in-waiting and not King Richard's kinswoman, but Joan was of an agreeable nature. She was tall and slender; some called her willowy. Her yellow hair, her pale complexion, her soft voice and quiet manners gave the impression that she was shy and even cold-natured. But her full and sensuous mouth belied this impression, and if one looked more closely, her eyes, though pale blue, were lighted from within with a warm light that lurked there and gave evidence of a passionate nature, held in check just now but waiting to burst forth at the right moment.

Although she affected friendship with her, Berengaria did

not like Lady Joan. She waved a hand impatiently and said, "Oh, never mind, I'm just a crosspatch this morning. It's this dreadful heat. I wonder that the heathens can stand it themselves."

"Perhaps the heathens don't have the same feelings as Christians," Clorise, one of the queen's ladies, offered.

Joan smiled faintly and said, in a respectful tone, "I should think rather that all men have the same feelings."

"Yes, don't be a fool, Clorise," the queen snapped. She drummed her fingers on the arms of her chair, her dark little eyes darting about the interior of the tent for some diversion. What a bore this had proven to be. They had come on this Third and, as everyone had said, most glorious of the crusades, to recapture the holy city from the infidels. Richard, only recently crowned king of England and her husband as well, had been the instigator of this journey. It had seemed such a grand idea for herself and the ladies to accompany him.

How was she to have known what an ordeal it would be? Why didn't someone warn her? All this heat, and the beastly food, and nothing, really nothing to do.

"Can't you think of some entertaining story to tell," she demanded of Joan. "No brave exploits to recite?"

Joan suppressed a sigh and again put aside her embroidery. "Since the truce there has been little activity," she said

"What about that Scottish knight you're always watching?" Berengaria asked, her eyes sparkling maliciously.

Joan blushed and cast her eyes down. "Royal Madame, I don't know whom you mean. I have watched all the knights in the tournaments."

"Don't play games with me. I mean the one they call the Falcon. I've seen your eyes following him around. You needn't think I'm a fool. Oh, this dreadful heat!"

Joan was glad that the queen had abandoned that subject. She was mortified to think that her interest in the Scottish knight had been observed; she must ever remember the queen's sharp eyes. Beset as they were now with boredom, they would be ever sharp, watching for some diversion.

With each passing day the young queen's boredom and her impatience increased. At first, despite the inconvenience of travel there had been a great air of excitement. King Richard had invited Philip Augustus of France to join him in the holy mission, and in time these two monarchs were joined by Leopold, Archduke of Austria, and by knights of every European country. There were also the Knights Templar and Knights Hospitaller of St. John of Jerusalem, so that a vast army was formed answerable to the Council of Princes of the Holy Crusade, but in actual fact commanded by the noblest of those princes, King Richard of the Lion Heart.

For a time there had been great tales to tell of the exploits of these knights and especially of King Richard: how the Saracens at Acre, who had besieged that town for nineteen months at the cost of many thousands of lives, surrendered a few weeks after Richard's arrival on the scene; and how, when the news came that Saladin, the Kurd sultan, had attacked Jaffa, Richard sailed at once with what troops he could muster and, arriving in the harbor, he leapt to his waist in the sea.

"Perish the hindmost," he cried, swinging his famous Danish ax, and he led his men into the city, clearing it of Moslem soldiery almost before Saladin could learn what had occurred.

As for Saladin, most of Christendom knew of him and had an image of him as an infidel dog, a heathen whose savagery and blasphemy beggared description; but since their arrival in the Holy Land, Joan had heard and seen much of this famed ruler who ruled, it might be said, the entire East; indeed, nearly all of the world that was not yet Christian. To the displeasure of Queen Berengaria, Joan had formed the opinion that while he was surely an infidel, the sultan was a gentleman.

When Richard's horse fell at Jaffa, Saladin himself sent the English king a charger. "It is a shame," he said through his messenger, "that such a gallant warrior should have to fight on foot."

The queen and her ladies had scoffed at the story when Joan had repeated it for them, but Joan was convinced of its authenticity.

Moreover, she had heard it said that this Moslem ruler was so lenient toward Christians who were his subjects that there were towns who invited his invasion to free themselves from Byzantine rulers.

Certainly nothing of the sort could be said of most of the Christian rulers Joan knew. It had often seemed to her so unjust that people of different faiths were persecuted so fiercely by the Christians. She thought of the Jews, many of whom currently followed the camp to work as tailors, carpenters, and doctors. They were restricted in the camp; laws controlled what work they could perform, where they could live, even what colors of clothing they could wear. She knew they were often the sport of rough soldiers and bullies; and yet hadn't Christ himself pleaded mercy, kindness and charity? The sort of kindness Saladin was said to show his subjects of whatever faith?

"Indeed," she had remarked one evening when she was with the queen, "it sometimes seems as if the Christian virtues are better exemplified in the Moorish sultan than in many a Christian king, making one wonder how so wrong a theology could produce so fine a man."

The queen was not pleased with the remark.

But all of these exploits had happened some time ago. It was now several weeks after that battle at Jaffa, which had ended indecisively. Richard had promised that his army would march in triumph into Jerusalem, and in this he might have succeeded had it not been for the jealousies of the Christian princes engaged in the crusade with him and the offense some of them took at the haughtiness—often remarked—of the English monarch. In truth, Richard often displayed an unveiled contempt for his brother sovereigns who, while equal in rank, were still far his inferiors in courage and military abilities.

Disputes and obstacles delayed every action while the ranks of the crusaders, even to Joan's feminine eye, were thinned daily. Saladin had learned well that his lightly armed soldiers were ill suited to close combat with the armored Europeans;

but Saladin had the advantage of numbers and the speed of his horsemen in the many little skirmishes that occurred.

As the army of the crusaders dwindled in numbers, Saladin's followers became bolder in their form of petty warfare. Clouds of light cavalry sometimes surrounded and almost besieged the Christian camp.

"They're like swarms of wasps," Richard complained. "Easily crushed when you can get hold of them, but their wings enable them to elude superior strength, and their stings can do great harm."

Valuable lives were lost in the perpetual warfare as Saracens picked off Christian foragers. Communications were cut off, convoys seized; the crusaders were forced to purchase the means of sustaining life by life itself.

In the queen's pavilion the hardship had been most felt in the deteriorating quality of their food. "We'll soon be eating no better than the poorest peasant in England," Berengaria complained, although she had no idea how any peasant lived.

The climate, too, was hard for men from the north, unused to the hot days and cold dews. Not even the iron constitution of Coeur de Lion could withstand the combined effects of the unwholesome climate and his ceaseless exertions, and he fell ill. Whatever victories the crusaders had enjoyed heretofore were Richard's victories, and the effects of his illness on the crusade and on the camp in general, were great. Saladin, who had so often displayed his admiration for Richard, readily agreed with the Council of Princes to a thirty days' truce, that Richard might recover.

When Richard's illness took on a serious aspect, however, the general tone of activity about the camp changed. Hope of a triumphant march into Jerusalem began to fade, and with it faded the numbers of the crusaders as well. Now desertion thinned the ranks still more as entire bands, ceasing to hope for success in their venture, withdrew from it and turned home-ward.

In the camp the interval of the truce was employed not as

might be expected, in recruiting new warriors, reanimating their courage and preparing for a speedy advance upon the Holy City; but rather in securing the camp with trenches and fortifications, so that it looked as if when the fighting began anew they prepared to repel the attack of a powerful enemy rather than assume the proud aspect of conquerors. A cloud of gloom descended.

"Well," Berengaria's voice intruded upon Joan's thoughts. "Your tongue is usually so quick, can you think of nothing to say to amuse me?"

Again Joan racked her brain for some subject of conversation that had not been already exhausted.

"This morning I heard talk of a holy man," she said, trying to make this news sound interesting, "a fanatic who lives in the desert near Engaddi."

"A Christian holy man?" Berengaria asked doubtfully. "Do you think the Saracens would let him live long unmolested?"

"I have heard they revere such men. They regard them as madmen and feel that a madman is possessed of special powers and special insights—even a Christian madman."

Berengaria was thoughtful for a moment and Joan was pleased that her little piece of information had provided the queen a moment's diversion. But she was less pleased with Berengaria's next remarks.

"But this is it!" the queen cried, her china-doll face radiant with childish delight. "A holy man, possessed of special powers. Why, we shall make a pilgrimage to him and pray for my husband's recovery."

She jumped up excitedly from her chair. Joan stood too, feeling anxious over the direction matters had taken.

"Noble madam," she said, "you cannot be serious. We are surrounded by Moslems and Engaddi, from what I can judge, is three, maybe four days' journey from here. Think of the danger of such a journey."

"God protects his pilgrims," was the queen's reply. "I'm going to ask my husband's permission right now. Come, Clorise."

With a frightened look, Clorise leapt up and hurried after her mistress. There was nothing Joan could do but follow in their wake. She knew the queen well enough by now to know that once she had gotten an idea in her head there was no dissuading her. The queen was little more than a child, and a badly pampered one at that. Joan's only hope was that Richard would forbid the journey in question, but it was a slim hope. Her kinsman was weakened by illness, and even when he had been in full health he was weak before his wife's entreaties.

"This is my fault," Joan thought unhappily. "If she goes to Engaddi, I will be duty bound to go with her."

CHAPTER TWO

...most like the roar
of some pain'd desert lion....
                              —Arnold

Not many people willingly approached the tent of King Richard these days. Confined to his bed, he fretted over the reports of inactivity in the camp, like a caged lion viewing his prey from behind his bars. He was by nature a man of violent passions, rash and impetuous, and now his temper had too little outlet. His attendants moved in terror of fresh outbursts, and even his doctors were loath to assume that authority that a good medical man must assume over his patient. Richard chafed, and when the frustration became too great for him he roared like his namesake, while those around him quaked.

Of all those in attendance upon the monarch, only one did not tremble at the sound of his voice and make every effort to avoid his vicinity; this was Sir Thomas de Multon, Lord of Gilsland in Cumberland. His nature was not unlike that of his monarch's and throughout Richard's illness he had quietly but firmly maintained a control over the invalid that no one else dared to assume. Sir Thomas was a blunt and careless soldier, taciturn to the point of sullenness and disdaining in speech and actions the courtly arts. But he was a well-battled soldier who had served Richard as well with his sword as he now did in sick attendance, and that the impatient monarch allowed de Multon's authority over him was a sign of the deep respect the two comrades-in-arms shared for one another.

Now, while the ladies approached, Richard lay on his sickbed, despising it. Sir Thomas, having just administered a potion, stood beside the bed. He was a man of giant proportions, and the contrast between his strapping figure and the wasted one of the sovereign was shocking.

"Well, is there no good news from the camp?" Richard asked impatiently after a long silence, his eyes sweeping the interior of his tent. On the floor a trio of greyhounds, his former hunting companions, eyed him with a look of curiosity at this unaccustomed inactivity they were forced to share.

"Things are much as they have been," Sir Thomas said, watching his king closely to see if the medicine had any more effect than the others had.

"All our knights behaving like women, in other words," Richard said. "The cream of Europe's knighthood, and not a spark of valor in evidence."

Richard's blue eyes, always gleaming brightly, had the sheen of fever now as they glanced from among the uncut and uncurled locks of yellow hair. His manly features were wasted by illness. His beard had not been trimmed for weeks, and now covered both lips and chin. He turned from side to side with impatient gestures that revealed the pent-up energy within him.

Again his eyes swept the tent; although it was the royal pavilion, it had more of an aspect of warfare than of elegance. Weapons were scattered about on the floor and the tent posts. The ground was strewn with rushes, covered with the skins of animals Richard had slain. Near the bed was a triangular shield of wrought steel with the emblem of three lions; close to that was the golden coronet and the purple velvet cloak that were the emblems of England's sovereignty. Beyond these was the mighty curtal ax, that would have weighed too much for most men's arms, but was Richard's famed weapon.

"The truce, milord, makes us men of inaction," Sir Thomas said. "Saladin has honored it on his side and it would hardly be right for us to dishonor it."

"Ay, the truce," Richard said. "I wish to God it were over and I could meet Saladin face to face. There is a worthy opponent." With that he lifted his arm above his head as if swinging his battle ax.

In an instant Sir Thomas was forcibly restoring him to a reclining position. "You heard the doctors, milord," he complained, "you must rest, and I must see that you do."

"What a nurse," Richard said, not without a smile. "You'd frighten most patients."

"We've both frightened many men, and will do so again when your fever's passed."

"My fever," Richard said scornfully, sitting up again. "Ay, and what is wrong with the others—King Philip, and that boorish Austrian, and the knights—the mightiest army of Christians in history, they all wilt and become false to their vows. They forget their promises to God."

"Sire, for the love of heaven, you must rest," de Multon protested. "Why do you aggravate yourself with such questions? Your own illness weakens the enterprise. Better an arrow without its bow than the Christian army without King Richard."

"You're a flatterer," Richard said, but he was not adverse to that sort of comment and he reclined on the bed again with a more contented expression.

The respite was only momentary though, for in a moment he was excited again. "Well, yes, this is smooth talk for a sick man. But why should they all droop with my sickness, the sickness of one man. Think of the monarchs here, the noble princes, the honorable knights. Why should my illness—my death even—halt an army of thirty thousand? Why don't they assemble and choose a new leader?"

"Milord, I have heard that there have been discussions on that very subject," Sir Thomas said.

His jealousy piqued, Richard exclaimed loudly, "Ha! I am forgotten already, before the spirit has even left my body. And whom have they chosen as my successor, pray tell me?"

De Multon shrugged and said, "They would hardly see fit to

consult me, my liege, but rank and dignity would seem to indicate the king of France."

"Oh, ay, Philip of France and Navarre," Richard said. "There is only one risk in being led by Denis Montjoie, His Most Christian Majesty—that he might mistake the word charge for retreat and lead the host back to Paris instead of to Jerusalem. By this time he has learned there is more gold to be gained by robbing his serfs."

"There's always the archduke of Austria," Sir Thomas said.

"What, Leopold? They'd choose him because he looks big and burly. Well, his head is the thickest part of him, and in all that mass of flesh there's no more courage to be found than in a wren. If they want to see him at his best, give him a flagon of wine to drink with his besotted landsknechts."

De Multon by this time had seen the wisdom of keeping his master's thoughts thus occupied for a while, and continued with the inventory of possible successors.

"Perhaps the Grand Master of the Templars," he suggested. "He has no kingdom of his own to distract him, and no one can question that he's brave in battle and sage in council."

"Yes, Brother Giles Amaury is both of those. But I ask you, good comrade, what is the wisdom in taking this Holy Land from Saladin, a man of many virtues, and giving it to Brother Giles, a worse pagan than any Turk, a devil worshiper, a necromancer—and we will not even discuss those other unnatural acts to which he is part. No, the Grand Master of the Templars is not the man to lead a Christian host."

"If not the Templars, then perhaps the Grand Master of the Hospitallers of St. John of Jerusalem. No one has accused him of magic nor unnatural acts."

"He's been accused of other things, though," Richard said quickly. "I have no proof of it, but I'm still sure he's sold favors to the infidels and in the doing cost us some victories. No, he's not a man to be trusted where there's any means to turn a profit."

Sir Thomas sighed and said, "I have only one other suggestion then. What do you think of Conrad, the Marquis of Montserrat?

It's said he's cunning and elegant."

Richard gave a derisive snort that said plainly what he thought of that suggestion. "Oh, yes, I'll grant you the marquis is elegant, in a lady's chamber, and as for his cunning, it is said you cannot guess his inward thoughts by his outward expressions. There's a man who can change his sails for any fresh wind. No, Conrad is no friend to the crusade, except as it can advance his own wealth or importance."

"Then I'm afraid we'll not pray at the Holy Sepulcher until King Richard has recovered and can lead us," said Sir Thomas.

This remark was made so gravely that Richard, seeing how he had been led through this conversation by his friend, burst out laughing.

"They say you're no courtier, Sir Thomas," he said, "but I think you handle your king well. You've brought me to the point where I must now confess my chief sin. I don't care a hang for the foibles of these men unless they intend to take my place as leader. But this is my ambition—I know the Christian camp has better knights in it than Richard of England, and it would be worthy to name one of them to lead the army."

Here Richard paused and raised himself from the bed, his eyes gleaming as they did when he was going into battle. "But," he went on, "so long as I'm unable to bear my fair share of that holy task, if one such man should plant the banner of the cross in Jerusalem, I tell you that as soon as I am able he would have to accept my challenge to mortal combat, for diminishing my fame and pressing in before me to my holy goal. But what is that disturbance in the outer chamber?"

There was a commotion outside and in a moment Queen Berengaria's voice could be heard demanding entrance to the king's chamber.

"His Majesty is resting, milady," one of the attendants could be heard to say.

"Fie, fie," she insisted. "His own wife can comfort him."

In another moment she had parted the curtains and come into the room, followed by Lady Clorise and Lady Joan. Richard propped himself up on one elbow, and for once de Multon did not take him to task for it. The king, looking annoyed at this unexpected intrusion, attempted to pull his bedclothes about him in a more seemly fashion.

Berengaria, however, although married to her husband only a short while before this journey was begun, already knew how to please this rough-mannered monarch. With a little frightened look she ran to the side of her husband's sickbed and, dropping upon her knees, seized the king's arm. She dragged it to her while he resisted, but faintly, until she was in possession of the arm that was the strength of Christendom, the dread of the infidel. Imprisoning its strength in her little hands, she bent her head and kissed it.

Richard was at first angry at the appearance of these ladies in his bedchamber unannounced. But beauty was something he admired only slightly less than glory, and it was not in his nature to look angrily for long upon this beautiful creature bent before him, or to feel without sympathy the tears which moistened his hand or the kisses that fell upon it. He turned his manly countenance upon her. His large blue eyes, so often gleaming with a fearsome light, were now soft as he caressed her cheek and raised her face so that he could kiss her forehead.

"And now, what does the lady of my heart seek in her knight's pavilion?" he asked gently.

"Milord, are you well?" Berengaria asked.

"Well enough to perform whatever task you seek of me," he replied. "What is it? Has someone offended your honor? I swear I shall challenge him."

She gave a little girl's smile and shook her head. "No, my liege, it is nothing so strenuous as that. I ask only a favor of you."

She hesitated and he said quickly, "Ask."

"I have learned that there is a holy man who lives near here, in a place called Engaddi."

"There is such a man, a hermit," he said. "Quite holy, they say, and a little mad in the bargain. But what does this have to do with you?"

"We would have your permission, my ladies and I, to make a pilgrimage to this holy man to pray for your recovery, my lord."

At this Richard withdrew his hand and put a stern expression on his face. "No, absolutely not. Think of the dangers that lie in that desert yonder, and it is many miles to the hermit's dwelling place. You hear, Sir Thomas, they would have me risk the richest gem and the fairest rose in all England," he said, indicating first his queen and second Lady Joan. "For the sake of my mere health. Why, it would take every knight in the camp to guard them properly. No, my lady, ask something else and it shall be granted."

"Something else," she sobbed, "something more precious than my husband's life? No such thing exists. But I shall die for you anyway, my husband. I shall die of grief that my prayers were not permitted to end your illness."

She paused and, suddenly rolling her eyes up at him, gave a little gasp. "Oh. Perhaps it's because you think my prayers are worthless, that I am not worthy in God's eyes."

"Oh, my precious," Richard murmured, stroking her brow fondly.

Berengaria began to cry noisily. Joan saw that these silly remarks had nonetheless softened the heart of her kinsman, and she had little doubt that Berengaria would have her way. She thought it best to mention now an idea that had occurred to her on the way here.

"My lord," she said, causing both king and queen to look in her direction. "I have an idea. Perhaps it would be safer if your lady and I traveled with fewer rather than more escorts."

"What, you'd have me entrust my queen and my cousin to a handful of knights?" he demanded.

"Not your queen and your kinswoman," she replied, "but a few ladies, in ordinary dress, on a pilgrimage, might be safe with a few knights, if their journey were not too much announced."

"Yes, yes, my liege," Berengaria cried delightedly, clapping her hands, "that's the very thing. We'll disguise ourselves as common women. I can wear something of Clorise's here," which remark brought her a quick frown from her lady-in-waiting, "and we'll slip out of the camp without anyone knowing about it."

"The idea has merit," Richard admitted reluctantly, "still...." But his answer was delayed, for just then he was struck by a pain that not even his iron will could ignore and with a sigh he sank back to his bed.

In an instant Sir Thomas was bending over him. "Summon the doctors," he said over his shoulder.

Berengaria and Clorise wrung their hands helplessly and stared aghast at the sickbed. This was the first either of them had actually witnessed of Richard's attacks. It was Joan who went through the curtains to the antechamber.

"His Majesty has need of his physician," she said to the attendants. In a twinkling they had vanished from the tent in search of the doctor.

Joan would have returned to the sickroom to help Sir Thomas, but at that moment someone entered the tent and she turned toward him, thinking it might be the doctor.

Her smile vanished when she saw that it was Conrad, the Marquis of Montserrat. She did not know quite what it was but there was something about this man that caused a quiver of fear inside her whenever she saw him; nor were her feelings assuaged by the evident admiration in which he held her. Often she would discover his eyes upon her, a hungry look upon his face, and she would barely be able to suppress a shudder at the thought of what he would like to do with her.

But he was an important member of the Council of Princes, and as Richard's cousin she could hardly afford to snub him. She stood motionless as he approached and, with a sly smile, made a little bow before her.

"My lady," he said, "how refreshing is the sight of your loveliness. You recall the scenes of our own lands; you are like a beautiful English flower set down to bloom in this desolate place."

"You flatter me, my lord," she said, her eyes downcast.

He moved closer and seized her hand in his firm grip, saying in a lower tone, "I would do more than flatter you, my lady."

She realized with a shock that he meant to kiss her, and the thought of his lips upon hers filled her with revulsion. "My lord," she protested, struggling against his efforts to take her into his arms.

The curtains to the inner chamber parted and Sir Thomas appeared. At once the marquis released Joan and stepped back. Sir Thomas fixed an angry look upon him, but he did not put his disapproval into words.

"Tell the attendants when they return that the spell was a brief one and that His Majesty is feeling better already," he said.

"Perhaps he is well enough to see me," Conrad said. Although he looked calm and unperturbed, he was seething inwardly at Joan's rejection of his advances and at de Multon's interruption.

"I think not now," Sir Thomas said. "He is in need of rest."

"Ah, I see the nature of his exhaustion," Conrad said as Berengaria and Clorise left the king's chamber.

"Joan, he has agreed to our little journey," the queen said gaily, coming to take Joan's hand. "We can leave in three days' time."

Conrad looked surprised and said, "What, are we to be deprived of the only solace this spot affords, the loveliest ladies of England?"

"We're going on a pilgrimage," Berengaria told him, "to a holy man at Engaddi, to pray for the king's recovery."

Joan frowned and added quickly, "The trip is to be unannounced, to minimize the danger. I trust you will keep this news to yourself, my lord."

"Indeed," he said smoothly. "I would be flattered to attend you on your pilgrimage if affairs of the council did not keep me here."

"His Majesty has promised us an escort of the bravest knights," Berengaria said.

Joan would have liked to suggest that the escort include the

Scottish knight known throughout the camp as the Falcon, for the emblem he wore on his shield. But the queen had already remarked on her admiration of the knight, and she did not want to call any further attention to him.

Instead she said, "Perhaps, my lady, we should return to our tent and plan what we shall wear."

"An excellent idea. Aren't you glad I thought of this?" Joan did not reply and Clorise looked terrified at the prospect of the trip that awaited them, but the queen never noticed. She was chatting gaily of their journey as they left the tent, bidding good day to the marquis.

De Multon had returned to the king, leaving Conrad alone in the anteroom for a moment. He stared after the departing ladies, wondering how best he could use this news. That it would be of interest to the Saracens was of little doubt; those two ladies would be a prize to catch, worthy of a great ransom.

Informing the Saracens of the news would present no difficulty, as he was already secretly in communication with the enemy for purposes of his own. In fact he had written Saladin without the knowledge of the council, offering to help him retake the city of Acre, in return for certain favors. He had no interest in recapturing the holy city for Christianity; he was concerned with what he could capture for his own profit.

"And, my little rose," he murmured, thinking again of Lady Joan, "you shall be glad one day to have me pluck your blossom."

CHAPTER THREE

There never was a time on the March parts yet
When Scottish with English met,
But it was a marvel if the red blood ran not
As the rain does in the street.
                              —Battle of Otterbourn

A large band of Scottish warriors had joined the crusaders and had placed themselves under the command of the English monarch. To some this seemed odd as there had been of late—indeed, always—some friction between the Scottish and the English; but they were all of Saxon and Norman descent, speaking a common language, and some of them were allied by blood and intermarriage as well.

Moreover they were now engaged in a common war, dear to them all because of their religion, and in this crusade Scots and Englishmen had fought side by side, their rivalry only serving to make both groups fight more bravely and more fiercely, each trying to outdo the other.

Richard was a rough but open commander who made no real distinction between his own subjects and those of William the Lion of Scotland, and this made it easier for the knights to work and fight together.

When the body is under the influence of illness, however, old wounds may break out anew. In just this manner, when Richard took ill and the circumstances of the crusaders became more critical, old frictions began to appear between the various bands of crusaders.

Both Scottish and English were jealous and high spirited, and the Scottish were quicker to take offense because they were the poorer and the weaker nation. The Scots would admit to no superiority over them and the English would admit no equality. As the truce forbade the warriors to wreak their vengeance upon the Saracens, they who had been good comrades in victory now turned on one another.

One of the Scottish knights, Sir Kenneth as he was called, was known also as the Falcon because on his surcoat and on his shield he wore the emblem of a sleek hawk, poised for flight, and beneath it the motto Swift and Terrible. Those who had seen him fight said that the emblem and the motto were fitting, for he fought with a savage intensity and a swiftness that belied his heavy armor.

Sir Kenneth had joined the crusade impulsively and for motives of his own, and being impetuous he had come ill supplied except for a few loyal followers. The wars and their deprivation, and their vow to give their lives in the crusade—a promise many of them had kept—had reduced his little band so that he now had for company only one old servant, and his dog Krouba, a magnificent deerhound, as fine a specimen of the breed as could be found.

Just now these two, Sir Kenneth and Krouba, were returning from the hunt. It had been necessary for the knight to find in nature the food he needed to keep himself and his little band alive and, as the animal life on this vast desert was limited, this had proven an increasingly difficult task. On this day he had found only a small bag full of rock partridges. The hills nearby sometimes supplied deer or wild pig, but he had not been lucky this time.

It was late afternoon and he was on his way back to the camp now. Beyond the crusaders' camp and in his path as he rode was a second camp, of the so-called "followers"; this was the camp of that second army of people who followed behind the knights and the royal court, depending mostly upon them for sustenance in one fashion or another. Here there were service people—tailors, tinkers, smiths and other diverse craftsmen; here too were people who made their living entertaining others—actors, jugglers, acrobats, dancers and troubadours. And of course there were the women—painted lovelies who strolled through the crusaders' camp at night plying their wares among the lonely knights.

It was a colorful little city, this second camp, made up as it was of various "colonies"—the area given over to the Jews, for instance, and another to the gypsies, while still another was filled with English freedmen. Like an Oriental city, one rode through it to a cacophony of sounds and impressions; music, from the plaintive wail of the Jew to the jingling tambourine of the gypsy; myriad languages; scents of varying cooking styles and methods, and the colorful costumes of the exotic inhabitants. There were even some Saracens in the camp, for the camp followers are mostly a nation unto themselves, owing loyalty first of all to the army they are following, at least until it is defeated, when they at once attach themselves to the victor.

As he rode now through this camp, Sir Kenneth was enjoying the varied sights and sounds, his quick eye everywhere, his ear picking up snatches of conversation in half a dozen different languages. Someone was roasting a pig and the delicious odor made his mouth water; he hadn't eaten since downing some moldy bread and some ale at daybreak, when he set out hunting. Krouba, who had caught some breed of desert rat, had fared better than he had.

Suddenly one sound penetrated the others, the cry of a woman in distress. "Help! Help me!" a voice cried.

Kenneth reined his horse to the right, following the sound. He rode past a group of gypsy tents and saw in the distance a young woman pursued by a handful of English knights, who were laughing and hooting with lustful glee.

"Help, for the love of God," she screamed, but the inhabitants of the camp were all too afraid of the armed knights to come to her aid.

Such sights were not uncommon here; indeed many of the women in this camp improved their desirability with a show of resistance. But this swarthy gypsy girl, as he recognized her to be, seemed genuinely frightened and desperate to escape her pursuers.

And of course, they were English, and Sir Kenneth was Scottish. He rode to the rescue, his armor clanging, his steed's hooves drumming the hard ground.

As the English knights were afoot, it was an easy matter to outdistance them and, despite his armor and mail, lean down and sweep the girl from her feet, onto his horse. Her bare feet still ran, treading the air, as he slowed his horse's gallop.

Thinking him to be another of her tormentors, she struggled in his arms and tried to strike him, but in her position, flung across the horse's shoulders, she could do little more than beat on that noble animal's body.

"English pig," she cried and would have thrown herself to the ground had he not held her firmly at the waist.

"Not English but Scottish," he said, laughing, "and not a pig but a falcon, if you will but see. Hold still now before I send you back to your suitors."

"Scotsman," one of the English knights cried, "find your own sport. That one's too pretty for the likes of you anyway."

"Ay, lass," another cried raucously. "Surely you wouldn't choose a Scot over a man." That brought a round of jeers and howls from his friends. Kenneth had reined in his horse now and turned toward them, and he saw at a glance that they were all fired up with drink.

"Begone, Englishers," he called to them. "Save your temper for the Turks, who might be frightened of it."

One of the knights had drawn his sword and he called, "Come closer with your friend, Scot. I've got something to stick in each of you."

If the man had been sober, Kenneth would no doubt have dismounted and accepted the challenge, but from the way the man staggered and swayed drunkenly, as if cast about by a mighty wind, he knew that it would be no fight at all. Instead, he drew his sword and rode closer, meaning only to disarm the man.

It was not necessary to do even that, though. The English knight swung with his sword before Sir Kenneth was within two horses' lengths of him and his sword slipped from his fingers to go crashing to the ground.

"Help me, lads," he cried to his companions but, looking over his shoulder, he discovered that they had chosen the better part of valor and were already running away. For a moment he hesitated, then he too turned and ran, disappearing quickly into the maze of tents and huts that made up the camp.

Kenneth looked after them and laughed at their drunken flight; but his laugh was suddenly cut short.

One of the rogues had not fled but stood off to the side, out of Kenneth's range of vision. Now, seeing Kenneth's back to him, he lifted his mace—a weighted ball on the end of a club—and, swinging it over his head, threw it at the Scotsman's head.

A warning cry from the gypsy girl, who saw the weapon thrown, brought Kenneth around in his saddle so that the blow, which might otherwise have opened his skull in an instant, was only a glancing one. Even so, it opened a gash alongside his head from which the blood began at once to spurt. He swayed dizzily in his saddle, his vision blurring as the ground seemed to rock and heave beneath him.

Had the villain who struck the cowardly blow followed up his advantage, it would have been no difficult matter to kill the knight on the spot; no doubt he would have done so had it not been for the intervention of Krouba, Kenneth's faithful dog. That creature, seeing his master struck, turned toward his attacker and with a terrifying snarl, leapt at him.

It was a brave man who could see that enraged beast setting upon him and not be frightened. This one gave a shriek of alarm and turned to run, tripping over his own feet and falling head-long.

In an instant Krouba was upon him, his snarls and growls

mingling with the man's terrified bleating and the laughter of the crowd that had gathered to watch the show.

It was not hard to judge what the outcome of this would have been had not Kenneth, never a vengeful man, called his dog back to his side, letting the English knight flee, his tunic and his pride in shreds.

The onlookers, convinced that the entertainment was over, began to drift away. For a moment Kenneth sat as he was, becoming gradually aware of the gypsy girl in his arms. She, discovering that he was no enemy but her protector, had ceased struggling against him and had managed to right herself, so that she now clung to him in the saddle. His arm remained about her waist, and he was aware of the feel of soft warm flesh beneath his hand. The scent of perfume drifted up from her dark curly hair, and when he looked down he found her gazing up into his face. Her eyes were green, a mysterious shadowy green like the surface of an English pond in the shade of the willows.

"You're wounded," she said in a low, throaty voice.

"It's nothing," he said. The ground had ceased its rocking motions and he would ignore the throbbing pain that pulsed from the wound through his entire head. "Show me which is your tent and I'll return you safely to it."

The gypsy girl, though, had been watching the knight throughout the incident. Once over her fear of him, she had discovered that here indeed was a fair "son of the cross." Although he wore his weapons and armor, his mail headpiece was back, revealing a handsome man with a ruggedly chiseled face. His hair was brown, but touched with highlights of red and gold as if it had absorbed the fiery sun of the desert.

Looking up into his handsome face, she decided that at the moment the solitary "safety" of her tent was the least of her desires.

She whimpered and pressed her face against a broad, powerful shoulder. "I'm frightened," she said in a whisper. "Suppose they come looking for me again. Who will protect me when you are gone?"

"Most of the women here are not so averse to a man's attention," he said frankly.

Her anger at his implication made her forget to be "afraid" and she tilted her face to look up at him again, her eye flashing like green fires.

"I'm not a whore," she said angrily. "Why do you think I was running from those English beasts?"

"It's a game I've seen played before," he said.

She gave a snarl, not unlike the snarl of the deer-hound, and lifted a hand to slap him. With a chuckle he caught her wrist in a powerful grip.

"In truth, I don't think you were playing," he said. His voice had such an obvious ring of sincerity that it was impossible not to accept what he said as fact, and her anger faded. For a moment more the two of them sat on the horse, looking at one another frankly.

"Who are you, and what do you do here?" he asked.

"My name is Elaine. I traveled originally with my father, but the journey proved too arduous for him and I buried him many miles back. Now I make my living pleasing men, but only with my singing and dancing."

"And those three were the first to demand more?" he asked.

She shrugged and said, "It's usually night when I entertain. The men drink ale or wine and there are other women among them, tending to their physical needs and emptying their purses. Usually when I have finished and collected the coins they throw, I slip away into the darkness."

"Usually?" He cocked an eyebrow.

She met his gaze openly and her brilliantly painted lips curved into a smile. "Yes, usually. I said I was not a whore, Sir Knight. But I'm no English virgin either."

He smiled back at her; the invitation in her eyes was obvious and her physical presence was no less inviting. She exuded a warm, womanly scent that mingled with her perfume and teased his senses.

"I could dress that wound for you," she said. "I'm very gifted with herbs and medicines."

"I'll bring you back to your tent later," he said, "when it's dark. Then you can elude whoever you want to."

It was nearing evening when they approached his camp. It was no more than a few miserable huts, hastily constructed of boughs and palm leaves and now mostly deserted. The central hut was his, as he was the leader of this almost extinguished band, and a swallow-tailed pennon on the point of a spear marked the hut as the chiefs. But no pages or squires waited by the pennon and that emblem of feudal power hung limply, as if sickening under the scorching Eastern sun. Only reputation defended this knightly emblem from insult, for it had no other guard.

The old servant came out to meet them as they rode up. If he was surprised to see his master accompanied by a woman he gave no sign of it, but helped the gypsy girl down as deferentially as if she were a highborn lady.

Kenneth dismounted more slowly. The blow to his head from the mace had been more serious than he had realized at first, and on the ride back he had found himself more than once on the brink of unconsciousness. Only an iron will had kept him in his saddle and so composed that the girl with him might never have guessed he had been injured except for the blood that still flowed from the ugly gash. She had tried to stop it with a piece torn from her own tunic, but her experienced eye told her the cut needed immediate and skilled attention.

As he got down from his horse, Kenneth's will finally failed him and before he could say a word to his servant he sank to the ground with a groan.

"That wound needs care," Elaine said, kneeling quickly over him. "Help me take him inside."

The servant, seeing the wound for the first time, wordlessly did as she bade. Between the two of them they managed to half drag, half carry him into the dark interior of the hut.

"Water," she ordered, "and if your bread has molded, bring me some of the mold."

With the servant's help she quickly gathered some wild plants and made a healing paste, applying it to the wound, which she then bandaged. The two of them undressed the still-unconscious knight and put him into his bed. This was not the first naked man she had ever seen, and she did not hesitate nor blush when his last garments had been removed and his body lay stretched naked before her. Indeed, her opinion as to his masculine beauty was only enhanced by the brief view before she covered him carefully. He had the lean, hard body of a pagan god; here, she thought, was a man indeed, and as she checked the wound's dressing, she began to hum a little song to herself.

"I'll spend the night with him," she said when the servant returned from fetching fresh water. "He may need a fresh bandage during the night."

He looked vaguely amused at the explanation but he did not quarrel with it and went outside to sleep. Krouba had remained in the hut beside his master's bed throughout Elaine's ministrations. She did not attempt to drive him out now; for one thing, she thought that although he had been quiet and docile, he might turn on her if she tried to separate him from the knight. Anyway, he would make good protection and notwithstanding the noble purpose of this expedition she knew from experience that a crusaders' camp was not the safest place to be at night.

The servant had cooked the fowl the knight brought back with him and now she nibbled on a leg, tossing the scraps to the dog. Then she stood and shed her tunic; she hesitated for a moment, then shed her chemise too and slipped into the bed beside the Scottish knight. The desert air turned cool once the sun had fallen, and she snuggled against him for warmth, quickly dropping asleep.

CHAPTER FOUR

...They, too, retired
To the wilderness, but 'twas with arms.
—Paradise Regained

Kenneth awoke slowly. He had been dreaming of the beautiful Lady Joan, the king's cousin. Since first laying eyes upon her, he had been in love with the beautiful noblewoman, with a love as hopeless as it was fervent—what chance had he, after all, with a kinswoman of the Lionhearted?

His dream became superimposed upon reality. He grew faintly aware of the feel of naked female flesh close against his body, and for a time in his dream it was Joan whom he held in his arms, turning now toward her and gently beginning to stroke the curve of her back, the voluptuous hill of her hip. In his mind's eye he saw her pale yellow hair falling across his shoulder; her eyes, as blue as the Scottish sky on a spring morn, gazed lovingly up into his.

Gradually sleep fled, the dream faded; but the reality of naked warmth in his arms, of womanly flesh against his flesh, these remained. He opened his eyes, half sitting up as he did. For a moment he looked with bewilderment at the woman with him. Certainly she was not Lady Joan, for this creature's hair was black, her complexion swarthy, and her eyes green. At first he could not think how she had come to be here; there was a dull ache in his head. Had he drunk too much—a rare occurrence—and picked up one of the whores from the followers' camp, so rare an occurrence it had never happened before?

He put a hand to his head and, feeling the bandage there, memory flooded back to him. "Elaine." He whispered her name.

She looked pleased that he remembered. "Does your head hurt?" she asked.

"Only a little," he said. "You are skilled with your medicines."

"I am skilled at caring for a man's needs," she said, a smile curving her lips.

He realized then, belatedly, why she had asked about his head. For a moment he thought again of Lady Joan. But that love was afar indeed, while this reality was very near. And she was very desirable too, in a ripe, overblown way. Her breasts, bared for his inspection, were like those big, delicious melons they had discovered in this foreign land, and looked as sweet.

The ache in his head was only a dull throb, after all, not enough to dampen a man's spirit; and as close as they were, as naked as they were, she was as aware as he that he was in every other way sound of limb.

"What is your name?" she asked.

"They call me The Falcon," he whispered. He lowered his mouth to hers. Her arms came up about him and her thighs parted in an ageless gesture of welcome.

* * * * * * *

Later she brought him breakfast—some cold roast fowl and some fruit that she had stolen from the followers' camp. He ate with gusto and while he ate she hummed to herself and mended a tear in his undertunic. She hadn't been so content in months; she knew herself well enough to know that she was never really satisfied without a man to fuss over. When her father had been alive, caring for him had filled the need to some extent, and of course there had been lovers.

She had been honest in telling the Scotsman that she was no virgin. She liked a bout of lovemaking now and again as well as any man, but she liked one man as a lover, and she liked to be able to care for him in every way—preparing his food, mending his clothes. In short, she wanted a husband, but none of the men she had met had suited her that far—none until now, anyway.

When he had eaten and dressed, he came to where she was sitting at the door of his hut. "I'll take you home," he said.

She shrugged and said, "There is no need. I can stay here and care for you."

He looked down at her for a moment. The feel of her body beneath his was still fresh in his memory, and he was tempted to agree; the memory was so pleasant.

But it was useless to confuse physical desire with love, and however futile, he loved another. To take this lusty gypsy girl for his woman would be false to both of them.

"I'm sorry, Elaine," he said, touching her raven hair with the tips of his fingers. "It would not do."

At first she was hurt and confused, then angry. "I can find my own way," she said when he again offered to return her to her own camp, and she flounced off with her head held high. He watched her walk away, his eyes following the swing of her wide hips, and was nearly tempted to call her back and tell her he had changed his mind.

Before he could do so, though, a messenger approached the Scottish camp, his eyes looking about him with an air of disapproval.

"I come from His Grace the Archbishop," he said, "with instructions to bring to him a knight from this camp, the Falcon, as he is known."

"I'm Sir Kenneth," the knight replied, surprised that so august a person as the archbishop could have need of his services. "Sometimes called the Falcon. What does His Grace want with me?"

The messenger, hardly more than a lad, gave a shrug of his shoulders and said, "I'm to bring you to the Council of Princes. They aren't likely to confide their plans in me."

"You more than I," Kenneth thought, but aloud he said, "Let's go then."

He was brought in short order to the tent in which the Council of Princes commonly met. A wide ring of open ground was kept around the tent and guarded by several sentries who seemed to know the messenger, as they were not hindered in their progress.

The archbishop waited just inside the vast tent. A throne, larger than any used by King Richard, was placed there for him, although at the arrival of Sir Kenneth and the messenger he was standing and pacing to and fro.

The boy showed Kenneth inside and then, with no word, disappeared, leaving the knight in the presence not only of the archbishop but of the many sovereigns of the crusade, who he could see seated about the tent.

Kenneth dropped to his knees before the archbishop.

"Are you the knight they call the Falcon?" the holy man demanded.

"I have been called that. Sir Kenneth, a Scots knight, at your service, Your Grace."

"Rise, Sir Kenneth," he said, "and be at ease. We have heard good report of you and stand in need of your services."

Kenneth was duly awed, not only by that unexpected remark but by the very presence of the holy man. This was the same William, Archbishop of Tyre, who had in part instigated this Third Crusade and who had blessed King Richard and Philip Augustus at Vezelay. He was a striking figure of commanding aspect. Kenneth had been told that in his youth William was very handsome, and even in age he was hardly less so. His episcopal dress was of very rich fashion, trimmed in precious fur and surrounded by a cope of elaborate needlework. On his fingers he wore rings worth a good barony, and the hood that he wore unclasped and thrown back, for it was stifling in the tent, had gold fastenings.

He had a long beard, now silver with age. He was served by two youthful and handsome acolytes, one of whom, in the Eastern fashion, held an umbrella of palm leaves over the archbishop's head while the other fanned him with a fan of peacock feathers, their brilliant colors winking in the sunlight coming through the opening of the tent.

"I will serve in any way I can, Your Grace," Kenneth replied, proud that he had been deemed worthy of such an honor.

"There lives at Engaddi, a few days' journey from here, a holy man, a hermit. We wish you to take this packet to him. Say that it is our understanding that he is on friendly terms with Saladin. And add your own pleas that, as he loves God and the Holy Church of Rome, he will intervene with the sultan on behalf of the request contained in these letters."

"If I am to plead the cause," Kenneth said boldly, for it was not his place to question God's representative upon this holy crusade, "might I not know the nature of the cause? Is it an extension of the truce?"

For a moment the archbishop's eyes flashed, but then he stroked his beard thoughtfully and said, "It will be better to tell you some of the truth than to spawn rumors. But, at peril of your immortal soul, I mark this secret between yourself and this council. We seek agreement from Saladin to a lasting peace, and the withdrawal of our armies from Palestine."

"Saint George," Kenneth said in astonishment, forgetting himself briefly. "But—"

"Good knight," the archbishop interrupted him wearily, "we have told you the nature of your mission. Do not tax our good nature too sorely."

Murmuring "My lord," Kenneth again bowed his head. "I will deliver your message and return at once, God willing."

"God is willing," the archbishop said dryly. He touched the knight faintly on the shoulder. "Bless you, my son, and God keep you."

Kenneth thought, going out, that he would need God's protection, for he knew well enough the hardships of the great desert, which would have made the journey treacherous even if the land were peopled by allies instead of by enemies.

* * * * * * *

By evening he had made arrangements to leave in the early morning hours. Before retiring, he checked the wound on his head and found it healing nicely, the pain almost completely gone. He smiled and thought of the gypsy wench; everything she had done for him she had done well. Perhaps he would see her again when he returned from his mission.

He shed his clothes and dropped to his bed. He had not quite drifted off to sleep when Krouba, sleeping on the floor beside him, roused him with a low, warning growl.

At once Kenneth grabbed his sword and called, "Who goes there?"

There was a rustle of movement near the door of his hut, and a throaty feminine voice said, "Hush, don't rouse the camp." In a moment Elaine had slipped into the bed with him.

"I thought you had gone back to your own camp," he said.

"What kind of doctor would I be if I did not check on my patient?" she asked in a petulant tone. "Perhaps you have a fever, Sir Knight. You are warm to the touch."

"And getting warmer," he said with a chuckle, drawing her nearer.

* * * * * * *

He left just at dawn the following day. Elaine did not awaken and he was loath to disturb her. He left Krouba in the care of his servant and set out while the camp was just beginning to stir.

He journeyed for that entire day and into the second. Syria's burning sun had again begun to descend to the horizon when he paced the sandy deserts which lie near the Dead Sea. There the waves of the Jordan pour themselves into an inland sea from which the waters do not escape.

He had toiled among cliffs and rock walls, and leaving those rocky regions had come to that great plain where in ancient days the accursed cities provoked the dreadful vengeance of the

Almighty.

The effort, the dangers, the thrust of his journey were forgotten in a burst of emotion as he viewed these scenes, long familiar to his imagination but now looked upon for the first time. There was the once fair and fertile valley of Siddim, now a parched and blighted waste, condemned to eternal sterility.

The sun shone upon this scene of desolation with almost intolerable splendor. All life seemed to have hidden itself from the burning rays but for his own solitary figure moving through the shifting sand at a slow pace and his horse, whom he was now leading.

He admitted again what he had already had ample occasion to realize, that the dress of the crusaders and the accoutrements of their horses were ill suited to the country through which they traveled.

He had donned full armor for the journey, not knowing what he might encounter. In the fashion of the day he wore not only a shirt and an undertunic, but a hauberk—a coat of linked mail—with mail gauntlets. As if this were not enough weight, there was in addition the triangular shield which hung round his neck and a barrel helmet of steel; under the helmet he wore a coif-de-mailles—a hood and collar of mail. His lower limbs too were sheathed in flexible mail, as were his feet.

Over all this he wore an embroidered surcoat, the purpose of which was to protect his armor from the burning rays of the sun.

As for weaponry, on one side he wore a stout quillon dagger and on the other a long, broad, single-edged falchion, its handle forming a cross. He carried a long, steel-headed lance, with one end resting on his stirrup and at the tip a little pennoncel to dally with whatever faint breeze might pass his way.

Nor was his horse clothed less weightily; he wore a heavy saddle hung with mail, covered in front with a peytrel of leather and mail and behind with a padded crupper to cover the loins. A mace hung from the saddlebow; the reins were secured by chainwork while the chamfroy over his face was in fact a steel plate, with openings for the eyes and nostrils and having in its middle a sharp spike which gave the beast the appearance of the famed unicorns, which some claimed to have seen here in Araby.

Many crusaders had died in the burning climate, their end no doubt hastened by the weight of their armor. But to Kenneth it was only an inconvenience.

The Good Lord he had come here to serve had cast his limbs in a mold of uncommon strength and endowed him with a constitution as strong as his limbs, which he took as a sure sign that he was to take up sword in His cause.

Traveling as he did alone, he had had time to ponder some matters that were much on his mind of late. Since coming to the Holy Land, his slender purse had melted away. Many of his fellow crusaders, as he well knew, made it a policy to replenish their wealth at the expense of the Palestinians, but he had exacted no gifts from the natives nor held any prisoners for ransom, both of which practices were common. The small party he had brought with him from Scotland had gradually dwindled. This alone did not particularly alarm him, as he was accustomed to think of his good sword as his safest escort and his own thought as his best companion.

Still it behooved him to face the fact that his straits were dire, and aside from spiritual privileges he saw no rewards that would come to himself as a result of this campaign. He had come without permission of his father, who had more than one reason to be offended, and so he could probably expect little welcome when he returned to Scotland.

Nature had begun to make demands for refreshment and repose, so he was glad when he saw two or three palm trees in the distance which he was sure marked the well he had been told to watch for. His good horse too, who had plodded forward with steady endurance, now lifted his head, expanded his nostrils, and quickened his pace.

Rest was not to be gained so easily however. As he gazed at the distant cluster of trees it seemed to him as if something was moving among them. The distant form separated itself from the trees and began to move toward him with a speed that soon indicated a mounted horseman. His turban, long spear and green caftan, which floated behind him in the wind, revealed that he was a Saracen cavalier.

"In the desert no man meets a friend," as an Eastern proverb has it. The Saracen, flying as if borne on the wings of an eagle, did not come as a friend. Kenneth mounted his horse, disengaging the lance from his saddle and, seizing it with his right hand, placed it in rest with its point half-elevated. He gathered up his reins in his left hand, put spurs to his horse and prepared to meet the charge of the stranger.

The Arabs are born horsemen, and this one was no exception. He came on at a speedy gallop, managing the horse more with his seat and the suggestions of his body than by use of the reins. He wore at his arm a lightweight round buckler—or shield—of rhinoceros skin, ornamented with silver loops, and he swung this as if he meant to defend himself with it against the knight's formidable lance. He carried his own long spear not couched, as was Kenneth's, but grasped by the middle in his right hand, and brandished it at arm's length above his head.

He approached at a full gallop as if he expected Kenneth to put his own horse to the gallop to encounter him. But Kenneth was well acquainted by this time with the wiles of these Saracen warriors, and had no intention of exhausting his good horse unnecessarily. He made a dead halt, confident that should the Saracen advance to the actual shock, his weight and that of his horse would give him the advantage.

Apparently the approaching Arab thought the same thing; when he had approached within two spear lengths, he wheeled his horse nimbly to the left and rode twice around the knight while Kenneth, wheeling, but presenting always his face to him, prevented any attack at an unguarded point. At last, reining in his horse, the Arab retreated to a distance of a hundred yards.

A second time he swooped down upon Kenneth, and a second time thought the better of a close struggle, and retreated to a distance.

Kenneth could see that this elusive warfare might serve in time to wear him out or at least make him careless and when the Arab approached the third time, Kenneth seized the mace hanging at his saddlebow and hurled it against the head of his enemy.

The Saracen, who had the look of a man of rank, saw the danger almost too late and although he raised his light buckler to the defense, it did not prevent a grazing blow on his turban, which brought him off his horse.

Kenneth had little opportunity to take the advantage, however, for before he could have even dismounted the Saracen had called his horse to his side and leapt astride him again, without even using the stirrups.

On the other hand, Kenneth had recovered his mace and the Arab, remembering how he had used it, was cautious to stay out of reach of that weapon and some distance from the knight.

Now the Arab produced a short bow and, once more galloping in a circle around the knight, shot several arrows at him that, had it not been for his heavy armor, would have produced as many wounds.

Kenneth perceived that something must be done to change the nature of the contest. Grasping his side where an arrow had struck, he fell from his horse. Instantly his enemy was at his side, bending over him.

His wound had been only a ruse, however, and now Kenneth seized the Saracen for close combat. But the Arab was saved by his quickness and his presence of mind. Unable to rise swiftly, Kenneth had seized him by the sword belt, thinking to hold him while he rose; but the Saracen unloosed the belt and was gone again. His faithful charger seemed to watch his master's movements with keen intelligence and understand all that transpired, and again he was there at the Saracen's side, and again the Saracen mounted and rode off.

But this time he suffered a disadvantage because he was without his sword and his quiver of arrows, which had been attached to the girdle he had been obliged to abandon. This disadvantage—or the stalemate they had reached—seemed to give the Saracen thought. He approached again, but this time slowly and with his right hand extended in what Kenneth recognized as a gesture of peace.

"There is a truce between our two countries," he said, using the lingua franca which was commonly used between the crusaders. "Therefore, why should we be at war? Why should there not be peace between us?"

"I have no objections to a peace," Kenneth said. "But what security do you offer that you will observe the truce between us?"

"The word of a follower of the Prophet is never broken," he said. "It is from you, brave Nazarene, that I would demand security, but for one thing. I know that treason is seldom combined in the same breast with such courage as you have displayed."

His words made Kenneth rather ashamed of his own doubts, for what he had said was undoubtedly true. Kenneth put his hand to his weapon, but this time not threateningly.

"By the cross of my sword," he said, "and by the cross that I follow, I will be a true companion, Saracen, while we are in company together."

"By Mohammed, Prophet of God, and by Allah, God of the Prophet, there is no treachery in my heart toward you. And now let us travel to yonder fountain. The hour of rest is at hand and the stream had barely cooled my lips when I was called to battle by your approach."

Kenneth yielded a ready and courteous assent, and at the side of his erstwhile foe, without any angry look or a gesture of doubt on either side, rode toward the little cluster of palm trees.

CHAPTER FIVE

'tis true that we are in great danger....
—King Henry V

"How on earth far is this dreadful place?" Berengaria made a disgusted face across at Joan.

"Another day's travel, they say," Joan replied, brushing a hand wearily across her brow. They were riding pillion behind two serving men; another time the queen would have ridden in a litter, but that would have made her identity too conspicuous for this journey. Behind them came the queen's ladies, Clorise, Callista and Amy, each riding the pillion seat behind a servant on horseback. Two knights and a bowman rode in front of them, and another such group behind them. The late afternoon sun glinted on the exposed metal of the knights' armor, hurting Joan's eyes.

It was late in the afternoon when they stopped to pitch camp. The servants set about putting up the tents for the ladies and building fires to cook supper, while the knights took up positions in a ring around the camp.

"What an awful place," Berengaria complained, her pretty lips forming a pout while she surveyed the rugged terrain. "I'm sorry we came. Why couldn't that holy man have come to see us? After all, I am the queen of England, am I not? Shouldn't that carry some weight?"

"Perhaps not with a man who has withdrawn from the world," Joan said patiently. "And the good bishop has said many times there is a special blessing upon those who make a holy pilgrimage."

"Well, the good bishop never had to spend days on end journeying through this godforsaken land."

Joan let her gaze go to the mountains rising up before them. The sun had turned the rocks into precious metals and gems; that outcropping there was gold, surely, and that ridge there burning crimson was carnelian, was it not? The heat had burned the blue of the sky to an almost white tint with no trace of a cloud. Here and there on the hills could be seen the green of grass and shrub, thickening as the terrain mounted higher. Not a dozen feet from where they stood, a snake slithered behind a rock with a faint, rustling sound.

It was a savage place, true, but she was willing to concede it a wild beauty that could not but stir something within her. Perhaps it was the lion's blood that ran in her kinsman's veins, and in some diluted part in hers as well. How tame, how simple and rustic, would England look after these dramatic vistas.

"If," she told herself, "I ever see England again."

For she had begun to consider what she would never have voiced to her companions; the possibility that they—that all of their vast entourage—might perish here in this desert. It was common talk outside of the royal tents that supplies were running perilously low, and soon they must either push forward to some place where they could seize new ones or retreat. If Richard were well, perhaps they would be able to push on; but without him she had begun to wonder if they would even be able to effect a safe retreat.

Once, as a girl, she had made her way down to the kitchens of her father's castle. In the kitchen yard she had watched the cook slaying fowl for their dinner. Cook began by severing their heads, then releasing the headless bodies. The poor creatures ran about the yard as if unaware their heads were gone, flapping their wings, their steps growing weaker; gradually they sank to the ground, making little kicking motions, and at last they were still.

Illness had removed the head of their army; if he did not recover, it would be permanent. In the meantime they were like the bodies of those poor fowl; for a time they continued in motion, as if alive. But gradually their efforts grew weaker, their lifeblood spilling from them, until they soon would be able to do nothing but sink wearily to the ground and, with a few futile kicks, die.

Her attention was brought sharply back to the present; something was happening. One of the knights had suddenly cried out and run toward his companions, his armor clanging.

"What is it?" Berengaria asked. She made a face as she took a step. "Oh, those fool horses, why couldn't I have ridden in a litter? What's happening, Joan?"

Joan had followed the knight's pointing finger; in the distance she saw a cloud of dust. Even as she watched it grew, drawing nearer, and she saw a flash of sunlight upon metal.

She felt a flash of something within herself too, a quickening of her senses. Too long had she sat in the royal tents, chafing with boredom and inactivity. Her nostrils flared as she seemed to catch the scent of danger blowing on the wind.

"I think, royal madam, that we are being attacked," she said aloud.

"Attacked?" There was a squeal from the other ladies, who had heard only the one word.

"What do you mean, Joan?" Berengaria demanded, her voice ascending on the last to a near shriek.

Joan pointed. "Surely those are Arab horsemen," she said. "See, you can make out their turbans now. And I think, with their javelins raised like that, they aren't coming in peace."

Berengaria and the ladies looked and their screams rent the air. "This is your fault," the queen berated Joan. "We could have been escorted by an army instead of half a dozen men."

"We could have stayed at home," Joan said smiling, "but travelers must be content."

The knight who was in charge, a burly fellow of Norman descent, came to where the ladies had gathered.

"Your Highness and royal ladies, I think it best if you retire to your tents," he said.

Berengaria and the others were quick to comply, running with little shrieks and sobs for the illusory safety of their cloth tents, but Joan remained where she was, staring toward the riders who now approached within the range of arrows. What did she care to hide in a tent? That would not protect her from Arab swords.

"Madam," the knight began, but she interrupted him.

"Go, defend us, and God be with you," she said, putting a gentle hand upon his mail-encased arm. "I will retire in good time."

He had scant time in which to argue with her. One of his fellows called to him, and with a last anxious glance at her, he turned and strode quickly to join the defense.

The knights had formed a semicircle between the camp and the approaching horsemen. The bowmen knelt behind the knights so that they were protected, but could still fire from between them upon the enemy.

By this time Joan had seen that there were perhaps two or three dozen Arabs in the attacking band. The little ring of knights and bowmen—six men in all—backed by the servants armed with knives and clubs, looked pitifully inadequate to withstand the attack.

"We should have stayed with Richard," she told herself; but even as she said it, she gave a little laugh of excitement. How she would have liked to be a man now! She put her hand down and felt the hilt of the dagger she had fastened to her belt. Let the Saracens come. One of them at least would taste the steel of her blade, and would know that an Englishwoman was more than fair hair and white thighs, as she had once heard a French knight say.

The fight had begun in earnest now. As quickly as they were able the bowmen loosed their arrows, while the English knights fought off with lance and broadsword the attacks of the bolder Arabs. The Arabs had begun to circle them on horse-back, sending their own arrows into the English camp, charging in singly with sword or javelin flashing to clash metal with a knight and then dashing back out of reach. The dust raised by their horses' hooves now choked the air, making Joan cough. As they fought, the Arabs let loose bloodcurdling cries that cut through the flesh as surely as any sword. Joan could smell blood and dust and the sweat of horses and men. Still she did not run to her tent but remained where she was, her eyes missing none of the action.

Even to her woman's eyes it was apparent that the tide was against the English knights. The great numbers of the Arabs, the mobility their horses gave them against the unmounted knights, and the lightning swiftness of their sallies were telling upon the armored knights. One of the knights and one of the bowmen had fallen, and another of the knights fought bravely with one arm while the other hung bleeding and useless at his side.

Suddenly one of the Arabs broke through the ranks of the defenders and, almost before Joan realized what was happening, he was charging down upon her. She could see the sweat glistening on his brow and the light of lust flashing in his eyes. Her hand went to her dagger.

Before she could draw it, though, the remaining bowman had turned and loosed an arrow that entered the man's back and came straight through, its point suddenly erupting from his chest in a gush of blood. The horse thundered past Joan, and the Arab, lifeless already, tumbled from the saddle to fall at her feet.

The English bowman, however, had given his life to save hers. He had turned his back upon the enemy and, before he could turn again and reload his weapon, an Arab sword had slashed across his shoulders, all but severing his head.

By now the fight was nearly over. Another knight had fallen and only two armored men, one of them severely wounded, and a handful of servants with sticks, stood to resist the charge of the horsemen. The Arabs regrouped their forces and with dreadful shouts and cries raced into the camp, flinging men aside, lashing left and right with their swords. The ground had turned to crimson mud.

Joan turned and walked rather than ran back to her tent, her head held high. Although her heart was pounding anyone who saw her might have thought she was out for a stroll in the keep of her father's castle. Her royal pride would not let her show her fear; she was cousin to Richard, the greatest king of England, and though she must die, she would die accordingly.

Behind her metal clanged and there was a stench of death in the air. She could hear the ladies and the queen, in the queen's tent, shrieking and sobbing with one another. She did not care to join them, desiring instead the solitude of her own little tent. It was dark and cool inside, and the silken walls muffled the sounds from without.

She had hardly entered the tent before there was a footstep from without and the curtain was ripped aside to reveal an Arab warrior. He paused in the opening, his dark eyes raking her hungrily. His lips were parted in a cruel grin, revealing teeth that gleamed in startling contrast to his darkened skin. He was tall, with the tawny coloring of a desert animal.

Now he strode boldly across the tent and put out a hand to seize her.

The blade of her knife cut through the air and slashed across the back of his hand.

He was quicker than she was, though, and jerked his hand aside so that the blade left only a superficial wound. In a twinkling he had leapt toward her and seized her wrist in a viselike grip. He was slim and looked somewhat puny, but she discovered now that his long, slender fingers possessed a wiry strength she would never have suspected. She fought against him, but despite her efforts the weapon was wrested from her and flung aside.

"And now, my beautiful English rose," he said. With an evil laugh he seized the fabric of her bliaut and tore it away from her shoulders. The cloth was like paper in his hands, nor did her undertunic and her chemise offer him any greater difficulty. In an instant her upper clothes had been ripped apart down to her girdle and hung like rags about her hips, leaving her body from the waist up naked to his hungry gaze.

"Our orders were to leave the queen unharmed," he said, running his tongue over his lips, "but we have no such orders regarding you. You will pay dearly for that scratch on my hand."

She tried vainly to cover her breasts with her hands. A shudder of terror went through her.

CHAPTER SIX

...the stern joy which warriors feel
In foemen worthy of their steel.
—The Lady of the Lake

Sir Kenneth and his Saracen companion, who had just a short time before been engaged in trying to kill one another, rode toward the distant oasis in respectful companionship. For some time they traveled in silence, each lost in his own thoughts.

It occurred to Kenneth that his horse was still lathered from his recent exertions, and his progress through the fine sand was a labored one, his hooves sinking deeper with each step. Pausing, Kenneth dismounted and began to lead the beast instead. The Saracen watched approvingly.

They arrived at the knot of palm trees where a fountain welled out in sparkling profusion. Kenneth paused for a moment in the welcome shade, grateful for the spot of beauty in this desolate land. No doubt anywhere else the scene would have been unremarkable, but as a single dot of green in a seemingly boundless desert, promising shade and fresh water, what would have seemed cheap where it was common made the little oasis a paradise.

Some helpful hand had long ago walled in and arched over the fountain, protecting it from being smothered by the blowing dust or absorbed into the earth. The arch by now was partly crumbled, but it still covered the water and shielded it from the sun's rays. While all else was blazing the water sparkled coolly, and what had spilled into the ground provided a carpet of green velvet.

The ruins of the well gave a sense of comfort to the Scottish knight, revealing that the hand of man had been here. It was a reminder to the thirsty and weary traveler that others had come this way, suffering the same discomforts, and here had found repose and refreshment to enable them to continue on their way to a more fertile country.

The two warriors relieved their horses of saddles and bits and reins and led the animals to drink first from the well before the men then refreshed themselves. Then they turned the animals loose, confident they would not stray far from the pure water and fresh grass.

Kenneth reflected, not for the first time, on the ease with which fighting men enjoyed these brief interludes of peace. It was, he thought, because war was the chief occupation of men these days and gave them ample opportunity to work out all their murderous impulses. The intervals of peace were thus made sweeter, and a knight who had just fought well against a worthy opponent and would again tomorrow was unlikely to harbor any continuing resentment against him.

Thus there was no resentment as the two sat down and each produced what would be his meal. There was a certain amount of curiosity; each had been given a unique opportunity for observation. The men knew one another as formidable opponents, and Kenneth had concluded that had he fallen it would have been by a noble hand.

Despite the time of travel and battle, this was the first chance he had ever had to observe a Saracen closely. He found the man's appearance in marked contrast to that of Europeans. He was shorter than Kenneth and at first glance looked somewhat frail; it was only on closer examination that Kenneth saw that he was as lean and hard and sinewy as a leather thong. His features were delicate, small and well formed; his nose was straight and regular, his eyes black and deep set, his skin deeply browned. He wore a black beard that had been trimmed with particular care.

The Saracen's manners were as grave as they were graceful. There was a sense of the restraint that men of warm temper often impose upon their natural impetuosity, and at the same time a feeling that his own sense of dignity caused a certain formality in his behavior.

Kenneth too had a feeling of superiority, but in him it resulted in a bold and even careless bearing; he gave the impression of a man too aware of his own worth to be concerned about the opinions of others. Both men were courteous, but from Kenneth it appeared to be a sense of what was due to others, while the Saracen's thoughts were more of what was expected from himself.

"Nazarene," the Saracen said as they brought out the provisions for their meal, "let me be forgiven for asking the name of one whom I have this day met in danger and in repose."

"It is hardly worth knowing," Kenneth said, "but among my fellow knights I am known as Kenneth, the Falcon. At home I have other titles, but they would only sound harsh to your ear. Tell me, Saracen, from which of the tribes of Arabia are you descended? And how are you known?"

"Sir Kenneth," the Saracen said. "I am grateful it is a name I can say with ease; those of the Franks defeat me, to tell the truth. As for me, I am no tribesman, although I come from a line no less wild nor less warlike. I am Sheerkohf, the Lion of the Mountain. I derive my descent from Kurdistan, which holds no family more noble than that of Seljook."

"I've heard that your greatest sultan, Saladin, claims his blood from the same source."

"Praises to the Prophet," Sheerkohf said, "that so honors our mountains as to send from their bosom he whose name is victory. But I am as dust beneath the feet of the king of Egypt and Syria, although in my own land my name may not be unknown."

The Saracen's meal was spartan—a handful of dates and a piece of some hard-looking bread, followed by a drink at the fountain behind them, as his religion forbade him liquor.

Kenneth's meal was coarse, but more generous. He had a piece of dried pork, which he ate ravenously, washing it down with wine from a leather pouch.

For some time Sheerkohf regarded with disapproval the keen appetite that carried the knight's meal on long after his own was finished. At length he said, "Brave knight, it is unseemly that one who fights like a man should feed like a dog."

Kenneth looked up in surprise at the unexpected criticism, but when he saw the Saracen's eyes upon the pork, he remembered that this too was forbidden to Saracens.

"I exercise my freedom, nothing more," he said. "My religion makes no prohibition regarding this food as yours does." As if to show his scorn for his companion's scruples, he took a long draft from his bottle.

"It is only freedom to feed like a beast and to drink a poisonous liquor which even the beasts refuse."

"You blaspheme the gifts of God," Kenneth said with a twinkle in his eye, "who gave man the gift of the grape to use wisely. It cheers the heart of man after his day's work is done, it refreshes him in sickness, and it comforts him in sorrow. And he who abuses the gifts of heaven is no greater fool in his drunkenness than you in your abstinence."

For a moment Sheerkohf bridled at this touch of sarcasm. Then he too relaxed and said, "Your words would create anger if they did not raise compassion. You boast of the liberty of your religion, but it restrains you in every way, even in marriage. It binds you to one mate only, whether she be sick or healthy, fruitful or barren, whether she brings comfort and joy or only clamor and strife to your table and your bed. I call that slavery, not freedom. On the other hand, to the faithful the Prophet gives the privileges of Abraham and of Solomon, the wisest of men, that we can have here a succession of beauty at our pleasure, and when we have departed this life, we have the black-eyed houris of Paradise."

Kenneth laughed and took another drink. "By heaven, now you've shown yourself for a blind and bewildered heathen, nothing more. Tell me, Sheerkohf, that diamond ring you wear on your finger—do you hold it of great value?"

"There is no match for it anywhere. But what has that got to do with it?"

"Much, if you'll only see. Let me take my ax and dash the stone into twenty pieces. Would each piece be as valuable as the original stone or would they all, even when collected together, equal even a part of its original value?"

"That is a child's question. The fragments of the stone would not equal a hundredth part of the entire jewel."

Kenneth shrugged and said, "There you have it. The love which binds a true knight to one only, fair and faithful, is the entire jewel. The affection you fling among your enslaved wives and half-wedded slaves is like the sparkling fragments of a broken gem."

"By the holy kaaba," Sheerkohf said, laughing, "you have shown yourself to be a madman. Look more closely, Nazarene. This ring of mine would be worth less if the diamond were not encircled with these lesser stones which grace and set it off. The central gem is man, firm and entire, his value dependent upon himself alone. And these lesser jewels surrounding him are his women, borrowing from his splendor, which he deals out to them as suits his pleasure, and in turn providing a setting for him and gracing his presence. If you took the central stone from the ring the diamond would still retain its value, while the ring and the lesser stones are of comparatively little worth without the diamond. This is the true reading of your parable."

But Kenneth could not take offense at this exchange of wit, and he had to admit the Saracen had given as good as he got. He said, "You speak like one who never saw a woman truly worthy of a soldier's love. Believe me, if you could look upon the fair ladies of our country, you would loathe forever the poor sensual slaves of your harem. It is the beauty and virtue of our ladies that gives point to our spears and edge to our swords. A knight who has no mistress of his affections will no more distinguish himself in battle than a lamp will shed light without kindling."

"I've heard of this madness among your knights," Sheerkohf said, no more offended than his companion had been, "and have accounted it as a symptom of the same insanity that brings you here to take possession of an empty sepulcher. But I would be pleased to behold with my own eyes these charms that transform such brave men into fools."

"If I were not on a mission to Engaddi I would be glad to accompany you to the camp of Richard of England, where you would see several of the fairest beauties of England and France."

"Now, by the Prophet, I will accept your invitation, if you will postpone your present journey and come back with me. And I advise you to do so, for to travel toward Jerusalem without a passport is to cast your life away."

Kenneth drew a parchment from his tunic. "I have a passport under Saladin's own signature," he said.

Sheerkohf showed his surprise as he recognized the seal. He kissed the paper with respect and pressed it to his forehead.

"You have sinned against my blood and mine for not showing me this when we met," he said, handing it back.

"You came at me threateningly. If a troop of Saracens had attacked me, it might have agreed with my honor to show the sultan's pass, but never to one man."

"One man was enough to interrupt your travels," Sheerkohf said haughtily.

"True, but there are few such as yourself. Such hawks shun the flocks and fly alone."

Pleased with the compliment, Sheerkohf said, "You do us justice. But it is well for me that I failed to kill you, with the safeguard of the king of kings upon your person."

"I'm glad to know it's so valuable. I've heard the road is infested with thieves who welcome any opportunity to plunder."

"You've heard correctly. But I swear to you by the turban of the Prophet, that should you suffer at the hands of any such villains I myself will revenge you. I will see every male of them slain and their women sent into such distant captivity that the name of their tribe will never again be heard here. I will pour salt upon the foundations of their village so that no living thing shall dwell there again."

"I would rather you take all that trouble to avenge someone more important than I," Kenneth said. "But the vow is recorded in heaven, for good or evil. I would be grateful to you now if you would show me the way to a resting place for tonight."

"You will sleep under the black covering of my father's tent," Sheerkohf said, indicating the sky overhead. "But why do you travel to Engaddi?"

"To see a holy man, Theodoric of Engaddi, who lives in the wilds there."

"I know the man and the place. I'll see you safely there."

"That would be pleasant company for me, but the hands of your people are already red with the blood of Christians. I wouldn't endanger the good man's safety by showing you where he lives."

"Sir Kenneth, it is taught to us, 'If you find holy men laboring with their hands and serving God in the desert, hurt them not, neither destroy their dwellings.' And such a man as the one you seek, even though the light of the true faith has not yet touched him, is safe in our country. Let us not defy one another, brother; we'll find plenty of Franks and Saracens to fight. This Theodoric is protected by the Christ he serves as well as by the—"

"By Our Lady," Kenneth interrupted him, "do not name in the same breath the camel driver of Mecca with—"

A look of anger illuminated Sheerkohf's face, but it was brief and was as quickly replaced by the same calm dignity he had shown before.

"Do not slander him whom you do not know," he said. "We venerate the founder of your religion while we condemn the doctrine your priests have spun from it. I will myself guide you to the cavern of the hermit, and on the way let us leave to philosophers to dispute the faiths, and content ourselves to talk on subjects that belong to young warriors—upon battles, upon beautiful women, upon sharp swords and upon bright armor."

They shook hands on this and rose from their place of rest,

courteously helping one another to replace their harnesses. Each man clearly possessed the confidence and affection of his horse, his constant companion in travel and warfare. The animals came willingly from their feeding and snuffled fondly round their masters.

Before they mounted, Kenneth again refreshed himself at the fountain. "Tell me," he said, "what is the name of this fountain?"

"It is called the Diamond of the Desert," Sheerkohf replied, mounting his horse.

"It is well named," Kenneth said. "At home there are a thousand springs, but I'll remember none of them more fondly than this one."

He mounted too, and they set off again on their journey across the sandy wastes. Evening was approaching and a light breeze somewhat relieved the desert heat. For a time they rode in silence, Sheerkohf guiding his companion. After a while he seemed more sure of their route and relaxed somewhat, again entering into conversation.

"Tell me, how many men came with you on this warfare?"

"I left rather quickly," Kenneth said, "but with the help of friends and kinsmen I was able to furnish some fifty men. Some have since deserted my pennon and others have fallen in battle. Several have died of disease. My little camp is virtually deserted now."

"Look," Sheerkohf said, pointing at a distant peak, "I have only to send a signal from that crest and fifteen thousand men would rise up to follow me. And I am only one of many leaders here. Yet you've come with fifty men to invade my land."

"My fifty were only a small part of the army," Kenneth replied. "And if you have so many followers, where are they? Why do you travel alone?"

"I travel to the camp of your English king," Sheerkohf said. "I hope that when you've finished your business in Engaddi you'll accompany me there and give me your welcome, as you've already indicated you would do."

"Gladly. But what's the nature of your journey?"

"I am physician to Saladin, the sultan of whom you spoke earlier. He's heard that King Richard is ill and, as he admires that monarch greatly, he's sent me to practice my meager skills upon him. I travel alone because it was feared that if I approached with a great entourage, we might be mistaken for an attacking army. My servants travel after me by day and will meet me there, if I've been welcomed."

"I'll vouch for your personal safety," Kenneth said.

"But with no men of your own, can you be sure Richard will honor the word of a lowly knight?"

"The name of a knight and the blood of a gentleman make my word as valid as Richard's," Kenneth said, "and he is duty bound to respect it."

"It must be a strange scene where any man with a suit of armor mixes freely with monarchs."

"Any knight with free blood and brave heart," Kenneth corrected him.

"And do you mix freely with the women of your chiefs?"

"The poorest knight is free to devote his hand and sword to the fairest princess, although he may not do more."

"From the way you described love, you must already have assigned yours to a lady both high and nobly born."

"Yes, most highly, most nobly," he said, an image of Joan appearing before his eyes. "But do not ask me her name."

"What of Richard?" Sheerkohf asked. "We hear much of this English monarch. Are you one of his subjects?"

"On this crusade I'm one of his followers, and it's an honor to serve him in this. And I'm of the same island too. But I am not born his subject."

"Do you have two kings, then, in one island?"

Kenneth nodded his head sadly. "Yes, and often at war. But we can rise together, as you see, for the right cause."

As they rode, the scene had begun to change around them. They were now approaching a range of steep and barren hills, and already the ground beneath their horses' hooves had taken on a more rocky aspect. They would soon have to make camp among these desolate hills.

Kenneth slowed his horse and pointed into the distance. "I think some of those robbers we were talking about are at work," he said.

They could barely make out a distant camp, and surrounding it, a band of Arab horsemen. It was evident that the little camp was under attack, and evident too who was winning the fight.

"That's no ordinary band of robbers," Sheerkohf said, shading his eyes with his hand. "There are too many of them; they're too well dressed and armed."

"So this is how the desert tribes honor Saladin's truce," Kenneth said angrily. "You'll have to make your journey alone, Saracen. My honor demands that I go to join the fracas, even if I fall in the course of it."

"Saladin's honor demands that I join you," Sheerkohf said simply.

"There are many of them and only two of us," Kenneth pointed out. "You'll die in the defense of Christians."

"In the defense of honor. And perhaps we won't die. My name is not unknown here, and it may prove a better weapon in this case than our swords. Come, and leave yours sheathed for now."

For a moment Kenneth hesitated; it was not his practice to ride into battle without his arms at the ready. But he trusted his companion and was willing to submit to his judgment, for the moment at least. It was true enough that their swords would not suffice to save them from death; if Sheerkohf's words could, and could save the camp of Christians too, it was worth the risk.

They rode swiftly toward the distant scene. As they neared, the sounds of battle filled their ears and they could see the blood that had turned the ground to crimson. By the time they reached the site the battle was all but ended, the Arabs cutting down a band of servants who made a last defense with sticks and clubs.

As the two warriors rode near and were detected, a shout went up and a handful of Arabs turned to meet their charge. There was some confusion as they discovered that one of the approaching riders was a Saracen and that neither of them was battle-ready; nonetheless the Arabs came to meet them with swords drawn.

Kenneth's hand went instinctively to the hilt of his sword, but again Sheerkohf cautioned him.

"Wait," he said; he shouted something in Arabic that Kenneth could not understand, although he caught the name of Saladin.

Whatever he shouted it caused some uncertainty, for the Arab horsemen slowed their gait and looked from one to the other with considerable uncertainty. Finally one of them called something back, and there ensued a shouted conversation which was rapidly carried to those Arabs who had overrun the camp. One by one at first, and then with growing haste, they laid down their arms.

To Kenneth's amazement they rode unmolested into the midst of the camp, where the fighting had now ceased; it was too late for most of these travelers. The knights who had defended the camp lay dead upon the ground.

Kenneth heard a feminine scream and looked toward the largest of the tents. A group of Arabs emerged, dragging with them several women; with a start of astonishment Kenneth recognized Richard's queen, Berengaria, and a number of her ladies, all dressed in common clothes.

"It's King Richard's wife," he said to Sheerkohf while he hastily dismounted.

The men who held the ladies, seeing the strangers, had again seized their weapons to fight, but Sheerkohf and their own fellows all began to shout and these Saracens too lowered their weapons as the others had done.

Kenneth approached to where the frightened and bewildered queen stood. She, so recently in the grip of a wild-eyed band of heathens, looked about her now in some confusion. Then her eyes fell upon the welcome sight of a knight approaching; at once she recognized him as the Scottish Knight, the Falcon.

"Noble lady," he said, falling upon one knee, "I've come too late to save your knights, but I thank God I'm in time to save you."

"And I thank Him too, and you," Berengaria said, recovering some of her poise. "Rest assured, Sir Knight, you will remain forever in my prayers for this miracle. I call it that because I was certain our end had come."

The other women too crowded forward to thank him, but someone asked, "Where is Lady Joan?"

At the mention of that name Kenneth's heart skipped a beat and he leapt to his feet. "Was she with you when the attack came?"

"Yes, yes, but—" the queen looked around again in confusion. "I don't know what's happened to her. Maybe in her tent—"

He followed her gaze and saw the tent, a little apart from the others. He went swiftly toward it, drawing his sword, for if she had been dishonored he meant to kill the guilty heathen and the truce be damned.

* * * * * * *

Within the tent Joan stood shuddering before the man who had ripped away her clothes, baring her bosom to his lustful gaze. He seized her in his arms and would have kissed her had she not fought against him. So intense was his desire for this beautiful Englishwoman that neither of them were aware of the change in activity outside the tent. Joan was intent only upon resisting his advances, and at the moment there was only one thing on his mind; thinking his men in full control of the camp he was completely confident that no one would interrupt him.

Suddenly the curtains parted and Kenneth entered the tent. It was dark inside after the glare of the desert sun and for a moment he stood blinking his eyes. In that moment the Arab had whirled about, startled; seeing a knight, he at once seized his sword and leapt forward.

By this time though Kenneth had seen the lady of his dreams, half-naked and being pawed by a heathen. His nostrils flared like those of an enraged beast and before the Arab could strike a single blow, Kenneth's great sword had parted the air and all but severed the man's head from his body.

Joan was too overcome by relief, too much yet in the throes of violent emotion, to think clearly. She reacted with a maiden's logic and flung herself into the arms of the knight who had saved her. For a moment Kenneth, panting with the force of his anger, found himself holding his beloved in his arms, her pale cheek pressed against his rough one. It was more than a man could bear with patience and calm and before he could weigh what he was doing he had covered those trembling lips with his hungry ones.

The kiss lasted only for a moment, but it was enough to be seared forever upon the memory of each of them.

Suddenly she whimpered and struggled against him, her hand pushing at his chest.

"Would you dishonor me as he meant to do?" she asked in a hoarse whisper.

"I killed him to save your honor," he said, looking away from her nakedness, "and I would sooner be killed myself than stain it. Cover yourself, my fair lady, and be assured no one will ever know from me how I found you."

"Then no one need know of that kiss," she said, grabbing a shawl to cover herself. "I think Richard would not be pleased to hear of it."

"For myself I would brave any sword, even Richard's, for the sake of your kiss," he said, smiling at the very thought of such a reward. "But I would not cause you shame."

"Then consider it a reward for your bravery, and our secret," she said. "Now go. I shall follow you out in a moment."

Bending down, he took the body of the dead Arab and, throwing it over his shoulder, left the tent. There was a great squealing and crying among the women at his appearance, and the queen came quickly up to him.

"Lady Joan, is she—?" She hesitated.

"Safe and untouched by this infidel," he said. "She asked for a moment to compose herself; that's all."

Their attention was diverted by the Arabs, who fell upon

the body of their dead chief with much wailing and shouting. Thus distracted, no one was really aware how long it was before Joan appeared, having hastily donned a new tunic. She looked shaken but in control of herself, and no one could say now that she had suffered any dishonor.

"Are you all right?" the queen asked, hurrying up to her.

"Entirely," Joan said, "thanks to this brave knight. A moment more and I shudder to think what might have happened."

Kenneth saw Berengaria look suspiciously from one to the other of them, and at a bruise on Joan's arm. He had no doubt that the queen did not entirely believe them, but she could hardly challenge them so long as they agreed upon their stories.

"How fortunate you were," Berengaria said, and meant it in more ways than one. She had long admired the Scottish knight, who had often been called to her attention for his exploits. A little flirtation with him would have been a most pleasant diversion, and she would have liked to think that those exploits might have been dedicated to her.

But it took no great shrewdness to see the light of love in his eyes when he looked at Joan. She felt a little surge of jealousy; if only it had been she in that tent with the Arab when the knight came to rescue her. She well knew how she would have rewarded him, and she rather thought Joan had, too.

"Very fortunate," she said again.

CHAPTER SEVEN

Nobly Wild, not mad....
—Ode for Ben Johnson

When the little English party, now composed mostly of women, moved on the following morning, it was in the company of Kenneth and Sheerkohf, who promised to see them safely to Engaddi. The queen had expressed some doubt as to trusting themselves to the care of a Saracen, but Kenneth had respectfully vouched for his companion's honor and pointed out to her that it was Sheerkohf and not himself who had saved them from the Arabs.

"But tell me, Saracen, what did you say that stopped the slaughter?" she asked.

Bowing from the waist he said, "I only told them my name, which is not unknown in these lands, and that my followers were but a few miles behind me. And they know I am Saladin's physician, and what Saladin would do to any who broke his truce."

"I wonder what their purpose was?" Kenneth said thoughtfully. "You yourself told me they were no ordinary robbers."

"I think," Joan said, "their purpose was to kidnap us, especially the queen. They knew who we were, at any rate."

"Impossible they could have known," the queen declared. "No one knew we were going on this journey, and we were quite well disguised."

"I doubt if any disguise would successfully hide your identity," Kenneth said. "Your beauty is famed, even here in this wasteland."

Berengaria preened at the compliment. "Do you think so?" she said.

"No, they hadn't even seen her yet," Joan said. "The queen and her ladies retired to her tent when the fighting began. Those men knew who we were before they attacked."

"How could they have known?" Berengaria asked, piqued that Joan hadn't been satisfied with the Scot's suggestion, which seemed to her a very sensible one.

"You yourself told Conrad of Montserrat. Perhaps you let it slip to someone else, or perhaps he did."

"Nonsense, Joan," Berengaria said. "You say that only because you are prejudiced against Conrad. He is a gentleman and a prince, and I am sure no word of our journey escaped his lips, nor did it mine."

"In any case," Kenneth said, "this is a matter that should be laid before King Richard."

"Be assured, brave knight, I will tell my husband the entire story as soon as I see him," Berengaria said. "And now, let us to bed. It has been a wearying day. Tomorrow you and the Saracen shall see us safely to our goal."

Joan was glad to retire to her tent for the night and glad too to know that Sir Kenneth slept outside to guard them from danger.

Yet she did not sleep as easily as she expected, for her thoughts kept turning to another kind of danger that threatened her. Long into the night she lay upon her bed and remembered the feel of Sir Kenneth's kiss. It was like a fire that had been lighted within her, and although the flames had died down, it smoldered still deep inside, waiting to leap into flame again.

It could never be, she told herself. She was a Plantagenet, a princess, a cousin of King Richard of England. However brave a knight he might be, he was still only a knight, who could never ask for her hand. They could never share a second kiss, for she would sacrifice her honor if she encouraged a love whose fulfillment was forbidden to them.

The desert air grew cool. A wild beast howled somewhere in the distance. A scent of smoke drifted to her tent from the fire the knight had lighted outside.

At last she slept.

* * * * * * *

In the morning they rode on. Now they were climbing into the hills; rocky eminences rose around them. In a short while they were following a steep path upward, past deep ravines and dark caverns. The two warriors who were now the party's entire guard were ever alert for the wild beasts and even wilder men who were known to inhabit this wilderness. Yet as they traveled, Kenneth was awed too by the knowledge that this was the very wilderness to which the Savior retired for forty days, to be tempted by the Devil.

Suddenly the Devil himself appeared—or if not the Devil, certainly one of his demons. A tall, thin man dressed in an animal skin suddenly leapt into the path before them, Sheerkohf, who alone was familiar with this terrain, was in the lead, and it was to his horse the apparition ran, seizing his bridle so that the horse stopped unexpectedly, reared up and nearly threw the Saracen to the ground.

"Infidel dog," the stranger cried, "why do you come here to trespass on holy ground?"

In a twinkling Kenneth had drawn his sword and pushed forward on his mount. He raised his weapon and would have struck a mighty blow had not Sheerkohf stayed his arm.

"No, do not strike," the Saracen said, and far from being frightened or alarmed he looked amused. "This is his way of greeting. He knows me well enough; we've had many a quarrel over our religions. And if you killed him you would have wasted your journey and that of our lovely companions, as this is the man you've come to see."

"This?" Kenneth stared in astonishment at the wild man on the path before him. "This the venerable Theodoric? You mock me, Saracen; this is a madman."

"It is a belief in our land that madmen are under the influence of immediate inspiration. When one eye is extinguished the other becomes more keen; when one hand is cut off the other becomes stronger. So, when our reason in human things is destroyed, our heavenly view becomes more perfect."

The wild man cried, "I am Theodoric of Engaddi, the firebrand of the desert, the friend of the Cross. Who are you, Sir Knight?"

"A lowly crusader, who escorts these pious ladies here to pray," Kenneth replied in a more respectful tone. "And I bring with me also a message from the Council of Princes of the Holy Crusade, if you can spare some time with me."

"I will spare the time," Theodoric said. "Follow me, and watch your step; this is wild country."

With that he leapt to a rock with the agility of a mountain goat and began to lead the way to the vast cave in which he dwelt.

* * * * * * *

Kenneth and Sheerkohf were not able to see the ladies again to bid them good-bye, as once they entered the cavern with its rooms carved from the stone they must abide by the holy rules imposed by Theodoric to see no one and to speak to no one.

Having delivered his message and received the hermit's reply, Kenneth was eager to be on his way back to the camp of the crusaders. Sheerkohf had promised that they would intercept the journey of his men and he would send from among them an escort to see the queen and her party safely back to Richard's camp. Having thus discharged his obligations to both king and queen, Kenneth bade good-bye to the holy man, whom he had found to be less mad than he affected, and that same afternoon the two warriors, Christian and Saracen, set out once more.

More familiar now with the trail and in the company of one familiar with the desert, Kenneth made the journey in three days where it had previously taken four. By the third afternoon, they were in sight of the camp of the crusaders.

Nor were they alone, for Sheerkohf had met his army as he said and, assured of entrance to the Christian camp by Kenneth's company, they approached a hundred strong.

They caused no little stir as they entered the camp, several of the men riding the peculiar-looking camels. They rode directly toward Kenneth's own camp, as Sheerkohf indicated that he wished to settle himself before requesting an audience with Richard.

"You'll find no luxury here," Kenneth warned the Saracen as they neared the little circle of huts that was his desert home.

"We are used to sleeping on the sand, with the sky for our tent. A good friend is all we ask in the way of luxury," Sheerkohf told him cheerfully.

At the sound of their approach Elaine came from Kenneth's hut and stared at them. When she recognized Kenneth, a delighted smile brightened her face.

Sheerkohf gave him a curious look. "Is this the object of your high and noble love?" he asked. Even to his Eastern eye, this was certainly not a lady of noble rank.

Kenneth blushed; he had completely forgotten the gypsy girl in the course of his adventures. He regretted now not making it more clear to her that she could not live with him.

"No, this is not she," he said. "This is only a wench who fancies herself in love with me."

Sheerkohf smiled and said, "Does the Scottish knight shatter his love, then, like the diamond he talked about in the desert?"

"Not my love," Kenneth said a bit sharply. "That is given elsewhere. This one is given a small bit of affection, nothing more."

"Something more, I think," Sheerkohf said, chuckling.

Embarrassed and annoyed, Kenneth said, "And does a Saracen never bed a woman just for the pleasure of it?"

Sheerkohf shrugged. "There is little need for me to do so. If I like a woman, I have only to marry her. As there is no limit to the number of wives I can have, there is thus no need to demean either myself or her."

The conversation ended as they reached their destination. Elaine came to help Kenneth from his horse, while Krouba raced out, barking deliriously.

Elaine was obviously happy to see him too, and even her happiness added to his annoyance. A few days ago he had been happy enough to lie with her; since then, though, he had held Joan in his arms, had kissed her lips. How could he be content with this earthy gypsy girl again?

"Where is my servant?" he asked, ignoring her greeting, and giving his attention to his dog.

She looked hurt and puzzled and took a few steps back from him.

"Ill," she said.

"What ails him?"

She shrugged and said, "The same fever that ails the English king."

"You advertised yourself as skilled in medicine," he said. "Haven't you been able to help him?"

"He's been abed since the day after you left, and I think he will soon lie in a deeper bed. This fever is beyond my knowledge."

"But not beyond mine, perhaps," Sheerkohf said. "Come, let's have a look at him. My servants will set up camp for me."

CHAPTER EIGHT

A wise physician, skill'd our wounds to heal,
Is more than armies to the common weal
—The Iliad

The disease that had afflicted Kenneth's servant continued to plague the English monarch. In his tent King Richard remained bedridden, not much better or worse than he had been for days.

While his strength failed him, however, his faculties remained keen and he continued to chafe at his forced inactivity. He plied with questions everyone who entered the tent for any reason: what was happening in the camp? Had there been any news of the Saracens? Any reports of skirmishes?

There were other questions that were reserved for de Multon. He could not ask most visitors, for instance, if there was any word of the queen, as hardly anyone knew she was gone. It had been given out that she too was feeling poorly, and for safety's sake her tent was under quarantine.

But it was with such questions as he asked that he was kept fairly well informed of goings-on in the camp, so that it was not long after Kenneth and Sheerkohf had arrived before Richard had learned that there was a party of Saracens in the Christian camp.

"I want to know what this is all about," he told Sir Thomas. "Go look into it for yourself and report back to me. This may be some message from Saladin, or it may be a Saracen trick."

Sir Thomas went out, bidding the servants in the outer

chamber to keep a sharp eye on their king. He had not gone far from the royal tent, though, when he saw a knight approaching whose grave and haughty demeanor revealed him to be either a Spaniard or a Scot; and when the man had advanced a little closer, he saw that he was the latter, the one known as the Falcon. Sir Thomas had observed him once or twice in battle, fighting well, considering that he was a Scot.

Of all the English nobles who had accompanied King Richard, none was more prejudiced against Scots than Sir Thomas de Multon. His own estates were close to the Border, and he had been engaged in battle with the Scots during most of his life, holding them as he did in little better respect than the Saracens he had come here to fight.

He would, then, have passed by the Scottish knight without a word had not Sir Kenneth moved directly into his path and spoken to him with formal courtesy.

"My Lord of Gilsland, may I speak with you?" he asked.

"With me?" the English lord asked, more than a little surprised. "Well, say your pleasure, but keep it brief. I'm on an errand for the king."

"My business concerns the king, too," Kenneth said, trying not to take offense at the unfriendly manner of the Englishman whose dislike of the Scots was well known among them. "More specifically it concerns his health."

"I did not know you were a leech too, Sir Scot It would be more appropriate if you brought the king of England some wealth."

"The health of King Richard is the wealth and glory of all Christendom. But time is passing. May I see the king?"

"I think not," Sir Thomas said, "unless you can explain your errand more clearly. The sick chamber of the king is not like a Scottish hostelry, open to all who inquire."

"My lord," Sir Kenneth said, bridling, "the Cross we both bear and the importance of my mission make me endure an attitude I am not accustomed to tolerating. I have come here in the company of a Saracen physician, who would like to treat the king."

"A Saracen physician? And who'll assure me he brings remedies and not poison? This is a specialty of doctors here."

"His own life is the guarantee. He offers his head as assurance."

De Multon shrugged. "I've known many a ruffian who valued his life little enough, and I've seen them troop to the gallows as gaily as if the hangman were to be their partner in a dance. It would take more than that to convince me."

"He comes from Saladin, whom even Richard admits is a man of honor. Saladin sends his own doctor, with a retinue and a guard that would suit a sultan, and with fresh fruits and snow for the king. He prays that King Richard will soon be recovered from his fever that they may meet again, with swords in hand."

"And who will vouch for Saladin's honor?" de Multon asked. "One stroke could rid him of his most powerful enemy."

"I myself will vouch for his honor," Kenneth said hotly. "With my honor, my life and my fortune."

"How did you happen to become involved in this matter anyway?" Sir Thomas asked.

"I was on a mission," Kenneth replied.

"To where?"

"To a holy man who lives in the desert."

"And what was the message you carried to him?"

"That I may not tell you, my lord," Kenneth said.

"I am of the secret council of England," Sir Thomas said haughtily.

"I owe no allegiance to England, as you well know," Kenneth said. "I voluntarily followed your king in this way and have served him honorably. But I was sent on this mission by the Council of Princes of the Holy Crusade, not by your king."

Sir Thomas's anger flared at this and he said, "So be it, messenger, but understand, no leech will approach the sickbed of King Richard of England."

He would have turned away then had not Kenneth placed himself again directly in his path. "Good Lord of Gilsland, do you esteem me a gentleman and a good knight?" he asked.

For a moment Sir Thomas hesitated; but for all his prejudice, he was an honest man and he said, "It would be a sin to say otherwise, for I have seen you well and bravely discharge your duties."

"Then," Kenneth said, satisfied with that answer, "let me swear to you, Thomas of Gilsland, as I am a true Scottish knight, and by the blessed cross I wear, that I desire only the safety of Richard Coeur de Lion in recommending this Saracen physician."

The Englishman was struck with the obvious sincerity of this plea, and when he spoke again it was in a kindlier tone. "Tell me, Sir Falcon, in a land where poisoning is as common as cooking, how can you be so sure of the wisdom of bringing this man to the most valuable invalid in Christendom?"

"My lord, I can tell you that this Saracen has treated honorably with me and with a band of Christians whom we found in the desert. And since we have arrived here, he's treated my own servant, who's suffering from the same fever as King Richard. Not two hours ago this same physician administered medicines to him, and at once he fell into a refreshing sleep. I feel confident that he can cure the fever. And that he wants to, I am convinced by the word of Saladin, who has always shown his deep regard for King Richard."

Sir Thomas cast his eyes downward and was thoughtful for a moment. Then he said, "May I see your sick servant?"

It was Kenneth's turn to hesitate for a moment; he blushed slightly before he spoke. The meanness of his quarters was an embarrassment to him, especially with an Englishman.

"Gladly, my lord, but you must remember," he said finally, "that the nobles and knights of Scotland do not feed so high nor sleep so soft as their southern neighbors."

Despite his prejudices, Sir Thomas was not a man to take pleasure in the mortification of a good knight and he was embarrassed by this remark, especially as he himself tended toward luxurious accommodations. He followed silently as Kenneth led him back to the Scottish camp.

Kenneth cast an embarrassed look about him as they approached his little hut; then he entered it, indicating that Sir Thomas should follow him. De Multon too cast around a dubious look before he stooped his lofty crest and entered the hut.

Inside were two beds. One was empty and spread with an antelope's hide. About it were spread pieces of armor and at the head was displayed a crucifix of silver. On the other bed lay the invalid servant, a man past his middle years, lean and harsh-featured. It was obvious at a glance that Sir Kenneth had given the servant his own bed and covered him with his own robes.

In the outward part of the hut Sir Thomas could see a girl, pretty but rudely attired in gypsy clothes, on her knees before a fire, cooking something. Part of an antelope was hanging from one of the props of the hut, and another glance told how it had been caught: a large deerhound, nobler even than those that guarded King Richard's bedside, lay on the ground watching the girl at the fire. As they came in the dog gave a low growl, like distant thunder, but when he saw his master he couched his head and wagged his tail. He made no further sound, as if his noble instincts told him noise was not appropriate to a sick chamber.

The Moorish physician of whom they had spoken sat on a cushion by the sickbed. Sir Thomas could tell little about him in the dim light, except that he sat cross-legged in the Eastern fashion, that he had a black beard and wore a cap and robe of a dark hue. He looked toward them and his piercing eyes could be seen. For a moment there was silence, broken only by the sound of deep and regular breathing on the part of the sick man.

"It's the first he's slept well in five days," Sir Kenneth said, "according to what the girl tells me."

"Something should be done about your gear," Sir Thomas said, placing a friendly hand upon Kenneth's shoulders. He spoke with his usual volume, his big voice booming through the hut. The sick man was disturbed by it.

"Master," he murmured in his sleep, "don't the waters of the

Clyde taste delicious after the brackish waters of Palestine?"

"He's dreaming of home," Kenneth said in a whisper.

The physician rose from the sickbed and, after pausing to check his patient's pulse, came quietly toward the two knights. He signaled them for silence and led them outside to the front of the hut.

"I beg you, good knights, do not disturb my patient's sleep," he said. "To awaken him now means death or the loss of all reason. But come back tomorrow at the hour when the muezzin from his minaret calls the faithful to prayer and I promise you if he has been undisturbed till then, this same man will be able to talk with you briefly without any harm to his health."

The two knights submitted to his instructions, each remembering the old proverb that says the physician is the king in the sick chamber, and the doctor returned inside.

The two remained where they were at the door of the hut for a moment more. Sir Kenneth expected his visitor to say farewell, but de Multon lingered. In the meantime the deerhound came out of the hut after them and coming up to his master thrust his long nose into Kenneth's hand, as if begging for some show of affection. Kenneth gave him a kind word and an affectionate pat and the dog, to show his gratitude and joy, flew off at full speed, galloping about the camp with outstretched tail, darting here and there, but always careful to stay within the boundaries of his master's camp.

After a brief gambol, the dog came back to his master with his usual sober manner, looking a little embarrassed that he should have departed from his usual gravity. The two knights regarded him with pleasure; Kenneth was justly proud of the animal, and Sir Thomas loved the chase and was a good judge of the animal's merits.

"A fine dog," he said. "I think King Richard does not have one that can match him. But in all honor and kindness, I must ask you, haven't you heard the proclamation that no one under the rank of earl is allowed to keep hunting dogs within the king's camp without a royal license? And speaking as Master of the Horse, Sir Kenneth, I do not think the royal license has been issued to you."

Kenneth said sternly, "I answer as a free Scottish knight, who follows England's banner for the present, but I do not remember that I ever subjected myself to England's forest laws, nor will I ever do so. When the trumpet sounds my foot is in my stirrup as quick as any man's, and my lance is not the last laid in the rest. But I do not think King Richard has any license to bar my recreation. My hours of liberty are my own."

"That may be," Sir Thomas said, "but it is not wise to ignore the king's ordinance. So, with your permission, I think I will send you a notice of protection for your friend here."

"I thank you, but within my camp I can protect him myself," Kenneth said coolly. Then, in a different tone he said, "But that is cold thanks for a well-meant kindness. My lord, I thank you most heartily. It is true someone might find Krouba at a disadvantage and do him some harm." He added with a smile, "You have had a look at my poor accommodations, and I think you will understand that Krouba is one of my principal purveyors of food. I hope King Richard will not be like the lion in the fable that went hunting and kept everything he found for himself. I do not think that noble man would begrudge a faithful follower his hour of sport and his bit of game, especially here where food has been hard to come by."

"You do the king justice," Sir Thomas said. "He is not a mean man. But the subject of hunting is a sore one just now with Englishmen."

"We've heard lately that your yeomen have formed a band in the shires of York and Nottingham, under the leadership of a man called Robin Hood. Maybe it would be wiser for King Richard to relax his forest code in England than to try to enforce it in the Holy Land."

"The world has gone mad," Sir Thomas said with a shrug, as if dismissing an unpleasant topic. "I'll leave you now, sir, but with your permission I'll return at vespers tomorrow and speak with this physician. In the meantime will you let me send you some provisions?"

"Again I thank you, but it is not necessary," the Scot said. "Krouba has stocked my larder."

The two men parted much better friends, Sir Thomas taking with him the letters of identification from Saladin, with which the physician had traveled.

CHAPTER NINE

This is the Prince of Leeches; fever, plague,
Cold rheum, and hot podagra, do but look on him,
And quit their grasp upon the tortured sinews.
                                    —Anon.

"It's a strange tale," King Richard said when Sir Thomas had related all this to him. "Would you say this Scot is a true man?"

"That I can't say, my lord," Sir Thomas replied. "I live too close to the Scots to have much faith in their honesty. But this man bears himself like a true man. In conscience I'd have to say that, even if he were a devil as well as a Scot, and as you know in my mind there isn't much difference."

"What about his carriage as a knight?"

"It is Your Majesty's province to notice men's behavior, and I expect you've noticed the manner in which this Knight called the Falcon has borne himself. Men speak well of him."

"And rightly so," the ailing monarch said. "Now that you call him by that name, I have indeed noticed him. One of my reasons for placing myself always in the front of battle is to see how our followers acquit themselves and not, as some men suggest, from a desire to accumulate glory. I know too well that the praise of man is nothing more than a vapor."

Sir Thomas might have been surprised by this statement, so in contradiction to the king's nature, had he not met the royal confessor on his way in; he shrewdly attributed this temporary self-deprecation to the reverend man's words, and thus made no reply to the king's remarks.

"Yes," Richard went on, hardly noticing that his companion had not replied, "I have noticed this knight. My crown would not be worth a fool's bauble if I hadn't. And I'd have rewarded him before now if it weren't that I've also noticed his audacious presumption. He is too proud a man, Sir Thomas, and a bit wild, for a holy knight."

"My lord, I'm afraid I have encouraged his presumption," Sir Thomas said. "Your Majesty will remember that I have the authority to grant certain men of gentle blood the right to keep a hound or two within the camp, and I have sent the Scot such a permission. It would have been a sin, my lord, to have allowed this gentleman's dog to come to any harm."

"Is it such a fine specimen?" Richard asked.

"The most perfect I've ever seen," Sir Thomas said. "One of the noble northern breed, with the thick chest and strong stern, black and brindled on the breast and legs—not white, mind, but just shaded into gray. He's got the swiftness of an antelope and the strength to bring down a bull."

King Richard laughed at the man's enthusiasm; de Multon's love for the animals of the field was well known to him. "Well, if you've given him the license, that's the end of it, but don't get too generous with your permissions. Now, as to this infidel leech, how did the Scot come to meet him?"

"According to his story, the Scot was sent on a mission to the old hermit at Engaddi—"

"On my blood," the king cried, interrupting him, "sent by whom and for what? Who dared send a knight there when our queen was on pilgrimage to the same spot?"

"He was sent by the Council of Princes," Sir Thomas said, "and he declined to tell me for what purpose. But I think, my lord, hardly anyone in the camp knew of the queen's pilgrimage and even the princes may have been ignorant of it."

"Well, it shall be investigated," Richard said grumpily. "So this Scottish knight, this special messenger to the council, met this wandering leech at Engaddi?"

"They met in the desert, apparently, where they had some battle as proof of valor, and finding one another worthy to bear brave men company, they traveled together to Engaddi and back here, as the physician was on his way to you, sent, he says, by Saladin."

"And have you examined his credentials?"

"I gave them to the interpreter, and here are their contents in English."

He gave Richard a scroll, which the king quickly read. It was from Saladin, identifying the bearer as Adonbec el Sheerkohf, Saladin's own doctor, skilled over all others. Saladin wished the English monarch a speedy recovery, so that they might bring their controversy to a more worthy end.

"Enough," Richard said, laying aside the scroll. "I will see this doctor; I will put myself into his hands. And I will repay Saladin for his generosity. We'll meet on the field again, and I will strike him to the earth with my battle ax. Then I'll convert him to the Holy Church and I will baptize him from my own helmet. Bring the doctor here."

"My lord," Sir Thomas said, "remember that the sultan is a pagan and you are his foremost enemy."

"All the more reason for him to be concerned with my health, lest a paltry fever end the quarrel between us in an ignominious fashion. I tell you he loves me as I love him, as a noble adversary, worthy of a man's valor. It would be a sin to doubt his good faith, de Multon."

"That may be, but wouldn't it be wise to wait and see the results of this man's medicines upon Sir Kenneth's servant?"

"Ummm, well spoken. All right, you suspicious mortal, go and watch this cure. I almost wish the man would either cure or kill me; I'm tired of lying here like a tethered ox while horses are stamping and trumpets are sounding."

* * * * * * *

The queen and her entourage returned the following day.

As there was now no need for secrecy, she arrived openly and escorted by a Saracen guard, which aroused no little excitement.

Soon after her arrival, Berengaria, accompanied by her ladies and Joan, came to see the king, where she told him of their adventures and misadventures in the desert.

"It's blood and death," Richard cried when he heard of their near escape. "This is treachery and someone shall pay for it. But you say the Scot and one Saracen quelled the entire horde of heathens?"

"Aye, my lord," Berengaria said. "The Saracen warned them, Sir Kenneth said, of what Saladin would do if they harmed us, and they surrendered their arms and rode away, leaving us in the company of the two knights."

"Was there any dishonor on your person?" Richard asked sharply, his eyes narrowed.

"None, my lord," Berengaria replied. "We had only been seized by the infidels when we were rescued. But," she paused meaningfully and cast a glance in Joan's direction, "I cannot speak of your kinswoman. She had been accosted by an Arab in her tent and was rescued there by the Scot."

All eyes turned toward Joan, who blushed but answered firmly. "My honor was rescued intact by the knight, who no doubt saved our lives as well. He deserves our gratitude rather than insinuations."

"Well spoken," Richard agreed. "And be assured he shall have my gratitude in person. I shall see to it today."

Berengaria knelt before her husband and acknowledged his gratitude for her safe return, but privately she was annoyed that she had not been able to direct Richard's wrath toward Lady Joan for whom she felt just now an unbearable jealousy.

"I will see the archbishop today," she said aloud, "and give thanks for our safe return."

* * * * * * *

At the moment, the Archbishop of Tyre was being visited

by Sir Thomas de Multon, who felt he needed some further advice regarding the Saracen physician. It was to the archbishop he confided his doubts, knowing that Richard both loved and honored the prelate, the same one who had blessed this holy crusade.

The archbishop listened with interest to Sir Thomas's story, especially his confession that he doubted that a Saracen could be skilled in medicine and whether it was in keeping with their holy mission to accept the services of such a man.

"Medicines are useful even though they may come from the basest material," the archbishop said. "And the same is true of mediciners. It is acceptable for men to use pagans and infidels, if they have need of them; thus we rightly make slaves of them, as an example. The early Christians obviously made use of pagans. When the blessed Apostle Paul sailed for Italy, the sailors were no doubt pagans, yet what did he say: 'Nisi hi in navi manserint, vos salvi fieri non potestis—unless these men abide in the ship, ye cannot be saved.' Thus it is perfectly all right to use non-Christians who can be useful—quod erat demonstrandum."

Sir Thomas was particularly moved by the Latin quotations, which he did not understand at all, and his mind was put at ease on that aspect of the problem.

But when he put to the archbishop the idea that the Saracen might take advantage of the opportunity to poison the king, the prelate was less confident. He read and reread the letter the physician had brought with him.

"One cannot help but suspect the possibility of poison," he admitted. "These people are highly skilled in its use and can prepare it so that it does not act on the victim for weeks, giving them plenty of time to escape. Why, it is said they can even impregnate cloth and paper, so that even this letter could be dangerous—here, Sir Thomas, take it quickly, please." So saying, he handed the paper at arm's length to the knight.

"But come," he said, "let us go to the hut of the sick man and see whether this Sheerkohf, as he calls himself, has succeeded in the cure that he boasted of. Then we can consider whether he should be allowed to minister to King Richard. But first, I will forearm myself against infection. I advise you, Sir Thomas, to use a little dried rosemary steeped in vinegar—you see, I too know something of the physician's art."

"Thank you, reverend lordship," Sir Thomas said, "but if I were going to get the fever I would have caught it long ago at my master's bedside."

"Even so," the archbishop said, blushing, as he had avoided King Richard's presence during the time of his illness.

As they approached the wretched hut in which Kenneth and his servant lived, the archbishop said to his companion, "You can see, de Multon, that these Scots care less for their servants than we do for our dogs. This Knight of the Falcon, as he is called, is said to be valiant in battle, and well thought of in peace, and yet he houses his servant in a hovel worse than any dog kennel in England. What can you say of such a man?"

"In this case, that he does well for his servant who lodges him in a home as fine as his own," de Multon said, and without explanation passed into the hut.

The archbishop came after him. Had de Multon looked, he would have seen that the prelate entered the hovel with a certain amount of reluctance, for although he was a man of courage in some respects, he combined that quality with a lively regard for his own well-being. But as he could not avoid this visit, he entered and at once assumed a stately manner intended, he hoped, to impose respect on the man within.

Sir Kenneth was out, and the Saracen physician was seated by the sickbed in the same cross-legged posture he had assumed the day before when Sir Thomas had first seen him. The patient was in deep slumber, and as they entered the doctor felt his pulse carefully. For some minutes the archbishop stood in silence, awaiting some salutation or at least some awareness of his impressive appearance; but Sheerkohf's attention was all for his patient, so that at length the archbishop was forced to speak first, greeting the man in the lingua franca.

"Salaam aleikum, peace be with you," Sheerkohf replied offhandedly, still without turning his head.

"Are you a physician, infidel?" the archbishop asked sharply, miffed at this unenthusiastic reception. "I would like to talk to you about your art."

"If you knew anything of medicine," Sheerkohf said, "you would know that doctors hold no debates in the sickroom of their patient."

From the other chamber the dog growled softly.

"Even the dog could teach you sense," Sheerkohf added. "His instincts teach him to suppress his bark in the sickroom. If you have something to say to me, come outside the hut." He stood and without waiting for a reply, led the way outside.

The Archbishop of Tyre was greatly annoyed at this rude reception; yet there was something about the physician's appearance that was striking and commanding. It was not his height, for he was barely of middle height, while the prelate himself was tall and de Multon was gigantic; and while they were dressed richly, the leech was in coarse garb. Nonetheless, the archbishop did as ordered without argument, following the Saracen outside. There he surveyed the doctor coldly, trying to think how best to open the conversation so that he would again gain the initiative that seemed to have been taken from him. He was struck by the apparent youth of the man before him, and as Sheerkohf still had not spoken, the archbishop demanded, "How old are you?"

"Ordinary men count their years by their wrinkles," Sheerkohf replied, "and sages by their studies. I dare not count myself older than a hundred revolutions of the Hegira."

Sir Thomas, who was not of a fanciful mind, took this to mean that the physician was literally a hundred years old and looked doubtfully at the prelate. The archbishop understood the words better, but as he could think of no suitable reply he settled for shaking his head mysteriously, a gesture he had found useful on more than one ecclesiastical occasion.

He resumed his air of importance and demanded, "What evidence can you show us of your medical skill?"

"You have the word of the mighty Saladin," Sheerkohf replied, "whose word was never falsely given to friend or foe. Would you demand more than that?"

"I would see proof with my own eyes. Without it you will not approach the bed of King Richard."

Sheerkohf shrugged and said, "The praise of the physician is in the health of his patient. Inside the hut there is a man whose blood has been burned by the fever which has filled your camp with skeletons and against which your Christian doctors have been helpless. Look at his fingers and arms, wasted like the claws of the crane. Yesterday morning death had him in his clutches, but I can tell you this, that had the angel of death been on one side of his bed and I on the other, his soul would still be within his body. Do not disturb me with your foolish questions but wait a few minutes more and behold in silent awe the miracle."

Having said this, the physician ignored them for a while and busied himself with his prayers, kneeling with his face turned toward Mecca. The archbishop and the English baron watched him with unveiled contempt and indignation, but neither interrupted his religious duties.

His prayers finished, Sheerkohf stood and walked into the hut, leaving them to follow or not as they chose. They both entered after him and saw him remove a cloth from a small, ornate box. This he put under the sleeper's nose, making him sneeze. At once the patient awoke and, looking wildly about, sat up naked on the couch.

He was a dreadful sight, his bones visible through the spare flesh that yet clung to him, his face wrinkled and ashen; but though his gaze wandered at first, it grew settled and looked not at all feverish. It came to rest on the archbishop and, realizing the importance of his visitor, he attempted feebly to cover himself and asked for his master.

"Do you know us?" Sir Thomas asked.

"Not fully, my lord," the servant replied in a weak voice. "I have been sleeping and I have dreamed much. But I can see that you are a great English lord and that this is a bishop of the church, whose blessing I beg on myself, a poor sinner."

"You have it," the archbishop said, then added, "Benedictio Domini sit vobiscum," and made the sign of the cross in the air, but he did not come any closer to the sickbed.

"You see for yourself," the Saracen said, "his fever has been subdued. He speaks calmly and clearly. His pulse is as steady as your own. Try it for yourself if you will."

The archbishop declined, but Sir Thomas, more determined, did so and satisfied himself that the man's pulse was indeed steady and the fever gone.

"The man is assuredly cured," he said. "This is indeed a miracle, Saracen. Your Reverence, I think I must conduct this man to King Richard's tent."

"Stay," the Saracen said, "let me finish one cure before I begin another. I am not yet finished with this patient."

He went to a chest that sat on the floor and opening it drew out several containers. In a cup he made a mixture of these, measuring each ingredient with painstaking care. It seemed to the onlookers as if some effervescence took place in the cup, but it was gone too quickly to say for sure that it had even been there.

Sheerkohf took the cup to the sick man and said, "Drink this. You will sleep some more and will awaken free of your illness."

"And with this simple draft you think you will cure the king of England?" the archbishop said.

"I have cured one of his humble followers. Are the kings of your land made of different clay?"

"Let us take him to the king when he is ready," Sir Thomas said. "He has shown to my satisfaction that he has the power to restore health. If he doesn't do so with the king, I'll be quick to put him beyond the power of any medicines."

They were about to leave the hut when the sick man called out, "My master. Tell me, where is my master?"

"He is on a distant mission," the prelate replied, "which may detain him for several days."

"What's the point of deceiving the poor fellow?" Sir Thomas said. "Friend, your master is in camp and will see you shortly."

The invalid smiled his thanks and, closing his eyes, fell almost at once into a deep sleep.

When they had gone out the archbishop said, "You were wiser than I, my friend. A pleasing falsehood may be better for a sick man than an unpleasant truth."

"I don't know what you mean," Sir Thomas said. "I wouldn't tell a falsehood to save a dozen men."

A look of alarm passed over the archbishop's face. "Why, you told him just now that his master was returned. It was the Knight of the Falcon of whom you spoke, was it not?"

"And he is back in camp," de Multon said. "I spoke with him yesterday afternoon. This Saracen doctor came with him."

"Holy Mother of God, why didn't you tell me this sooner?" the prelate asked in obvious consternation.

"Didn't I say that the Knight returned in company with the leech—I thought I did," Sir Thomas said in an offhand manner. "But his return was of no great importance. It was the doctor and the cure of King Richard that I was concerned with."

"Important. Yes, it is important," the archbishop said, clenching and unclenching his fists. "But where is he now? God be with me, this may be a grave mistake."

Puzzled by his companion's manner, de Multon looked around and said, "There's the gypsy girl that keeps him company. Probably she can tell us where he's gone."

The girl was summoned and in a petulant tone she gave them to understand that an officer had come to summon the Scottish knight to the royal tent.

At this the archbishop's alarm seemed to grow worse, and at the same time his efforts to keep it to himself increased. He mumbled some words of parting and hurried away, leaving de Multon to look after him with some bewilderment.

CHAPTER TEN

Now change the scene—and let the trumpets sound,
For we must rouse the lion from his lair.
                                        —Old Play

Having welcomed back his queen and taken leave of her, Richard was bored. Between the impatience of the fever and that which was natural to him, he murmured that Sir Thomas was not in attendance and that he had had no further word on the skills of this Saracen leech. He tired the attendants by demanding amusement from them, had recourse to the priest, and even to the harp of his favorite minstrel, but nothing satisfied him.

At length, impelled by curiosity and a desire to learn the truth of the stories he had heard, he sent a messenger commanding the presence of the Knight known as the Falcon in the royal tent.

Sir Kenneth in due time arrived, entering the royal presence as one who was no stranger to such settings. He was scarcely known to the king, who gazed sternly on the knight as he approached the bedside. Sir Kenneth bent his knee briefly, then rose and stood before him in a posture of deference, but not of subservience.

"You are called Sir Kenneth, are you not?" Richard asked; Kenneth replied in the affirmative. "From whom did you have your degree of knighthood?"

"From the sword of William the Lion, King of Scotland," Kenneth answered.

Richard nodded his approval and said, "A weapon worthy of conferring honor. And I think it has been laid on a deserving shoulder. I have seen you bear yourself gallantly and valiantly in battle. I've also seen that you have such presumption that the best reward I could confer on you might be to pardon your transgressions. What do you say to that?"

Kenneth started to reply, then hesitated. He was suddenly conscious of his too-ambitious love for Lady Joan and wondered if his emotions had somehow been read by her kinsman. The keen glance of Coeur de Lion seemed to penetrate his inmost thoughts.

"And yet," the king went on when no reply was forthcoming, "although our commands ought to be obeyed, we can forgive a good soldier a greater offense than the keeping of a single hound."

Watching the Scot's face closely, Richard saw the relief produced by this last remark and smiled inwardly.

"And it please you, my lord," Kenneth said, "Your Majesty must be kind to us poor Scottish knights in this respect. We are far from home, without income and unable to support ourselves as your wealthy nobles do. We can fight the Saracens with more energy if we occasionally eat a piece of venison."

Richard shrugged and said, "It's hardly worth asking my leave anyway, since Sir Thomas de Multon, who does as everyone else around me and pleases himself, has already given you permission. But enough of this. What I want to know of you, Sir Knight, is why and by whose orders you took this recent trip of yours to Engaddi?"

"By order of the Council of Princes of the Holy Crusade."

"And how dared anyone give such orders when I was not acquainted with them? Surely I am not the least important member of that council?"

"And it please Your Highness," Kenneth said, "it was surely not my place to question their orders. I'm a soldier of the cross, serving for the present under Your Majesty's banner, and proud of the right to do so. But I've taken an oath and am bound to obey without question the commands of the council. Like all good Christians I lament that illness has taken you for a time from the council, but as a soldier I must still obey the council's commands or set an evil example."

"Well, you acquit yourself nicely," Richard said grudgingly. "I have to admit the blame rests not with you, but with those who sent you. And when heaven raises me from this accursed bed I'll reckon with them roundly. Now, tell me, what was the substance of your mission?"

"Your Majesty," Kenneth said, "I can only tell you the outward form of my mission; there are others who can tell you more of its purpose and who really should answer your questions."

"Do not split straws with me, Sir Scot," the irritable king snapped. "It does not bode well for your safety."

"My safety, my lord, I cast aside as worthless when I pledged myself to this crusade. I look rather for my immortal welfare."

"By the Holy Mother, you are a brave fellow," Richard said. "Now listen to me. I love the Scottish people, no mind what the chroniclers say. They are hardy and stubborn and, in my opinion, true men for the most part. I deserve some love in return from them too, for I have done voluntarily what arms could not force me or my predecessors to do. I have restored your ancient boundaries and renounced a claim to homage upon the crown of England. I have tried, in short, to make honorable and independent friends of the Scots, while the kings before me only tried to make of you unwilling vassals."

"What you say is just, my lord," Kenneth replied. "And it is because of these things that you have had with you Scottish soldiers who might otherwise be ravaging your borders. It's true that their numbers are few now, but that's because their lives have been freely wasted."

"True, true," Richard said. "And for the good deeds I have done your land, I ask you now to remember that as a principal member of the Christian League I have a right to know what negotiations my confederates are conducting. Now, do me the justice to tell me what I have a right to know and what I will surely know more honestly from you than from some others."

"My lord, asked like that I must tell you the truth; and I believe your motives on this crusade are single-hearted and honest, which is more than I would say for some others. My orders were to see the hermit of Engaddi, a holy man respected and protected by Saladin himself—"

"And propose a continuation of the truce, I suppose," Richard interrupted him.

"No, by Saint Andrew," Kenneth said, "I was to tell him that the council wished to consider with Saladin the establishment of a permanent peace and the withdrawal of all our armies from Palestine."

"Saint George," the king cried in astonishment. "I could never have dreamed them capable of such dishonor. And what were the conditions of this peace?"

"They were not entrusted to me, my lord, I delivered them in a sealed letter to the hermit."

Richard was thoughtful for a moment. Then he asked, "How did you regard this hermit—as a madman, a fool, a traitor or a saint?"

"He does act foolish, sire, but I think that is an act to win the favor and protection of the Saracens, who regard madmen as inspired of heaven. I think his mind is shrewd enough."

"A wise answer," Richard said, laying back on the couch from which he had half-risen. "And what do you think of his policies?"

"I think he despairs of the security of Palestine and of his own salvation now that Richard of England has ceased fighting."

"And so the cowardly policy of this hermit is the same as that of those miserable princes. They forget their knighthood and their faith and are only determined upon retreat. Rather than fighting the Saracen, they would trample a dying ally in their flight."

"My lord, if I may presume," Kenneth said gently, "I think this conversation is aggravating your illness, which is an enemy the Christians fear more than the armies of the infidels."

In his agitation Richard had grown more flushed and his actions were more feverish. His fists were clenched, his eyes flashed; he seemed to suffer bodily pain equal to his mental vexation. But he spoke now as if contemptuous of both.

"You flatter me, Sir Knight, but you will not escape me so easily. I want to know more from you. Tell me, on this journey, you met my royal consort, did you not?"

Kenneth lowered his gaze. "It was my good fortune, Your Majesty, to come upon her party at a time when she had need of a good Christian knight,"

"You were in the company of a Saracen, were you not?"

"I had met up with a Saracen, who traveled subsequently with me. He was with me at that time, yes."

"And how did he conduct himself? Was there any fighting?"

"Not when we arrived, Your Majesty. He spoke with the Arabs in their own tongue, which I understand not at all, and they laid down their arms. He said he had warned them what Saladin would do to them if they harmed the queen."

"Or made some better deal with them, perhaps," Richard murmured, more to himself than to his audience. "But what I want to know from you, Sir Scot, and I charge you tell me everything in truth, was my queen dishonored in this incident?"

"My lord, I will answer as if in the confessional. When I arrived the infidels had laid hands upon her and brought her from her tent to the out-of-doors. But she was not dishonored, and her bearing was every inch that of a queen of England and the wife of King Richard."

"You recognized her at once?"

"Yes, my lord, and knelt before her."

"Good, good, and I am grateful to you, Sir Knight. Richard will find the right time and the right means to show his gratitude. But tell me something more—was there any other lady present whom you recognized?"

Kenneth stood silently, his eyes downcast.

"I ask you," Richard said sternly, raising himself up on one elbow, "if you knew any of the other ladies?"

"My lord, I've seen them all at the tourneys. I might guess at their names."

"And I can make some guesses of my own. Was Lady Joan among the women?"

"She was not among them when I first arrived," Kenneth said.

"Where was she?"

"In her tent, my lord, confronted by the leader of the Arabs."

"Now tell me true, Sir Scot, was my kinswoman dishonored?"

"Your Majesty, the Arab had such intentions, but my sword removed them—and his head—before he could carry them out."

Richard stared coldly at the knight for a moment, but he decided that the answer satisfied him. He had noted, though, the knight's confusion regarding his fair cousin and he thought a word to the wise might suffice on that subject.

"Enough," he said. "But hawk that you are, Sir Kenneth, do not tempt the lion's paw. Remember what I tell you, that to become enamored of the moon would be a foolish act; but to leap from the turret in the wild hope of reaching her sphere is self-destructive madness. Not even the wild falcon flies so high."

At this moment some noise was heard in the outer apartment and the king said, "Very well, you may go now. Find de Multon and tell him to bring the Saracen physician to me. I will trust the word of Saladin. Ha, I wish he would abjure his false faith. With him at my side we would drive the French and Austrian scum from his land and I would think Palestine as well ruled by him as when her kings were appointed by Heaven."

Kenneth retired and in a moment the chamberlain came in to announce that a deputation had come from the council to wait upon His Majesty of England.

"Well, so they acknowledge that I am alive, at least," Richard said. "I'm grateful for that much anyway. Who are the reverend ambassadors?"

"The Grand Master of the Templars and the Marquis of Montserrat."

"I thought perhaps Philip had come," Richard said. "Had he been sick I'd have been to see him long before this. But our fair brother of France doesn't like sickbeds, I suppose. Jocelyn, straighten up the couch; it looks like a stormy sea. Hand me my mirror and pass a comb through my beard and hair—they really do look like a lion's mane just now. And bring me water."

"My lord," the chamberlain said timidly, "the doctors say that cold water may be dangerous to you."

"To the devil with them," Richard snapped. "If they can't cure me, I won't let them torment me either."

He made his preparations, washing his face, combing his hair and straightening his bed and his clothes as best he could.

"Now, then," he said when he was finished, "show the worshipful envoys in. I think they'll see that disease hasn't made Richard negligent."

The envoys were ushered in. The Grand Master of the Templars, Brother Giles Amaury, was a tall, thin man with a war-worn look. He had a penetrating eye and his brow was stamped with a thousand dark intrigues. He was at the head of his order, of whom it was said they sought the advancement of their power even at the cost of the very religion they had been formed to protect; the Knights Templar had been accused of heresy and witchcraft, suspected of secret negotiations with the infidels and in general regarded as men of dark actions. The character of the order and especially of their mysterious master was a riddle at which most men shuddered.

Conrad of Montserrat was less fearsome to see; he was generally regarded as handsome, bold in the field, shrewd in council and gay with the ladies. Those who distrusted him—and they were legion—said that he was also as changeable as a chameleon where his own interests were concerned and ambitious to a sin.

The men exchanged greetings and Conrad explained that they were sent by the Council of Princes to "inquire into the health and well being of our noble ally, the king of England."

"We are glad our health is important to the council," Richard replied. "It must have caused them much pain to suppress their concern for it for fourteen days. No doubt they must have feared aggravating our illness by showing their anxiety."

The marquis's flow of words was checked by this remark and he was thrown into some confusion. But the Grand Master was not easily perturbed and he took up the conversation.

"We come from the council," he said, "to pray in their name that the king of England will not suffer his health to be subject to the tamperings of a heathen physician, rumored to be dispatched by Saladin, until the council has had the opportunity to confirm or remove their suspicions regarding the enterprise."

"Grand Master and most noble marquis," Richard replied, "if it will please you to retire into the adjoining apartment, you will see shortly what answer I give to the council."

Somewhat puzzled by this vague reply, the two envoys retired accordingly to the outer room. When they had waited there some minutes, the Eastern doctor came in accompanied by Sir Kenneth. Sir Thomas had come with them, but he paused for a minute or two to issue some orders outside.

Sheerkohf, noting the dignified appearance and clothing of the two nobles, made his obeisance to them. The Grand Master returned the salutation coolly, but Conrad was noted for his courtesy and he replied with more warmth. There was an awkward pause as Kenneth waited for Sir Thomas before entering the chamber of the king of England.

"Infidel," the Grand Master greeted the doctor, "do you have the courage to practice your art on the person of the appointed leader of the Christian hosts?"

"The sun of Allah shines on the Christian as well as the true believer," Sheerkohf replied, "and as his servant, I cannot make a distinction between them but must practice the art of healing upon all who need me."

"Misbeliever," the Grand Master said sternly, "do you know that should the king die under your care, you will be torn asunder by wild horses?"

"It seems a hard justice," Sheerkohf replied, not without a trace of amusement, "since I can only use human means, and the outcome is already written in the book of light."

"Reverend Grand Master," Conrad interrupted him, "this learned man is perhaps not acquainted with the order of things here. Physician, your wisest course would be to come with us to the Council of Princes of the Holy Crusade, to be examined by such doctors as the council may appoint, concerning the means with which you intend to treat the king. In this fashion you will escape the danger which accompanies your taking such a critical matter upon your sole judgment."

"My lords," Sheerkohf answered, "I understand you, but I am here at the command of my sovereign, Saladin, to heal this Christian king. If I fail, you wear swords that are thirsting for the blood of the faithful, and I will offer my body to them. But I will not argue with one uncircumcised leech upon the virtue of the medicine I use through the grace of Allah, and I beg you not to delay me in my efforts."

"What's this about delay?" Sir Thomas asked, coming into the tent. "There'll be no delay; we've had too much of that already. Lord of Montserrat, Grand Master, I salute you both, but I must now pass into my master's chamber with this physician."

"My lord," the marquis said, "we came on behalf of the council to argue against risking the health of Richard to the tamperings of an Eastern physician."

"Noble marquis," Sir Thomas said bluntly, "I'm not much good with words, or with listening to them, to tell the truth. But I'm ready to believe what my eyes have seen, and I'm satisfied this heathen can cure King Richard, and will try to do so. Time is precious, though, so I give you good evening, gentlemen."

"No," Conrad said, "we have the king's word that we should be present when the physician treated him."

Sir Thomas spoke in a whisper to the chamberlain, who told him that King Richard had said something to that effect.

"Very well," Sir Thomas said aloud, "you're welcome to enter with us. But I must warn you both that if you interfere by action or by threat I'll remove you from the room without respect to your high person. I'm so well convinced of the worth of this man's medicines that if Richard himself were to refuse to take them, I think I would be inclined to force him to do so. Saracen, come with me."

The Grand Master looked darkly upon Sir Thomas but at a glance from the marquis he put on as calm a face as he could manage and followed Sir Thomas and the physician into the king's chamber. Kenneth, not sure what was expected of him, followed these gentlemen in, but out of consciousness of his inferior rank, he stood apart from the others.

Seeing them enter, Richard said, "Ah, a goodly group come to see Richard take a leap in the dark. Noble friends, I greet you again as representatives of the council and tell you now, Richard will soon be among you again or you shall bear to the grave what remains of him. De Multon, you have the thanks of your king whether he lives or dies. There's someone else here, but the fever has weakened my sight—ah, the bold Scot, who would reach the heights without a ladder. You're welcome too, sir. Come, physician, get on with it."

Sheerkohf, who had already been studying the king's condition, now approached and felt his pulse. Then he knelt over the chest he carried with him and, as before, prepared a potion. The Grand Master stood on tiptoe trying to see what the ingredients were, but Sheerkohf carefully kept his actions concealed from them. He brought the potion to the king and offered it to him.

"Wait," Richard said. "You've felt my pulse, let me feel yours. I know a little something of your art too."

The Saracen yielded his hand without pause and Richard's large hand enfolded the slender, dark one.

"His blood is beating as calmly as a baby's," Richard said, releasing the hand. "Men who are going to poison princes are not so at ease. Sir Thomas, whether I live or die after this, release this physician with honor and safety. Saracen, commend us to the noble Saladin. If I die it is surely not his intention. If I live, I will thank him as a warrior would wish to be thanked."

Richard raised himself up on the bed and took the cup in both hands. He turned to the marquis and the Grand Master.

"A toast, gentlemen, to the everlasting honor of the first crusader to strike the gate of Jerusalem with his sword, and to the eternal shame of the man who turns back."

With that he lifted the cup and drained it. Then, handing it back to Sheerkohf, he sank back upon the cushions, closing his eyes wearily.

The doctor silently motioned for the others to leave, and they did so, except Sir Thomas, whom nothing could persuade to leave. In a moment the two of them were alone with the king, who was sleeping already.

CHAPTER ELEVEN

And now I will unclasp a secret book,
And, to your quick conceiving discontent,
I'll read you matter deep and dangerous.
—Henry IV, Part I

The Marquis of Montserrat and the Grand Master of the Knights Templar came out of the royal tent together. The Grand Master was in a bad temper. His chief interest was the advancement of his order, and he had long resented the offhand way the king of England had dealt with them on this crusade. He especially chafed at the rude welcome they had gotten just now from Richard. While others praised that monarch as the crown of Christendom, to Giles Amaury he was more a crown of thorns.

"The evening breeze is cool and refreshing after the heat of the day," Conrad said as they approached the spot where their pages and esquires waited; their horses were there too, prancing impatiently. "Let's dismiss these fellows and walk home through the camp."

The Grand Master nearly declined; he was not a man who sought exercise unnecessarily, but something in Conrad's manner suggested to him that the marquis had more in mind than an evening stroll.

"Very well," he said; they both dismissed their attendants, who went off glad for the free time. The two noblemen began to stroll. The Grand Master observed that, while the marquis did give the impression of a casual stroller, he led them along a route that soon left behind the more inhabited parts of that tent city and took them instead along the broad path which lay between the tents and the outside rim of defense. Here men could talk in privacy, unnoticed except for the sentries they passed.

Conrad spoke for a while about the defense of the camp and other military matters. Giles Amaury answered without any great enthusiasm. This was only a prelude to some other conversation, he was sure, and he would as soon know the real purpose of this stroll.

At length the conversation died, and there was a brief silence between them. Conrad stopped abruptly, turning so that he was face to face with his companion. Giles Amaury stopped too and returned the gaze, but his countenance revealed nothing but polite expectancy.

"Sir Giles," Conrad said, "I want to ask you to lay aside the dark mask you wear over your thoughts and to talk frankly with a friend."

"There are all kinds of masks," Giles said, a half-smile on his lips. "I do not know that mine is any darker than any other man's."

"Quite true," Conrad said. He put a hand to his face in a gesture as if removing a mask. "There, I have put aside my mask and will talk openly. Tell me, from the standpoint of your order's interests, what do you think of the prospects of this crusade?"

"It seems more as though you wish to remove the mask from my thoughts than from yours," the Grand Master said. "But I'll reply with a story: there was a man who complained he hadn't enough rain to keep his crops growing right and he cursed God for not sending him the rain. The following day the rains came and there was a flood. The river overflowed and swept away everything the farmer had."

"And we are like the farmer," Conrad said, nodding his head, "who prayed for a crusade and may now be destroyed in the flood. I wish the ocean had swallowed all but a few of these knights. With the ones who remained we might be in a better position so far as the Latin kingdom in Jerusalem and the

Christian nobles of Palestine. As things were, we could have bent to the wind or persuaded Saladin to grant us peace and protection; he is a tolerant man."

"But this army is too great a threat," the Grand Master said, echoing Conrad's thoughts. "When this war is done we cannot think Saladin will grant any of us territories, and certainly he will not tolerate the military orders such as mine. We've caused him too much grief in this crusade."

"Exactly," Conrad said. "This crusade leads us to grief."

"Unless," Giles said, "it succeeds and Jerusalem becomes a Christian city again."

Conrad shrugged and said, "And what will that gain either of us, friend?"

"Conrad, Marquis of Montserrat might become Conrad, King of Jerusalem."

"That has a certain ring to it, I'll admit. But let me be honest, I don't think it likely. Others—Guy de Lusignan, for instance— have a better claim. I tell you frankly I would rather have real power over my small territory than have a tenuous chance at a throne like that. I hold Tyre now. I may lose that and gain nothing."

The Grand Master smiled warmly and put out his hand for the other to clasp. "You've convinced me of your sincerity," he said. "No doubt others have similar thoughts, but you are the only one who has dared admit that he desires being master of his own small portion more than seeing the kingdom of Jerusalem restored."

"You won't betray my confidence, I trust," Conrad said sharply. "Let me warn you, my tongue will never betray me and my hand is ever ready to defend against any charges. If I should ever be charged, I'll deny everything and meet the man who charges me in combat."

"Nervous words for so bold a man," Giles said. "But rest easy—I swear to you by the Holy Temple that I will keep your confidence like a true friend."

"We are friends," Conrad said with a sly smile. "In the truest sense, because our interests bind us together. If these princes were to recover Jerusalem and restore the kingdom, do you think they would allow either your order or my marquisate to remain as independent as they are? I would be like another vassal, and as for your knights—they would be spreading plasters and dressing sores in the hospitals. You would become men-at-arms again at best."

"We are an order, and have rank, privilege and opulence," the Grand Master said, drawing himself up haughtily.

"Yes, indeed, and men complain of it loudly. You know as well as I do that if the princes were successful in this crusade, their first step would be to curtail the power and independence of your order. You are protected now by the pope and by the need for your valor in the conquest. But give them success, and you will be tossed aside as a broken sword is thrown out after the war."

"You may be right," Giles admitted. "But what is the advantage if the allies withdraw and leave Palestine to Saladin?"

"Better," Conrad said. "I'm going to tell you what no one else knows. I've already been in communication with Saladin. I've suggested to him the advantage, should the crusaders withdraw, of having several provinces maintained with a body of good knights. A number of such armies, joined with his own, could retake Acre for him—it is my understanding he wants that back."

"Fight against other Christians," the Grand Master said thoughtfully. "What have you asked in return?"

"Beirut and Sidon," Conrad said. "To hold as fiefs from him. Of course this would only be temporary, for the sultan's lifetime. But here in the East empires have a way of occurring overnight, almost. Suppose Saladin dies sometime in the future, as he must. Suppose we have meanwhile strengthened our position with a constant stream of the best soldiers from Europe. Uncontrolled by these princes of the crusade, there is nothing we might not achieve. But if they remain here and have their way, we'll be in degradation and dependence."

The Grand Master was thoughtful for a moment, not out of any scruples, but because he did not like to agree too quickly to any proposition; it made men too confident, and he liked others a little uncertain of him.

"You speak wisely," he said finally, "and your thoughts echo my own to a great extent. But we must be cautious in anything we attempt. Some of the princes are wise men; Philip of France, for instance, is no fool."

"So much the better. He was urged into this crusade by the archbishop and King Richard. He's jealous of the English king who is, after all, his natural enemy. Those two countries have always been at sword's point. And Philip has other goals to pursue closer to Paris. No, give Philip any good reason and he will turn his back on a project that is only wasting his resources."

"There is the Austrian archduke," Giles said.

"The archduke's conceit and foolishness will lead him to the same conclusions as Philip's wisdom. The archduke sees himself as poorly treated because everyone around him sings the praises of Richard. Leopold hates and fears Richard, and would be happy to see the English king suffer. Have you ever seen a pack of dogs set on by wolves? There's always one cur that, when he sees the leader caught by a wolf, attacks him from behind rather than coming to his aid. Leopold is like that. All of the princes would be willing to break up this league and return home, except for Richard."

"But that one exception is a force to be reckoned with. If this Saracen heals Richard, he'll soon be taking up the banner again and the others will have to follow him, if only for shame."

"Perhaps," Conrad said, nodding sagely, "but before Richard can be cured, it may be possible that some friction will break out among the princes—between Richard and Philip perhaps, or Richard and Leopold, and Richard may rise from his bed to command nothing more than his own troops."

"You have a will, but it stops too short of the mark," the Grand Master said. He paused and looked suspiciously around, as if to ascertain that there was no one within listening distance.

Then, taking Conrad by the hand, he said in a lowered voice, "Richard cured? Conrad, my friend, our plans would be better served if Richard never rose from his bed."

The marquis started as if his companion had pressed a thorn into his palm. His face grew pale in the moonlight and his knees shook. "What are you saying?" he gasped. "You speak of Richard, King of England."

Giles Amaury looked back at him with an expression of amused contempt. "Do you know what you look like just now, Sir Conrad? Not the wise and brave marquis of Montserrat, not the man who would direct princes and guide empires—no, you look like a novice sorcerer who has by accident conjured from his master's book and now stands in terror before the demon he has raised."

Conrad made an effort to regain his composure. "I'll grant you," he said, "that the road you suggest is the most direct one to our goal. But Blessed Mother, we would become the curse of Christendom; the raggedest beggar would give thanks to God that his name was not Giles Amaury or Conrad of Montserrat."

The Grand Master shrugged; throughout the interview his relaxed composure had not varied and now with no particular passion he said, "If you feel that way, let's forget this entire scene. Let us say we have dreamed, we have spoken in our sleep, and now we are awakened and the dream is gone."

He turned as if to go, but Conrad said, "The dream can never depart."

"It must remain a dream if a man is not bold enough to seize it for reality."

They stood regarding one another steadily for a moment. It was Conrad who broke the silence first. "Well, let me try my way, to create friction between the princes."

The Grand Master said, "As you wish," and strode away.

Conrad remained where he was looking after the man's flowing white cloak until it had disappeared amid the darkness of the Eastern night.

The turn of the conversation had disturbed him more than he

had been willing to show. It was true he was proud and ambitious, in many ways unscrupulous. It was he who had plotted to have the queen kidnapped on her pilgrimage, thinking to use this as a lever to force Richard to a peace.

But he was not cruel by nature. He was a voluptuary, and like most such men had little liking for inflicting pain or witnessing cruelty. Too, he had the best of all consciences—a respect for his own reputation.

It had been his intention to enlist the Grand Master's support in his schemes to undo the crusade—but sly connivance was his style, not murder.

And yet, that was the surest method, as the Grand Master had pointed out.

"I have raised the devil with a vengeance," he said, still staring in the direction where he had seen the last slight movement of the Templar's cloak. "Who would have thought that stern ascetic man would be willing to do more for the advancement of his order than I for my own profit?"

His reverie was interrupted by a voice that suddenly cried in the darkness, "Remember the Holy Sepulcher!"

It was the cry the sentinels used on their watch, and it was echoed now from post to post. Conrad was familiar with the cry and had heard that warning voice time and time again.

But somehow it touched a different nerve this night. It seemed a voice from Heaven, warning him. He glanced around instinctively, as if expecting to see some prophet of old standing nearby. He wished that like the prophet, he could find a ram in a thicket to offer as a substitute for the sacrifice he and Giles were preparing to offer, not to God, but to the devil of their own ambition.

As he glanced about, the breeze caught in the folds of an English banner. It had been placed by Richard himself on a high mound in the center of the camp, so that it rose above the banners of the other princes of the crusade.

Conrad's quick and wily mind grasped at an idea, and at the same time his nervousness and uncertainty dropped away from him. He walked toward his own camp with a more confident step. He would follow his own idea and see if their purpose couldn't be advanced by mild means before they turned to the more desperate ones.

CHAPTER TWELVE

...Envy, that follows on such eminence,
as comes the lyme-hound on the roebuck's trace,
Shall pull them down each one.
—Sir David Lindsay

Leopold, Archduke of Austria, was all in all a weak and vain man. He was tall and handsome to look at, with a ruddy complexion and long, flowing blond hair. But there was a certain clumsiness to his manner; it was not only his movements, which lacked the sort of elegant grace that marked other princes; it was his dress as well which, however costly, never quite seemed to suit him. And it was his attitude toward his underlings, with whom he was sometimes too familiar, and toward himself, which often lacked appropriate dignity for a person of his rank.

He lacked knowledge of the proper way to assert his authority and as a result frequently resorted to quarrels and complaints, and even violence, none of which would have been necessary had he handled the situation properly at the start.

Had these qualities remained invisible to the man himself, he might have been a boor, but a happy one. But he had a dim consciousness of his inabilities as a ruler and leader of men, and this resulted in a dangerous sensitivity; he suspected, sometimes justly, that others were laughing at him and was ever on the alert for some offense.

When he had first announced his intention to join in this crusade, it had been his idea to establish a friendship with

King Richard, whom he had greatly admired, and he had made advances in that direction.

Coeur de Lion, however, had soon sized up the man and found him, to his standards, wanting; he held him in contempt for his lack of valor on the field. More, while Richard was a man of lusty appetites, he knew how to contain them and balanced them with moderation, while Leopold was overindulgent with food and wine, often to the point of drunkenness, or just this side of it.

Richard was not one to hide his feelings, and he made his contempt for the archduke apparent. Hurt and ever suspicious of affront, Leopold responded with a passionate hatred toward the English monarch and a grave distrust of him.

As to the other major prince, Philip of France was anything but a fool. Philip was in actuality Richard's liege lord regarding England's continental domains, and he could not help but resent the dictatorial attitude that Richard assumed toward him; he too had suspicions of Richard, who could be all overpowering.

It had been Philip's policy to fan the fires of discord between Leopold and Richard, keeping Leopold as his own ally against the English monarch.

This was the atmosphere of discord that Conrad of Montserrat had decided to play upon in his scheme to undermine the crusade. The following day at noon he came to visit the archduke, bringing him a gift of some Cyprian wine that had recently come into his possession. He had sent a message in advance, and had received an invitation to join the archduke for his meal. In the meantime, the archduke had prepared what he thought was a splendid meal, but which impressed the marquis as cumbersome.

Sitting at Leopold's table, Conrad's senses were stunned by the Teutonic clamor assaulting him on all sides. The Germans were not so engrossed in the niceties of chivalry nor the prescribed rules of society that, to the English and French, expressed the height of civilization. The Germans wore their beards long, which was out of fashion in Western Europe, and they wore short jerkins of various bright colors, cut and fringed.

Behind the dignitaries at the table stood numerous dependents of all ages and descriptions; these individuals joined freely in the noisy conversation and accepted from their masters the scraps of food from the table, which they ate greedily as they stood behind the company. There were also jesters and minstrels in great numbers, noisier than they were allowed to be in better society. They were allowed to share in the free-flowing wine too, with the result that their license grew as the meal progressed.

It was the sort of scene, Conrad thought, that would have suited a German tavern or a fair better than the tent of a sovereign.

In the midst of it all, Leopold had attempted to impress the marquis with the elegance of his service and his etiquette. He was dressed richly, his mantle trimmed in ermine. He wore poulaines—velvet shoes that ended in elaborate curled points and that, peaks included, measured nearly two feet; they were so cumbersome that they rested upon a silver footstool. He was served by pages of noble blood, who knelt to offer him lavish dishes from rich platters of silver and gold, and he drank his wines from a cup of gold.

Yet it showed the character of the man that, for all his efforts to impress Conrad, Leopold had more conversation with his jester, who stood behind him, than with the marquis. The jester made almost as much noise with his bells and his fool's cap as did the nobles seated at the table.

This individual, leaning over the archduke's shoulder, threw out a stream of remarks that were alternately grave and silly. Leopold laughed or applauded them, while at the same time watching Conrad out of the corner of his eye to see how his distinguished guest was impressed with this show of Austrian wit and eloquence.

Conrad took pains to see that his real feelings were not revealed. He displayed nothing but pleasure with what he heard and saw; he laughed and applauded as enthusiastically as the archduke, and always at the same points.

It was not long before the jester gave Conrad the opening he had been waiting for by referring laughingly to Richard Plantagenet.

"The genesta, or broom plant, from which Richard's name derives, is the symbol of humility," he explained. "In this instance I would say it was misapplied."

"Richard does receive his share of honor," Conrad said to Leopold, choosing his words carefully. "And he is due honor, certainly. But I can't help thinking he sometimes receives the share of others as well. You never hear minstrels sing of anyone else anymore. Why have I never heard a song in praise of our noble entertainer, the royal archduke of Austria, for instance?"

He had hardly spoken when three minstrels stepped forward, each offering to supply the need. The jester motioned two of them away and the third began to sing in German some stanzas which Conrad was unable to follow. Leopold translated for him, with no attempt to match the rhyme.

"Which brave chief," he said, speaking loud to be heard over the minstrel's singing, "should lead the armies of the holy legions? It should be the best of them, the finest horseman, the highest head and tallest feather."

"He means you, royal master," the jester cried, rattling his bells.

Leopold feigned embarrassment and lowered his head, although a great smile spread across his face. "Tush," he said, "I'm only translating what the man says. Let's see, now.... 'Do not ask why Austria, among princes, still raises her banner the highest. You might as well ask why the eagle flies the nearest to Heaven!'"

"The eagle," the jester interjected unnecessarily, "is the emblem of our noble lord, the archduke."

There was a round of applause when the song was finished, which Conrad joined in enthusiastically. But when it had died away and the minstrel had retired, he said, "It's unfortunate the lion has leapt above the eagle."

This remark was greeted with cold silence; the archduke, who had consumed no little amount of wine, turned red in the face.

"Are you jesting, sir?" he asked. "Do you think that Richard of England has any preeminence over the free princes who are, voluntarily I say, his allies in this crusade?"

"I only say what is on display," Conrad remarked nonchalantly. "His banner stands alone on a hill in the center of the camp; to a stranger it would certainly look as if he were the king of all of us."

"And do you endure this implied insult so calmly?" Leopold asked.

"I? I'm only a poor marquis," Conrad said in feigned surprise. "I could hardly be dishonored if such princes as those of Austria and France see no insult in it."

Leopold banged on the table with his fist. "I've told Philip about this," he cried. "I've said we have to protect the lesser princes from this islander. If we don't stand up for your rights, who will? And all he does is put me off."

"Philip is wise and has his reasons," Conrad said. "After all, their relationship is that of lord and vassal, and politics may dictate that he maintain peace between them. As for your reasons for submitting to English mastery, why, no doubt you have them."

"Submit? To English mastery?" Leopold demanded, his voice rising. "I, the archduke of Austria, part of the Holy Roman Empire, submit myself to this petty monarch, this king of half an island, this Norman bastard's grandson?"

"Very well, sire," Conrad said quickly, as if to soothe the troubled waters, "I retract my statement. Let me say only that the Austrian banner submits."

"Never!" Leopold cried, springing to his feet. "I shall show the camp—the whole world—that Austria yields not an inch to the English dogs. Up, my merry men, and follow me. We'll place the Austrian eagle where she will soar above the English lion cubs."

He made for the door of his pavilion and, to a roar of applause and cheering, seized the Austrian banner which stood nearby.

"No, I beg you, my lord," Conrad cried, moving as if to block his path. "Lions have sharp teeth. Surely it would be wiser to bend your knee for the present to this upstart."

"Never, not a moment longer," Leopold shouted. "Eagles have claws. Come, my men." With that he marched in the direction of the mound on which stood the banner of England. His shouting attendants made a noisy procession behind him that roused much of the Christian camp.

Conrad, in the meantime, had drifted away, but not before expressing to several people his regret that Leopold should have chosen this hour and this means to redress any wrongs he might think he had suffered.

* * * * * * *

Despite the illness that had preyed on him for two weeks, the constitution of Richard Coeur de Lion was so strong that, with the aid of Sheerkohf's medicine he was already on his way to recovery. He had slept through the night and the morning, and now was awake. The physician checked his pulse and made an examination of him.

"The fever has left him," he announced to Sir Thomas, who had remained at the king's bedside throughout. "He will not even need a second dose of medicine."

Richard sat up and rubbed his eyes. Although he felt a bit sleepy and still weak he did indeed feel that the fever had left him.

"De Multon, how much money is in the royal coffers?" he asked suddenly.

"Without looking I don't know the exact amount," Sir Thomas replied.

"It doesn't matter," Richard said. "Whatever amount it is, give it to this doctor."

"Great prince," Sheerkohf said, bowing before him, "your

gesture is appreciated, but I do not sell the wisdom Allah has given me. I have been told that the medicine would lose its effectiveness if I took gold for it."

"A doctor refuses money!" Sir Thomas said, astonished. "This is even more remarkable than his being a hundred years old."

"Sir Thomas," Richard said, "you know courage and virtue like few men, but I tell you, this Saracen could set an example to the so-called flowers of knighthood."

"Your gratitude is reward enough for me," Sheerkohf said. "But now let me beg you to again rest, for too early exertion of your strength would not be wise."

"I'm bound to obey you, physician," Richard said, reluctantly lowering himself to the bed again. "But I feel so well just now that I'd face any man's sword without hesitation—even with gladness. But what's that distant racket I hear? De Multon, go see what's happening."

Sir Thomas went out and returned a moment later. Although he had seen clearly what was happening, he remembered the physician's warning to King Richard regarding the exertion of his strength and now Sir Thomas carefully censored his report.

"It's only the Archduke Leopold, making some drunken procession through the camp," he said.

"The fool!" Richard exclaimed contemptuously. "Can't he at least keep his drunken revelry within his own tent, must he make an ass of himself before all Christendom? What do you say, Sir Marquis," he added, addressing Conrad, who had just entered.

"I say I'm happy to see Your Majesty so well recovered," Conrad replied. "And that's a lot to say after having a meal with the archduke. He pours wine most freely."

"You, dining with the Teutonic wineskin?" Richard said. "Well, maybe you can tell us what this nonsense is in the camp?"

Sir Thomas stepped back where the king could not see him and tried to signal to the marquis; Conrad, however, apparently did not see the signals.

"What he is doing," he said, "is showing his wine. And everyone will recognize it for what it is. Still, even drunk, I wouldn't have thought he'd go so far."

"So far as what?" Richard demanded suspiciously.

"Why, he's pulling down the English banner that stands on the mound in the center of camp and putting up the Austrian banner instead."

"What are you saying?" Richard cried in a voice that must have roused the dead.

"No, don't let it upset you," Conrad said, "that a fool should act foolish. Let—"

"No!" Richard shouted, springing from his bed. "Not another word, don't speak to me, Lord Marquis! De Multon, I command you, not a word, he that breathes a word is no friend of Richard Plantagenet—Sheerkohf, silence, I charge you!"

As he threw these commands at them Richard was hastily pulling on his clothes and now he snatched up his great sword and, without any other armor or even calling for his attendants, he rushed from the tent. Conrad, throwing up his hands as if in bewilderment, would have started a conversation with Sir Thomas, but that loyal knight pushed him rudely aside and followed in his king's wake.

In the other apartment he paused long enough to bark an order at one of the royal equerries. "Run to Lord Salisbury's quarters, tell him to get his men together at once and follow me to the mound where the banner is displayed. Tell him the king's fever has left his chest and settled in his head."

The knight was gone before the equerry could get his wits together and ask for a clearer message. He had only half heard, less understood, the orders and now he rushed hastily to the tent of Lord Salisbury, spreading an alarm as he went. But the alarm was so vague that the entire English camp was in an uproar in minutes.

The English lords, roused from the noontime sleep they had adopted as habit, asked one another the cause of the alarm and as quickly supplied numerous answers. Some cried that the

Saracens were attacking, others that the king had died of his fever, while someone said Richard had been assassinated by Leopold of Austria. The officers labored to get their men under command while from every quarter came the cries, "Bows and bills! Bows and bills!" and "Saint George for Merry England!"

In the other camps men were likewise aroused to a confused uproar and began to gather together, arms ready.

Heedless of the tumult thickening behind him, Richard made his way with the utmost haste toward the mound, his dress in disarray and his sword ready. Sir Thomas rushed to keep up with him, outracing even the alarm he had given; they passed most of the quarters, even Sir Thomas's own, before the disturbance had reached them.

By chance Sir Kenneth was outside his hut and was astonished to see the king, whom he thought was still ill, rush by followed by de Multon. It took only a glimpse of Richard's angry face to tell Kenneth that something critical was happening and in a moment he had snatched up his sword and shield and was rushing to catch up to de Multon. There was neither time nor breath for explanation, and Kenneth hurried along, now side by side with Sir Thomas, in Richard's rapid steps.

The area surrounding the mound was crowded with men. There was no little resentment of the English in the camp, and by now the Austrians had been joined by cheering onlookers as well as the merely curious. Leopold, uncertain to the last, had refrained from flinging the English banner down and had contented himself with placing the Austrian banner so that it blew over the English one. This act brought cheers and shouting from the crowd which made the archduke swell with pride despite a certain nervousness he was experiencing.

Suddenly the mob parted before the approaching English king. The summit of the mound was a level platform of land, where Leopold stood with his retinue. Into this circle burst Richard, followed by Sir Thomas and the Scottish knight.

"Who has dared to place this paltry rag beside the banner of England?" Richard demanded in a voice that boomed through the camp and immediately silenced the uproar.

Leopold, for all his foolishness, was not without a certain amount of courage. But he was so astonished by the sight of the English king, whom he thought still on his sickbed, and so awed by Richard's commanding presence, that the question was repeated a second time before he found the voice to answer, with as much confidence as he could assume, "I did. Leopold of Austria."

"Then," Richard said, "Leopold of Austria can see how his banner is regarded by Richard of England."

With that Richard seized the standard, splintered it, and throwing the Austrian banner to the ground, put his foot upon it.

"So much for your banner," he said. "Is there a knight among you who will dare to challenge me?"

His act so stunned the crowd that there was a long moment of silence. But there are no braver men than the Germans, and cries of "I" and "I" began to fill the air, Leopold's among them.

The Earl of Wallenrode, a valiant warrior from the Hungarian frontier, leapt forward. "Countrymen," he cried, "this man's foot stands upon your honor. Down with the pride of England!"

He raised his sword and, before Richard could even turn toward him, struck a blow at the English king.

Only Kenneth's quick movement saved him; he raised his shield and intercepted the blow.

Richard turned his angry gaze upon the earl, and his voice rang out over the uproar that had again erupted. "I've sworn never to strike with my sword a knight of the Holy Cross," he said, "otherwise your life would be ended by now. But you will live to remember Richard Plantagenet."

With that he seized the Hungarian and, with the strength of a bull, flung him backward with such force that the earl toppled from the mound and rolled down its side. At the bottom, knocked unconscious, he lay like a dead man.

This display of Richard's strength did not encourage any others to follow the earl's example. Some of those further back did clash their swords and cry "Down with the English dogs," but those who were nearer began to cry, "Peace, peace, the peace of the holy cross, in God's name."

The three men of the British Isles stood alone surrounded by a veritable army; but while the crowd showed its irresolution Richard glowered around him with an angry eye from which his enemies shrank as from a roaring lion. Sir Thomas and Sir Kenneth stood at his back, and it was apparent they meant to defend him to the last. Moreover, in the distance the Earl of Salisbury could be seen approaching with his men, bows already bended, bills and partisans ready.

It was at this moment of turmoil that Philip of France arrived on the scene. He was duly surprised to see, first, Richard out of his sickbed and second, the two allies confronting one another in a threatening manner.

"Your posture is both threatening and insulting," Philip said, indicating Richard's foot, still on the Austrian banner.

Richard felt embarrassed at being found like this by Philip, whose wisdom he respected almost as much as he disliked his person. He had to admit, now that his temper had cooled a little, that his posture was hardly becoming a monarch or a crusader, and he removed his foot from the trampled flag, assuming a look of some indifference. Leopold, too, tried to assume an attitude of calm; he was mortified that Philip should have found him passively submitting to Richard's insults.

Philip was not unhappy at this opportunity to play matchmaker. He was a clever and sagacious man, more a politician than a warrior. This crusade had not been his choice, but honor and the Church had forced him to accompany Richard. In some milder age Philip might have stood higher in men's eyes than Richard, but the crusade was in itself an unreasonable enterprise and the men who undertook it scorned discretion.

Philip suffered silently the fact that men regarded the adventurous Coeur de Lion more highly than they did himself, and he was not displeased with this chance to show himself in advantageous contrast to his rival.

"What is this quarrel between the allies of the Holy Cross?" he demanded. "The royal king of England and the noble Archduke Leopold—how are these leaders of our crusade—"

"No sermons," Richard interrupted him, further annoyed that Leopold had been given a suggested equality with himself. "This duke, or prince, or what you will, has been insolent, and I have merely shown him the error of his ways."

"Majesty of France," Leopold said, "this English monarch has pulled down my banner and trampled on it."

"Because he had the audacity to display it with mine," Richard said.

"My rank is equal to yours," Leopold said, growing more confident now that Philip was here.

"Tell me that your person is equal to mine," Richard said, "and by Saint George, I'll treat you as I did your embroidered kerchief there—fit only for a man to blow his nose on."

"No, patience, brother of England," Philip said, holding up a hand for silence. "I will explain his error to the archduke. Noble duke, you must not think that in permitting the English standard to occupy this high mound, we other sovereigns acknowledge any inferiority. Even the oriflamme of France, to which in certain respects Richard is subject, stands below the English lions. But as sworn champions of the cross, we and the other princes accorded Richard the rank of our leader and gave him a precedence which in other circumstances would not be granted. I am sure that when Your Royal Highness has thought about this, you will apologize to the English monarch and Richard will in turn express his regret for the insult he has given you."

The archduke, who had counted on Philip's unqualified sympathy, said petulantly, "I'll refer my quarrel to the Council of Princes."

Richard said, "Noble French brother, forgive me, I am a bit weak still with the fever. You know that I'm a man of few words and as to this matter I'll submit to no council or man a matter touching the honor of England. Here is my flag. If any pennon is placed within three butts' length of it—yes, even if it were the oriflamme you were just speaking of—it shall be treated like that dishonored rag on the ground there. And the only satisfaction I'll give anyone on that matter is what I can give in contest if any man wants to challenge me. Or any five men, for that matter, against me alone."

"I haven't come to start new quarrels," Philip said. "We are here under a holy oath. You and I will part as brothers should part, and our only quarrel shall be who is most fierce against the heathens."

"Well spoken, royal brother," Richard said, offering his hand with all the frank good nature that went with his rash but generous character. "And may we soon have the opportunity to test that quarrel."

"Come, noble duke," Philip said, addressing Leopold, "join us in the friendship of this moment." Sullenly the archduke approached and offered Philip his hand.

"I do not linger on matters of foolishness," Richard said, meaning to be accommodating. Leopold refused Richard's hand though, turning his back on him, and walked away, followed by his retinue.

Philip took a more cordial leave; when Richard and his followers were left alone on the mound, he looked after the archduke.

"There is a kind of courage," he said thoughtfully, "that like the firefly only shines at night. By daylight I've no doubt this flag will be safe enough, but nighttime is another matter."

He turned to Kenneth, who had stood by him throughout the incident. "Brave Scot, I owe you for my life perhaps and before that for my queen's life, and I'll pay you richly, all in good time. But for now, there stands England's banner, and her honor. Watch it as a bitch does her pups, defend it against injury or insult. If more than three at once come at you, sound the alarm. Will you take this charge?"

"Gladly," Kenneth said. "I'll go now to arm myself properly and when I return I'll guard it with my life until morning."

The crowds had mostly dispersed by this time, each placing the blame according to his own prejudices—some said that the archduke had started the quarrel, others that Richard had been unbearably haughty.

"Already, you see," the marquis of Montserrat said to Giles Amaury, with whom he had watched the scene from the distance, "subtle forces are at work that will make your violence unnecessary. These scepters and lances are held together with the clumsiest of knots, and I will untie them."

"It would have worked better," the Grand Master said, "if there had been one man among the Austrians brave enough to sever the bonds you speak of with his sword. If you untie a knot it may be tied again, but not when the cord has been cut into pieces."

CHAPTER THIRTEEN

And when a lady's in the case,
You know all other things give place.
   —Fables: *The Hare and Many Friends*

Berengaria, Richard's queen, was both highborn and beautiful. She was slight in form, and that, combined with her youthful features, made her look even younger than her one-and-twenty years. With these she combined a childish behavior, petulant and willful. She was good-humored by nature, and so long as she received what she regarded as her due share of homage and admiration she was friendly and for the most part easy to get along with.

But she was like a despot who, having had certain powers voluntarily granted to her, desired always to extend her influence. Sometimes she simply chose to be out of spirits. She would be afflicted with imaginary illness, and her doctors would have the difficult job of creating names for her ailments. Her ladies must ever invent new games, new gossip, new diversions to cheer her through these unpleasant moods.

More often than not, the diversion these ladies resorted to was to suggest some trick or piece of mischief to be practiced upon someone under the queen's sway. This rarely failed to whet the queen's interest, and she little considered whether such frolics might be beneath her own dignity or painful to the victims. She was like the lioness who sports with others, unaware of the weight of her paws upon them.

For all her shallowness Berengaria very much loved her husband, and likewise very much feared his roughness and his loftiness. Richard enjoyed the company and conversation of his cousin Lady Joan and often spent time talking to her. Berengaria, who knew that she was not Richard's intellectual equal, was not especially pleased with this friendship between the cousins, and although she did not exactly hate Joan for it, the ladies had found that a joke at Joan's expense was a certain way to revive the queen's low spirits.

For a long time their jests were limited to such things as a carelessly arranged head veil, but the ladies had not long remained ignorant of the Scots knight's silent adoration of Lady Joan and her equally furtive response. Sir Kenneth's liveries, his feats of arms, his motto and emblem—all had provided them with occasion for passing jest.

But their pilgrimage to Engaddi, with its harrowing misadventure and a suspected intimacy between Lady Joan and her admirer had provided Berengaria with a delicious safeguard against boredom or ennui.

The stories of the quarrel between Leopold and Richard traveled throughout the Christian camp and were not long in reaching Berengaria's royal tent. She listened with relish to the accounts that described, as the tellers had it, Richard's complete triumph over the archduke.

"And the Scottish knight," she asked, "the same one who rescued us, he's been put to guard the banner?"

"Then I consider the banner well guarded," Joan said.

The queen shot her an annoyed glance; she was not at all pleased with the smug way Joan had been bearing herself since the incident in the desert.

"You mustn't think, just because this knight happened along at the right minute," she said, "that he is a saint and not a man like any other."

"More honorable, I think, than many others," Joan said.

"Fiddle-dee-dee," Berengaria laughed, "a man with weaknesses like any other. I'll warrant he'd defend the banner bravely enough against attack—but there are ways to coax any man from his duty if the coaxer only knows the right one to use."

"I think nothing short of death would coax this knight from the duty your husband has given him tonight," Joan insisted. She rose, preparing to retire for the night.

"Well, if you're as sure as all that, perhaps we can have a little wager," Berengaria said, "say, your ruby ring there against this gold bracelet you've admired so often—that this knight can be coaxed away from his post."

"I don't think it's maidenly to make such a wager," Joan replied, suspicious of the queen's mischievous nature.

"Oh, tush," the queen cried, leaping up. She seized Joan's hand and before she could remove it had slipped the ruby ring from Joan's finger. "Here, Clorise will hold the jewelry. Here's my bracelet."

The ladies had laughed gaily at the queen's remarks, but Joan did not consider the subject a very funny one. She was about to argue further, but on second thought held her tongue. What did it matter anyway? Not for a moment did she believe anyone could lure the Scottish knight from his post and by morning the queen's joke would have gone quite flat.

"It is late," she said, ignoring the subject of the wager altogether. "I shall bid you good night, Your Majesty."

She swept gracefully from the room; for a moment Berengaria looked after her with a look of malice. Then she turned to her ladies.

"Clorise, Amy, Clothilde, come closer; this is what we're going to do."

The ladies talked in whispers for some minutes, with much giggling and muffled squeals of delight.

"Perhaps this," Berengaria said at length, "will bring Lady High-and-Mighty down a bit."

* * * * * * *

It was nearly midnight. The moon floated high and watchful

in the sky. On the ground Kenneth stood guard beside the English banner.

Like the moon, Kenneth's thoughts floated high. He could not but think he had won some favor in the eyes of King Richard, who before now had apparently not distinguished him among the other knights fighting under him. He would not have been placed on a post so important to the king if he were not an object of royal regard.

His love for Lady Joan was the spark that lighted the fire of his military enthusiasm. He knew that his attachment was hopeless under any circumstances, but recent events had at least lessened the distance between himself and Joan. Richard had given him the honor of guarding the English banner, and he was no longer a poor adventurer but someone a princess might at least notice.

He was as far from her level as ever, of course, and their love had no hope of fulfillment; but at least he would not now suffer an unknown fate. If he died—especially if he died on this duty—Richard must weep for him and avenge him, and Joan would weep for him too.

In short, he could no longer die a fool's death.

These were the thoughts that occupied him through the lonely hours since he had taken up his post. Around him every-thing now slept in the cool moonlight and the deep shadows. All about him were the long rows of tents, some glittering in the pale lights, others darkening in the shade. They were as silent and still as the streets of a ghost city.

At his feet lay Krouba, whom he trusted to give him early warning of the approach of any footsteps, however stealthy. His companion seemed to understand the purpose of their vigilance; from time to time the deerhound would look up at the banner, and when the cry of the sentinels could be heard in the distance he would answer them with one low bark, as if to announce that he too was at his post and all was well. When Kenneth happened to pass him as he took turns about the mound, Krouba would lower his head and wag his tail, and when the knight stood motionless and silent, lost in his thoughts, Krouba would thrust a rough muzzle into his hand to solicit a caress.

For most of the evening nothing out of the way had happened. Now, suddenly the dog began to bark furiously and look as if he were going to dash forward into the darkest shadows, but he waited for a command from his master.

"Who goes there?" Kenneth called; he could just make out something moving in the shadows at the foot of the mount, too indistinct to see clearly.

"In the name of Merlin," a hoarse voice called back, "tie up that fanged demon there or I'll come no closer."

"Who are you? And why do you approach here? Be warned, I am here on a life-or-death stance."

He lifted his long lance and held it as if to throw it like a javelin at some object that he could just discern beneath him.

The shadows parted and into the moonlight stepped a dwarf, a stunted and decrepit figure. He came toward the mound like an actor stepping onto the stage.

Kenneth knew him at once as Ectabanus, the dwarf who traveled in the queen's retinue and sometimes amused her. He lowered his lance and gave his dog a command; with a low snarl Krouba returned to lie beside the standard.

The ascent to the mound was laborious for the dwarf, and he was panting furiously when he reached the top. He stood there in a dignified attitude for a moment.

"Sir knight, this is a cold welcome for one of the queen's retinue," he said in a frosty voice.

"Noble Ectabanus," Kenneth replied, willing to humor the poor creature, "forgive me, but I am here as a soldier, a guard, and you failed to identify yourself."

"Your pardon is accepted," Ectabanus said. "So long as you attend me now and accompany me to the presence of those who have sent me for you."

"That I cannot do either. My orders are to remain here until sunrise, and you must excuse me until then."

Kenneth turned and would have resumed his pacing of the

mound, but the dwarf stepped into his path. "You must obey and come with me," he said. "I come from one whose beauty could call the moon down from her flight and pale the luster of the stars."

A wild thought suddenly burst into Kenneth's mind—that Lady Joan might have sent this messenger for him, but at once he rejected it. It was impossible.

Still his voice quavered a little as he said, "Ectabanus, you are making a fool of me. This fair lady you speak of is no more than some dancing girl. Perhaps it is only Elaine, and you've somehow gotten acquainted with her."

"You doubt what I say?" Ectabanus said. "Well, then, look at this and if you know this token, obey or refuse the commands of her who sends me."

Reaching out he placed in Kenneth's hand a ruby ring which the knight recognized at once as one he had seen on Lady Joan's finger. Even if he had been able to ignore the ring, he couldn't ignore the ribbon of pale blue, her favorite color, tied to it. He was struck dumb for a moment.

When at last he recovered his voice he said, "In the name of everything holy, who gave you this? Tell me who sent you here and take care; this is no matter for foolery."

"Foolish knight," Ectabanus said, "do you need to know more than this, that you are honored with the commands of a princess? I will not argue with you further except to command you, in the name of that ring, to follow me to her who sent it. Every second you hesitate here is a treason against her."

"Think, Ectabanus, can this lady know what duty I'm engaged upon tonight? Doesn't she know that my life—more than my life, my honor—depends upon staying here on guard for the rest of the night? Can she wish me to betray that trust, even to see her? This is impossible of such a noble lady. She is making merry with you, or with me."

"Oh, well, keep your trust," the dwarf said, turning to leave. "What difference is it to me whether you are true or false to this lady? Good-bye, sir knight."

"Wait," Kenneth cried, putting a hand on his shoulder, "answer me one question—is the lady who sent you near to here?"

"What does that matter," Ectabanus answered scornfully. "Does faithfulness measure the miles—this close I will be true, but further than this and I am false? But, you poor soul of suspicion, unworthy vassal without courage or truth, since you must know I'll tell you that she's no further than the range of an arrow."

Kenneth's eyes lingered on the ring, as if it would somehow answer the questions in his heart. "Does this lady want my presence for any length of time?"

"Time?" The dwarf spat the word out. "A knight's time is measured in the acts of valor he performs for God and his lady."

"There's truth in that," Kenneth muttered, wavering in his resolution. He was sworn to stay and guard this banner until daybreak; yet he was sworn too to honor Lady Joan, if only in his own heart. Which oath must he honor now?

"This lady," he said aloud, "wants me to perform some task in her name, but could it not wait the few hours until daybreak?"

"She needs you instantly, cowardly knight. We've wasted too much time already. She says, 'The lips that kiss in the desert will know how to meet again.'"

This reminder of their meeting in the desert sent a hundred memories spinning through Kenneth's brain, and convinced him finally that the dwarf's message must be genuine.

"Who am I," he asked himself, "a slave or a subject to King Richard? No, I'm a free knight here on crusade. And whom have I come to honor? Our holy crusade and Lady Joan. What if the Saracens were to attack us now, would I stay here like a vassal and see that King Richard's pride suffered no defeat, or hasten to the battle and fight for the cross? Surely I'd leave the post and fight. And next to the holy cause I owe allegiance to my sworn lady. A duty can be forsworn if a greater duty calls."

"Unworthy knight," Ectabanus cried impatiently, "give me the ring. Give it back, I say."

"Wait a minute more, and I'll go with you," Kenneth said.

He threw his cloak down beside the standard. "Here, Krouba," he commanded the dog, "watch and let no one come near."

Krouba looked into his master's face as if to be sure he understood the order. Then he sat beside the cloak, ears erect, head up, ready to watch. Kenneth would hear him if anything happened; once he had reached the lady he would throw himself at her feet and beg her leave to return to his post until morning.

"Ectabanus," he said to the dwarf, "lead me to her, and hurry."

"Nonsense," Ectabanus said, following in his footsteps, "I can't take such long strides."

Kenneth was impatient now to finish his mission, and not much inclined to waste time or breath arguing. He leaned down and snatched the dwarf from the ground, carrying him easily along in the direction he had indicated despite Ectabanus's cries and entreaties.

"Here, put me down here," Ectabanus cried. "This is the place."

Kenneth saw that they were near the queen's pavilion; he could see the usual small guard of soldiers outside the entrance. He lowered Ectabanus to the ground so that the dwarf could show him what to do next. The dwarf stood panting for a moment. He was both angry and frightened but he was wary of provoking the knight to any further displays of strength. He had found himself lifted as easily and as surely as a rabbit in the claws of a falcon.

Wordlessly he turned and made his way among the labyrinth of tents, signaling Kenneth to follow. He led them around to the back of the pavilion where they were in shadow and concealed from the watching eyes of the guards.

Here Ectabanus lifted a part of the tent and motioned for Kenneth to climb under and enter. For a moment Kenneth hesitated; it seemed immodest, at the least, to enter in such a clandestine manner the tent which was obviously erected here for the privacy of noble ladies.

"It is not for you to question the wishes of your lady,"

Ectabanus whispered.

Obediently Kenneth stooped and crept beneath the cloth enclosure. He was in darkness; a lingering scent of perfume reminded him that this chamber was used to more feminine inhabitants.

"Wait here until I call you," Ectabanus hissed from outside. Then he was gone.

CHAPTER FOURTEEN

You talk of Gaiety and Innocence!
The moment when the fatal fruit was eaten,
They parted ne'er to meet again; and Malice
Has ever since been playmate to light Gaiety,
From the first moment when the smiling infant
Destroys the flower or butterfly he toys with,
To the last chuckle of the dying miser,
Who on his deathbed laughs his last to hear
His wealthy neighbor has become a bankrupt.
                                        —Old Play

For a moment Kenneth stood in the darkness. He was already beginning to wish he hadn't let himself be persuaded to come on this errand; but he had no intention now of leaving without seeing Lady Joan. For her sake he had been seduced from his military post, and he would at least have the pleasure of hearing the reason from her own lips.

In the meantime, however, he could not help being uneasy. It took no great insight to realize what the outcome would be if he were found concealed within the queen's pavilion in the middle of the night.

As his senses became accustomed to the room, he found that he could distinguish the sound of whispered voices coming from the opposite side. He went in that direction. His eyes could now distinguish a faint light on the other side of the canvas wall, so that the shadows of those in that room were cast faintly upon it. He could see several persons and now that he was closer and they less careful to keep their voices low, he found himself over-hearing a conversation in which he figured prominently.

"Call her," a woman's voice said with much giggling. "Ectabanus, for this you'll be made an ambassador."

Kenneth heard the dwarf's shrill voice, but it was so low that he could not make out what was said, only that it provoked still more laughter.

"Royal Madame," another woman's voice said, "how shall we get rid of this insolent knight errant, who can be so easily convinced that highborn ladies have need of his overbearing valor?"

Kenneth's cheeks turned crimson as he realized he had been made a fool of by the queen and her ladies for some purpose of their own. He whirled about and would have made a hasty escape from the tent but the next remarks made him pause.

"No, truly," the queen's own voice said, "our cousin Joan must learn for herself how this knight has conducted himself. She must see that he's failed in his sworn duty. I think, Clorise, she's let this northern adventurer sit closer to her heart than wisdom would warrant."

"But Lady Joan is prudent," someone said.

"Prudent?" the queen said sharply. "That's only her pride and her desire to seem better than the rest of us. No, I mean to teach her a lesson. You know as well as I do that when any of us are at fault Joan is apt to point out our errors, however politely—hush, here she comes."

Another shadow was cast on the wall as someone entered the apartment. It glided slowly along the canvas until it stood with the others.

Despite his bitterness, despite the insult he had suffered, Kenneth felt a gladness in his heart that his lady had had no part in it. His curiosity made him linger to see what would happen next.

In the meantime Joan had said nothing; she had been roused from her sleep to be summoned before the queen and now she found that lady holding a hand over her mouth as if to smother her laughter while her ladies tittered and giggled behind her.

"Your Majesty is certainly in a happy mood," Joan said finally, "though at this hour I would think a sleepy mood more appropriate. I was asleep when I had your command to attend you."

"I won't keep you from your sleep for long, cousin," Berengaria said, composing herself with an effort. "Although I'm afraid you'll sleep less soundly when I tell you you've lost the wager."

Joan sighed and said, "Royal Madame, I think we've dwelt overlong on this joke, which is worn out. I made no bet with you, although perhaps it pleased you to think so."

"Now, now, dear cousin, remember we've just been on a pilgrimage. You bet me your ruby ring against my gold bracelet that this knight of yours could not be seduced from his post."

"Your Majesty, it was you who proposed such a bet and you who took the ring from my finger." Joan suppressed her anger. She did not like her interest in the knight to be an object of merriment. Since their meeting in the desert the very thought of Sir Kenneth was enough to make her heart beat a little faster; yet she knew all too well that it was a hopeless love and one that must be snuffed out from the beginning.

"But, Joan," Amy said, "you have to admit you've expressed favorable opinions of this knight's honor."

"And what if I did?" Joan said sharply. "I spoke of him as men speak of him who've seen him in the field. In a camp such as this one what have women to speak of but men and their deeds?"

"Lady Joan has never forgiven us for saying that her eyes light up when she sees the knight," Clorise said with a smirk.

Joan gave her an icy look and turned back to the queen. "If Your Majesty has no commands for me except to listen to the chaffing of your ladies, I would like your permission to return to my bed."

"Clorise, be quiet," the queen said. "We indulge you, but

don't forget that Lady Joan is the king's cousin. And you, Joan, must you be so stern? We've spent so much time weeping and worrying, surely you won't begrudge us a moment's laughter."

"I think a man's honor is a poor subject for laughter," Joan said.

"Oh, forgive me," Berengaria said, still laughing gaily. "But what great harm is done? A young knight has been coaxed from his post, which no one will bother in his absence, coaxed for the sake of a pretty lady. I must give you credit. Ectabanus could not conjure him away in any name but yours."

"Your Majesty," Joan cried, "you cannot mean what you say? Gracious heaven, with respect for your own honor and mine, say you're joking. Forgive me for thinking for a moment you could be serious."

"Lady Joan regrets that we've won her ring," the queen said, quite displeased at this fervent reaction to her little jest. "You must not begrudge us a little moment of triumph, Joan."

"A triumph? The only triumph will be with Saladin when he hears that the queen of England can make a joke of the reputation of her husband's cousin."

"I'll give you the ring back," Berengaria said. She was becoming quite angry at these accusations that she hadn't acted wisely, especially when she had begun to suspect there was some truth in the charge.

"Madam, I'd give a hundred such rings rather than have my name used to bring a brave knight to disgrace and punishment."

"Ah, now we have the truth," Berengaria said triumphantly. "You're worried about your brave knight's punishment. But you forget who I am, fair cousin. You rate me too low when you suggest that a life could be ruined as a result of some mischief of mine. You're not the only woman who can influence the iron breast of a warrior."

"For the love of the Holy Mother," Joan cried, flinging herself at the queen's feet, "for the love of all the saints, madam, take care what you do. You've only been married to Richard a short time. You don't know him as I do. He'll never pardon a military offense, certainly not one on which his pride and honor hinge. You'll find yourself facing the wild west wind. For God's sake send this knight back to his post before anything happens."

"Arise, dear Joan," Berengaria said graciously, pleased with this little show of humility on the part of one usually so proud. "Everything will work out, I promise you. I'm sorry if my little joke with this knight for whom you care so deeply—oh, don't look so angry at me—if you like I'll agree you don't care for him at all, anything rather than have you look at me like that— all right, this knight with whom you are acquainted, I'll send Ectabanus to dismiss him back to his post and at some time in the future I'll grace him to make up for his trouble. I expect he's lying hidden in some neighboring tent?" She addressed this last to the dwarf, who had watched the scene with malicious delight, for he liked nothing more than to see people in a stew.

"Your Majesty is mistaken," he said, "he's here, just beyond that canvas wall."

"And where he could hear every word we've spoken," Berengaria cried in dismay. She whirled about and slapped the dwarf sharply on his cheek. "Get out, you monster, you perpetrator of evil."

The dwarf fled with a yell caused more by fear than by pain. The queen stared angrily after him, sorry she hadn't administered some still more violent punishment.

After a moment's thought, though, her attention came back to the man beyond the partition. "What can we do?" she asked Joan in a whisper.

"We've little choice, I should say," Joan replied. "We shall have to see this knight and place ourselves at his mercy." She went to the cords that held the curtain in place and began to undo them.

"Good heavens, wait," the queen said, "this is my apartment, we're not dressed, think of our honor—"

Joan gave the cord a yank and the curtain fell, revealing Kenneth standing just beyond, where he had indeed heard every word. He had listened with a mixture of shame and pride in the way Joan had defended him.

It was a warm Eastern night and the ladies, hardly expecting a male visitor, were in rather a state of undress. The queen shrieked and flew from the apartment, followed by her ladies, all in confusion.

Only Joan remained. Although she herself was hardly clothed properly for such a meeting and her hair was disheveled, she felt that someone owed Kenneth some sort of explanation and apology.

Kenneth found himself once again alone with his lady love. It was an intimate moment. Her long yellow hair fell in charming disarray about her shoulders; she was dressed in a flimsy garment of pink silk and a pair of Oriental slippers. About her shoulders she had thrown a scarf. Her face was flushed now with shame and confusion, and he thought she had never looked more desirable. Only a supreme effort of restraint kept him from going to her, seizing her, and once again tasting those ruby lips.

Recovering some semblance of her usual poise, Joan drew her scarf about her more tightly and came a step or two toward him.

"Return to your post, Sir Knight," she said. "Ask no questions. You've been deceived in being brought here."

"I don't need to ask questions," he said with a frank smile. All his humiliation and anger had fallen away at the first glimpse of her.

"You've heard everything, then? It's to be expected. But go, then; every second threatens you with dishonor."

"I am aware of that," he said. "And what do I care what punishment happens to me? I want only one thing and then I'll go out to see if the blood of the heathens won't wash away the stain of dishonor."

"If you hurry back to your post everything may still be all right," she said impatiently. "No one may ever know except us."

"Do you care about my life then?" he asked, his voice low and charged with feeling.

"I value you, yes—that is, I value every crusader—but hurry, please go."

He was almost recompensed for his disgrace by the concern she showed for him. He could no longer restrain his manly desire and with a quick movement he had come to her and taken her in his arms.

"This is what I came for and what I want before I leave," he said.

He kissed her. This time she did not struggle nor push him away. Her arms came up about him and she kissed him back; she did not care that it was wrong, that there was no hope for them. The sight of him standing there, so handsome, so proud, the knowledge of what he had risked for her, erased every other consideration from her mind.

"You came for my sake," she whispered when his lips had released hers.

"I would cross the entire desert for your sake," he said, again kissing her lips, her cheek, her throat. "There is no ocean could keep me from you."

"There is an ocean," she said, shaking her head sadly. "There is a desert that cannot be crossed between us. No, this is no time to argue it. Go, quickly, for my sake as well as your own."

For a moment more he held her to him. Then, obedient to her commands, he released her and took a step back from her. She gave him a tremulous smile and, taking up the lamp the queen had left behind, she turned and hurried from the chamber.

When she was gone, Kenneth went back to the place where he had entered the tent. It would take time to leave the same way he entered and instead he cut the canvas with his sword—let the queen explain that rent in the morning.

Outside the cool night air stirred his senses; it had been a singular and confusing event, but now he must do as Joan had ordered and hurry back to his post. But for now he was entangled in tent ropes and a confusion of tents and he must move cautiously until he found the path; he didn't want to attract the guards in front of the pavilion. A cloud had crossed over the front of the moon, deepening the darkness and making his way all the more difficult.

Suddenly he heard a cry, a fierce, angry bark that he recognized as Krouba's. Hardly had that sound faded than it was followed by another yell, but this one was a cry of agony. It sounded to Kenneth's ears like a death cry.

With a gasp Kenneth leapt over a rope in his way and, finding the path back to the mound, began to run toward it. In a moment or so he had climbed the steep side and was on the mound.

The straggling cloud moved on, freeing the moon. Its pale light revealed the broken standard that had held the English banner. The banner itself was gone, and beside the broken spear lay his faithful dog, dying.

CHAPTER FIFTEEN

...All my long arrear of honour lost,
Heap'd up in youth, and hoarded up for age!
— Don Sebastian

For a moment the torrent of conflicting emotions left Kenneth stunned. There was no trace of the villains who had done these deeds and he did not go looking for them but rather knelt to examine his faithful friend.

The wound appeared mortal, and it shamed Kenneth that he had got it in defending the post his master had been seduced into abandoning. He held the dying animal on his lap; Krouba seemed to forget his own pain in the delight of being with his master. Despite the low groans that expressed his pain, he wagged his tail and licked his master's hand.

Kenneth tried to remove the fragment of lance still in the animal's side. Krouba gave a pained yelp and then, as if afraid he had offended his master, redoubled his licking. The dying creature's devotion to him only enhanced Kenneth's sense of shame and desolation. He had become an object for the contempt of all mankind, and now his only friend was being taken from him. He gave a groan and held the dog close.

A nearby voice intruded upon his grief, saying, "Misfortune is like the period of the cold rain, which is unfriendly but from which is born the flower and the fruit."

Kenneth raised his eyes and saw Sheerkohf, who had approached unheard. Ashamed at being found displaying his grief in a womanish fashion, Kenneth wiped away his tears and returned his attention to the animal in his arms.

"As the poet said, the ox is best suited for the field and the camel is designed for the desert," Sheerkohf said. "Perhaps the hands of a doctor could do more for those wounds than the hand of a knight."

"I'm afraid this patient is beyond your help," Kenneth said.

"Let me examine him."

Kenneth put the dog gently on the ground and stepped back a little so that Sheerkohf could examine the wound, his hands as gentle as if they were treating a human. He produced a little case of instruments from his robe and, using the right pincers, gently withdrew the fragment of weapon from the dog's shoulder. Styptics and bandages were skillfully applied to the gash. Krouba all the while lay motionless and silent, except for an occasional whimper.

"He may live," Sheerkohf said finally, "if you will let me take him to my tent and treat him properly."

"Take him," Kenneth said. "I give him to you freely if he lives. I owe you a reward for curing my servant, and it's all I have to pay with. For myself, after this night I will have no further need of that noble beast."

Sheerkohf clapped his hands together and instantly, as if by magic, two slaves appeared from the shadows. He gave them orders in a tongue unfamiliar to Kenneth and they lifted Krouba between them, handling him gently. The dog's eyes sought his master, but he was too weak to struggle.

"Good-bye," Kenneth whispered, "good-bye, my last and best friend."

As the slaves disappeared with the animal, Kenneth said, "I wish I could exchange places with him."

"He is dying and a dog," Sheerkohf said. "You are alive and a man."

"It is better to be a dog who dies doing his duty than a man who abandons his," Kenneth said. "Leave me, Sheerkohf, my wounds are of the spirit."

"Perhaps I may have a cure for them, if you'll tell me their nature," the Saracen said.

"A cure?" Kenneth said scornfully. "You see that broken standard there? Last night it was used to display the banner of England. I was the appointed guardian of that banner. Morning is now breaking and the banner is gone."

"Yet you are alive," Sheerkohf said, puzzled, "even unharmed. There is no blood on your weapons. But every man who knows you speaks of your valor—ah, you have been seduced from your duty, surely, seduced by one of those pale-eyed houris you Nazarenes honor so highly. It has been so always, since man first fell."

"And if it were so, how can you cure that?"

"Knowledge is power," Sheerkohf said. "Listen to me; your own writings say that when you are persecuted in one city, you should flee to another. Our Mohammed, the Prophet, fled to Medina when he was driven from Mecca."

"What are you saying?"

"That the wise man flees before an approaching storm. Come with me, away from Richard's vengeance, to the camp of Saladin, where you will be safe."

"You are kind, Sheerkohf, but I would rather lie alone in the desert, letting the sun dry my features into dust, than to add dishonor to dishonor."

"You speak foolishly. Saladin is wise and powerful, and I tell you this crusade, as you call it, is doomed anyway. Princes on all sides court him, and there are some whose offers have been treacherous to your cause. Only Richard is regarded by Saladin as honorable and it is for this reason—I tell you this in confidence—that Saladin will marry a Christian maiden, a cousin to King Richard. Her name is Lady Joan—"

"What!" Kenneth cried, starting up. He had been only half listening to the Moslem's remarks but now he was jarred from his apathy. "You are mistaken. No Christian would agree to marry a Christian maiden to a Saracen."

"You are bigoted, Nazarene. In Spain there are many such

marriages without any scandal. And I can tell you that Saladin will grant the English maid full freedom of religion. The truth is, he realizes it is not of much importance what religion females serve. And he has agreed to give her rank over all his wives, so that she will be in effect his true queen, in the English custom. Surely this should make her happy."

"Foolish Saracen, do you think Richard would give his high-born and virtuous cousin to be the chief concubine in Saladin's harem? Any Christian would laugh at such a suggestion."

"Many of them have not—Philip of France, for instance, and Henry of Champagne, have promised to support the proposal. The holy man from Tyre has carried the scheme to Richard and given it his approval. So you see I know what I'm talking about. Come, good friend—for you have been that to me—come with me. I'll give you a message to Saladin and you'll be welcomed as a prince. You'll be useful to him too, since you can give him much good advice, especially how to please a Christian wife. And when the truce is established, Saladin can persuade Richard to give you a pardon, so you won't be abandoning your own people permanently."

"Sheerkohf," Kenneth said, speaking slowly and sternly, "you've saved the life of my servant and of King Richard, and I am grateful for the care you showed my dog. But what you suggest is a cowardly act I regret now giving my animal to a man who could suggest it."

"A gift that is regretted is already recalled," Sheerkohf said. "If the dog recovers, I will return him to you."

Kenneth gave his head a shake as if to throw off the unhappy thoughts that plagued him. "What does it really matter when there's no more than an hour or two of life left to me? Leave me, so that I can conclude my affairs and reconcile myself."

"I go as you command," Sheerkohf said. "To the man who is doomed to fall the mist hides the cliff."

He went slowly, looking back from time to time as if he hoped Kenneth might change his mind and call him back. But no such signal came and at last the physician was gone among the shadows, that were lightening now with the approach of dawn.

But his conversation had had one effect, it had changed Kenneth's emotion from grief to anger at the very thought of Lady Joan wedded to a heathen sultan. This hateful suggestion at least he could deny.

First, though, he must conclude his own affairs. He stood for a moment more staring down at the broken standard on the ground. Then, flinging aside his helmet, he strode toward his own camp.

Elaine was just stirring when he came into the hut. She smiled sleepily at him and opened her arms in a gesture of welcome.

"It's early yet, my lord," she said, "and you've earned a rest."

"What I've earned I'll soon enough go to collect," he said. "I'll tell you good-bye now, pretty one. After today I'll be dead or sold into slavery."

"Dead? Slavery?" Elaine sat up, her eyes wide; but at once her mind, accustomed to dealing with problems and dangers, turned to practical matters. "We must escape," she said, leaping naked from the bed. "I'll collect our things."

"You don't even know what my crime is, and yet you speak of escape," he said sadly.

"Crime, what do I care about crime?" she cried, running to him and flinging her arms about him. "What man hasn't got a crime or two to his credit? You're alive, that's what matters— and maybe we can still escape before the alarm's given."

"That's already been suggested," he said, gently pushing her aside. "And I'll tell you what I told him. I've already stained my honor; I'll not abandon it altogether by escaping my just punishment."

"Your honor!" she spat the words at his back. "What do I care about your honor? What good will that do me? Can I sleep with your honor? Will your honor hunt food for me, or protect me? They speak of honor who have everything else. Honor is a luxury a desperate person can't afford."

"But a resigned one can," Kenneth said. Ignoring her sudden

burst of tears, he went into the other chamber and roused his servant, explaining to him briefly that he was giving him his freedom and giving him as well the few coins he had left in his purse.

Having said his good-byes and done his duty by his old and faithful servant, who wept as he shook his hand, Kenneth set out sadly but determinedly for the pavilion of King Richard.

CHAPTER SIXTEEN

Shame and ruin wait for you.
                                        —Boadicea

It was just the hour of sunrise. Sir Thomas was sleeping beside his master's bed when a slow footstep approaching aroused him from his light sleep. He had just sat up and said, "Who goes there?" when Sir Kenneth entered the tent with a gloomy countenance.

"This is a bold intrusion, sir knight," de Multon said, rising quickly.

"It's all right," Richard said, awakening also. "Sir Kenneth has been at a post assigned by us and has come now to render an account of the night—a general's tent is always open to such a visit."

He rose up on one elbow and turned his shrewd gaze upon the Scot. "Speak, sir. Do you come to tell me of a safe and honorable vigil? I have no doubt the lions on the English banner were enough to guard it without the assistance of a knight as honorable as you."

"As honorable as I once was known but will not be again," Kenneth said. "My watch has been neither safe nor honorable, royal sir. The English banner is gone from the mound."

"What?" Richard cried in a voice of incredulity. "And you're alive to tell me of it? You're not even scratched. Don't stand there silently; tell me the truth. It's foolish to jest like this with a king—but I'll forgive you for that. Is this a jest?"

"I wish to God it were," Kenneth cried. "But it's the truth."

"By all the saints," Richard said, his disbelief becoming a passionate anger; yet he checked it still. "Sir Thomas, go see where the banner was; see if it's gone or not. Perhaps the fever has gotten to this man and affected his brain. This can't be true—this man's courage is too well known; I've seen it myself. This can't be."

But before Sir Thomas could do as ordered one of the king's attendants burst wide-eyed into the chamber.

"The banner's gone," he cried, "and the knight who was guarding it is dead."

"What makes you say he's dead?" Sir Thomas asked.

"He's gone and there's a pool of blood where the standard lay. Surely that—but—here he is."

"Yes, here is the traitor," King Richard said. He leapt to his feet and seized his nearby battle ax. "And you shall see him die like a traitor."

He raised the weapon to strike. Kenneth stood before him as motionless as a statue and nearly as white. His eyes were cast down and his lips moved slightly in prayer as he waited the fatal blow.

For a second or two Richard stood with the ax poised. Then he let the weapon sink toward the ground. "You say there was blood on the ground? Sir Scot, listen to me, I know you were brave, I've seen you fight before. Tell me that you killed two villains defending the banner. Say that you've killed one—that you struck one good blow on my behalf—and then leave the camp with your life and your shame intact."

"My lord," Kenneth said, "I would not have you believe better of me than the truth. There was blood shed in defending your honor but it was the blood of a poor hound who was more faithful than his master. I'm afraid he's died in the effort."

"And a dog has served me better, more honorably, than a Scotsman," Richard roared. Again he raised his ax but this time Sir Thomas stopped him.

"Royal master," he said, "this can't be—not by your own

hand. There have been enough mistakes for one night, among them entrusting your honor to a Scot."

"You've said they were false, Sir Thomas," Richard admitted. "I shouldn't have been such a fool. I forgot how that fox William deceived me regarding this very crusade."

"My lord," Kenneth said, speaking with passion for the first time since he had entered the tent, "heap whatever abuse you will on me, but do not insult the good name of William of Scotland."

"Be still, you shameless fool," Richard said. "You dirty the name of a prince by even speaking it."

He turned his back on the knight, but after a pause he said, "Yet, de Multon, it is puzzling. Could a coward or a traitor have stood like that, without flinching, when my ax was raised to open his head? I might have been preparing to confer knighthood on him for all the fear he showed. If he had given the slightest sign of fear I'd have shattered his head, but how can you strike a man who neither resists nor fears you?"

"Your Majesty," Kenneth said.

"So, you've got your voice back—no doubt to beg forgiveness."

"I do not seek forgiveness of mortal men. I beg for a moment to speak frankly with Your Majesty on a matter which touches your honor."

"Speak," Richard said, expecting some confession regarding the loss of the banner. "What do you want to talk about?"

"Treason," Kenneth said.

"You make a good example of that yourself," Richard said.

"I've heard talk of another treason that will mar your honor more than losing a hundred banners. The Lady Joan—"

"What?" Richard cried, drawing himself up to his full height and fixing a stern gaze on the man before him. "What has she to do with this?"

"With the banner, nothing," Kenneth said, perhaps a little too hotly. "But I've heard talk of a scheme to disgrace the name of Plantagenet by marrying the Lady Joan to Saladin and so buy peace at a price shameful to England and to all Christendom."

Richard's reaction to these comments was violent. The English king was the sort of man who would not serve God if it was the devil who asked him to. He reacted to information and advice according to his feelings for the one who offered it. The mention of Lady Joan had reminded him of Kenneth's presumption, as he considered it, in fixing his affection on one so far above himself. Even when Kenneth had stood honorably in the rolls of chivalry, the king had disapproved of this attachment and in the present state of affairs it was an insult that further roused Richard's fury.

"Speak no more," he roared. "I'll have your tongue pulled out with red-hot tongs, for even mentioning the name of a noble Christian maiden. Infamous traitor, I saw long ago to what height you dared to raise your eyes and although it was insolent, I bore with it. But your lips are blistered with your confession, and with them you dare not name my kinswoman. It's nothing to you if she marries a Saracen. What is it to you, a coward, a traitor, if I choose to ally myself to Saladin?"

"It is little to me," Kenneth said, "as I shall certainly soon be dead. But even though you tear out my tongue I must tell you that if you marry Lady Joan—"

"Do not use her name," Richard commanded, again lifting his ax, "don't even think of her.

Kenneth's spirits, stunned by his misfortune, had begun to recover somewhat, and this command was like a slap in the face.

"I will name her," he said boldly. "By the Holy Cross, I promise you that her name will be the last word on my lips. Use your famous ax on me and see if you can prevent that."

"He drives me mad," Richard said, lowering his ax.

At that moment voices were heard outside and among them could be heard the voice of Queen Berengaria.

"Tell the lady she must wait," the king called to his attendants. In a lower voice he added, "This traitor is not a sight for ladies to see. De Multon, take him out the back way; guard him. He's going to die, but in the proper way and in the proper time.

And let him die in his belt and spurs, knight-like. He may be treacherous, but he is surely bold. And see that he has a holy man to make confession to."

Sir Thomas escorted the prisoner out, to a separate tent where the provost officers disarmed him and put him in fetters.

When Sir Thomas and the Scot were alone, Sir Thomas said, "It is the king's command that you die like a knight."

"I'm grateful," Kenneth said in a low voice. "At least my family won't hear the worst. Oh, my father!"

This last outbreak was so filled with heartache that even the rough heart of Sir Thomas was touched.

"It is the king's pleasure too that you should have a holy man; the hermit from Engaddi is here at the invitation of the council. I'll send him to you whenever you're ready."

"Let it be at once," Kenneth said.

"It's as well," Sir Thomas said. "I think the king would rather it be done soon."

"God's will and the king's be done."

Sir Thomas went slowly toward the exit, but there he paused and looked back. He was touched by the forlorn appearance of this man whom yesterday he would have called a true and valiant knight. He came back on an impulse and put his hand on Kenneth's shoulder.

"Sir Kenneth," he said in as soft a voice as he had, "you are still a young man. You have a father, as I have a son. Yesterday I would have said I would be glad to see my son bear his manhood as well as you bear yours. Is there nothing you can say in your defense?"

"Nothing," Kenneth said sadly. "I abandoned my post. What more needs to be said?"

"God have mercy. I wish to heaven I'd taken that post myself. There's some mystery here, young man. A coward? No, I can swear you aren't. A traitor? No traitor ever died so calmly. You've been lured from your post, by a maiden perhaps. Which of us hasn't succumbed to such persuasion at one time or another? Come, tell me the truth. When his mood is calmed down Richard is merciful, but your silence prevents mercy. Can't you tell me anything more?"

"No, nothing," Kenneth said, turning his face away.

Sir Thomas was not a man of words and having exhausted his powers of persuasion, he rose and left the tent, but he went sadly.

"It is true he's only a Scot," he said to himself as he went, "but I had come to think of him as almost a brother."

CHAPTER SEVENTEEN

Ruin seize thee, ruthless King!
Confusion on thy banners wait.
                    —The Bard

Joan's first act on rising that morning after a restless sleep was to send someone to bring her word of the English banner. When word came back that the standard was broken and the knight disappeared, Joan went straightaway to the queen's apartment.

"Royal madam, rise and go at once to the king's tent," she cried. "You must avert the evil consequences of your mischief."

The queen was frightened in turn by Joan's news. As was her custom, she blamed the folly on her ladies who, she said, had persuaded her to it against her own best judgment. She tried too to calm Joan with a dozen inconsistent arguments.

"I'm sure no harm has been done, however," she said, wringing her hands at the same time. "The knight is just sleeping, I fancy. After all, he had a long night watch. What if he did desert his post, after all, it was only a piece of silk. He's a shabby adventurer, that's my opinion of him. Oh, perhaps he's been put under confinement for a while, but what's the harm in that? I'll soon coax Richard to pardon him. It's just a matter of letting his temper calm down."

She talked on and on like this, trying to still her own fears as well as Joan's. In her heart she now bitterly regretted this folly.

Joan had meantime sent her friend for further information

and now that lady entered the apartment. One look at the horror on her face and Joan would have sunk to the floor in a faint were it not for her strong self-control.

"My lady," she addressed the queen, her voice choking, "there's no time left to talk of saving life. If we act quickly we may just be able to do it."

"He's been brought before the king," her friend said. "He's condemned to die."

There was a confusion of weeping, a shrieking among the ladies, and the queen's voice was the loudest.

"I'll give golden candlesticks to the Church," she cried, kneeling and lifting her eyes heavenward. "I'll build a special chapel back in England."

"Madam, for the love of God," Joan said, seizing the queen's shoulders and attempting to drag her to her feet. "Get up and be your own best saint."

"Indeed, mistress," Clorise said, "Lady Joan is right. Let us go to the king's tent and beg for this poor knight's life."

"I'll go, I'll go at once," the queen said, rising to her feet with their aid. She was trembling frightfully and her ladies, as agitated as herself, were scarcely able to help her get dressed. It was Joan alone who, calm and composed although as pale as death, helped her queen with her toilet.

"Tavern wenches," the queen scolded her ladies, her lovely voice going shrill as it did when she was frightened, "does Joan have to do everything? There, you see, Joan, they're hopeless, I'll never be dressed in time. I'll send for the archbishop and send him as my advocate."

"No, no," Joan cried, "you must go yourself, madam, it was you who did the harm, you must make the amends."

"I'll go, I'll go," Berengaria said, fresh tears streaming from her eyes. "But you know Richard. If he's in his temper I wouldn't dare speak to him, he'd kill me too."

"You must go, noble mistress," Clorise, who knew better than anyone else how to handle her mistress, said. "Not even the enraged lion could look upon someone as lovely as you and retain a trace of anger, let alone a true-love knight like Richard, to whom your slightest wish is a heavenly command."

"Do you think so, Clorise," the queen asked, brightening at once. "Oh, you little know him, the stories I could tell you...but I will go; you're right. Oh, but look—you see, you've dressed me in green, you know he detests that color. Someone get me a blue dress and you, see if you can find that ruby coronet—the one from Cyprus—it's in the steel casket or, let me see, no, it's somewhere else. Amy, my hair looks dreadful, you must—"

"Madam, a man's life is at stake and you prate about dresses and coronets," Joan cried impatiently. "This is beyond human endurance. No," she added, for the queen had lifted her hand imperiously, "no, don't command me to silence. Be at ease, all of you, I'll go to King Richard myself. I am involved, after all, and I must know whether my poor honor is so little valued that my name can be used to seduce a brave knight, bring him to ruin and death and make the name Plantagenet a laughingstock throughout Christendom."

She turned to go while Berengaria looked at her with a stunned look of fear and astonishment, as no one had ever dared before to defy her or upbraid her like this. But as Joan was about to leave she said, in a hoarse voice, "Stop her, someone."

"Yes, you must stop, Joan," Clorise said, holding her arm. "And you, mistress, must go without further delay. If Joan goes to the king alone, he'll be all the more furious, and it will take more than one life to appease him then."

"I'll go," the queen said again, but faintly.

Now the preparations were as quick as anyone could have wished. The queen threw a flowing mantle about herself to hide any deficiencies in her dress and in a moment more had swept from her tent, accompanied by Joan and all her ladies. The guards outside, startled by this sudden expedition, hastened to accompany the women.

Thus they burst into the royal tent, where the chamberlain in the most respectful manner possible, restrained them. They heard the king's command from within as clearly as he did.

"There, you see, Joan," the queen said, flinging her hands out in a gesture of helplessness, "I knew it. He won't even see us; we may as well go back to my apartment and wait the outcome of all this."

"Madam, we will wait," Joan said. "And I pray the wait is not a long one."

From within they heard sounds of movement and voices, although muted. A word or two could be distinguished from time to time—the walls were only canvas. Someone went out and a short time later someone came in. Richard could be heard giving some kind of instructions. The women clearly heard a reference to the royal executioner.

At these words the ladies grew paler and more frightened than ever, and the queen looked as if she would bolt and fly back to her own pavilion. She might have done so had not Joan acted.

"Your Majesty," she said to the queen, "if you do not make your own way, I'll make it for you. Chamberlains, the queen wishes to see King Richard. The wife means to speak with her husband."

"Noble lady, it grieves me to forbid you," the chamberlain said. "But His Majesty is dealing now with matters of life and death."

"And so are we," Joan said. "I will make entrance for Her Majesty, Berengaria, Queen of England."

She stepped past the terrified chamberlain and seizing the curtains, flung them aside. The chamberlain, defeated, stepped helplessly out of the way and Berengaria, entrance made for her, was obliged to enter Richard's chamber.

Richard was half-reclining upon his couch, having just dismissed the royal executioner. Looking angry at having his orders disobeyed, he leapt up, dragging his cloak about him as the queen and her ladies entered and gathered about his couch.

Berengaria came directly to him and flinging herself on her knees threw her arms about his powerful legs, crying, "Mercy, my lord, mercy."

Richard, his anger fading as usual at the sight of his lovely queen, asked, "Foolish woman, what do you want?"

"Pardon, my lord," she said, still without looking up.

"Pardon? Pardon for what?" he asked.

"First, for coming too boldly into your apartment," she said, hesitating.

"You? The sun might as well seek forgiveness for entering his rays into a poor wretch's prison. But I was busy at work unfit for your tender presence. What else do you want?"

"A life," the queen said in a tiny voice; the king's smile vanished. "This poor Scottish knight—"

"Madame, do not speak of him," Richard commanded. "He is condemned to die. The judgment is fixed."

"No, no, my royal liege, I beg you," she cried, turning her tearful face up to him. "It was a silk banner that was lost, nothing more. I'll give you another one, embroidered by my own hand. I'll bedeck it with every pearl I own and with each pearl shall fall a tear of gratefulness for my beloved king and husband."

"Madame, you don't know what you're talking about," Richard said angrily. "England's honor is sullied and you talk about pearls and embroidery. All the pearls of the East couldn't pay for England's honor. The tears of Heaven aren't enough to wash away a stain on my good name. This is what comes of women interfering in man's business. Go back to your apartments, madam, and mind your proper place and business."

"You hear, Joan?" Berengaria said in a whisper. "It's hopeless."

"Even so," Joan said, stepping forward. "My lord, as I am your kinswoman, I beg not for mercy but for justice. And a king's heart must always be open to justice at any place and in any business."

"Cousin, you speak kinglike," Richard said. "And I will listen kinglike, but do not make a request unworthy of either of us."

Joan was a beautiful woman in an entirely different, perhaps less showy way than the queen; but now her concern for the knight, her determination, had given her a glow and a dignity that impressed even Richard to listen to her when his nature and his mood would rather have commanded her to silence.

"My noble cousin," she said, "this knight whose life you mean to take has served the Holy Cross well; we both know that, all the camp knows that. True, he's fallen from his duty, but a trick was played upon him, a message was sent in the name of one—oh, why don't I say it?—was sent to him in my name and with it he was persuaded to leave his post for a moment. What knight might not have been likewise seduced?"

"And you saw this knight?" Richard asked, angrier than ever at this suggestion.

"Yes, my lord, I did," Joan said.

"And where did you do him this honor?"

Joan hesitated, but her only hope of persuading Richard lay in complete honesty. "In Her Majesty's tent," she said.

"Her Majesty's tent?" Richard cried. "Our royal consort? Now, by Saint George, by every one of the saints, this is too insolent. I have overlooked this knight's audacious affection for one so high above him, and I told myself it was as well that one of my blood should shed her light on him as the sun sheds light on the earth far below. But by all the heavens that you, a Plantagenet, should have stooped to an assignation with him, in the middle of the night, in Her Majesty's tent, and you dare to tell me this is the excuse for his desertion. Joan, you shall regret this for the rest of your life in a convent."

"My lord," Joan said proudly, holding her chin still higher, "your greatness perhaps gives you the right to practice tyranny, but I tell you this: my honor is as unstained as yours, perhaps more so, and my lady the queen can confirm that if she chooses. But I am not here to excuse myself or to blame others, only to ask you to give mercy to one whose sin was the result of great temptation, as you yourself must one day beg for mercy from a greater King and for faults perhaps no worse than this."

Richard put a hand to his head and said bitterly, "There must be some mistake. Can this be Joan—Lady Joan, my cousin, the wise and the noble? Or is this some lovesick wench who places the life of her paramour above her own honor? I have half a mind to have the villain's skull brought and fixed as a perpetual ornament in your cell."

"Do so, then," Joan said hotly, "and when anyone asks I shall say it is a relic of a good knight, a gentleman, cruelly and unfairly put to death by a tyrant—"

"A tyrant?" Richard roared.

"—By one who should have better rewarded his chivalry. You call him a villain? He was indeed my lover—the truest sort— who was content to save my life, my honor, and to speed to me when he thought that I had some urgent need of his services. And for these deeds men must die?"

"Oh, silence," Berengaria pleaded in an urgent whisper, plucking at Joan's sleeve. "You're only making him angrier."

"I don't care," Joan said, thrusting her hand away. "The spotless virgin does not fear the raging lion. Work your will, king, on this valiant knight. Joan, the maiden for whom he dies, will know how to honor his memory. And don't speak to me again about political alliances requiring this poor maiden's hand. Had the Scot lived I could not—I would not—have been his bride; our rank was too different. But death bridges the gap and I tell you, from this day forward I am married to the grave."

This tirade had so fired Richard's anger that he might almost have struck his royal cousin had not they been interrupted just then by the appearance of a monk who entered the chamber hastily. His head and person were covered by a long mantle and hood of coarse cloth so that hardly anything could be seen but his hands extending from the sleeves. He rushed directly to the king and flung himself to his knees before him.

"Majesty, noble king," he cried, "I beg you by every holy word and sign to halt this execution."

"By the holy saints," Richard cried, rolling his eyes upward, "the world is conspired to drive me crazy. Every fool, woman and monk in the place is trying to tell me how to run my business. How is it, monk, that this knight is still alive? He should have been dead by now."

"King, I begged the Lord of Gilsland to stay the execution

until I had thrown myself at your royal feet."

"And he did as you asked? That does not please me either. But what is your plea—for Heaven's sake, say it and get it over with."

"My lord, there is a secret here, revealed to me under confession, so that I cannot repeat it. I swear to you by my holy order, by the habit I wear, that this young knight has revealed something which, if I could tell it to you, would at once stay the executioner's ax."

"Holy father," Richard said, "my life and the arms I bear give witness that I love the Church. But if you want to influence me in this matter, you'll have to tell me this secret of which you hint."

"My lord," the holy man said, throwing back his hood to reveal to the ladies the hermit they had gone to Engaddi to pray to, "I am Theodoric of Engaddi, here at the invitation of the Council of Princes. For twenty years I have lived in a miserable cave in the desert, doing penance for a great sin. I am dead to the world, to all who knew and loved me. Do you think then that I would lie to save a life? I tell you this secret exists, but I cannot betray the oath of the confessional."

"Then the knight shall die."

"King, you are setting afoot trouble that you will afterward wish you had stopped."

"Do not threaten me, hermit," Richard commanded haughtily.

"Threaten?" the hermit cried, drawing himself up to his full height, "Threaten? It is God's voice that threatens you, mighty king. You have refused the counsel of the Church and mocked the sacred oath of the confessional. I will warn you again: do not take this life. And good-bye, haughty man, we shall not meet again."

With that he whirled about and left the tent, leaving an ominous silence in his wake.

"And you, ladies," Richard said, "the day is wasting away and still the honor of England goes unavenged. Leave, if you don't want to hear orders displeasing to you."

Joan started to speak but Richard's anger flared, silencing her. "Does no one bend to my wishes in anything?" he roared. "Berengaria, leave. Joan, leave with her—no, don't renew your pleas. I grant you this much: the execution shall be delayed until noon. Now go; I command you."

This last he said with such a look that even Joan's courageous heart faltered. The ladies withdrew, Berengaria and her women forgetting rank and ceremony and huddling together like a flock of wild fowl whom the dogs have just raised.

CHAPTER EIGHTEEN

The Devil watches all opportunities.
—The Old Bachelor.

Conrad of Montserrat felt more than a little pleased with himself. It had been his idea to watch the mound where the English banner stood to see if he couldn't in some way further inflame the passions that the earlier dispute had raised. He had posted servants to observe the banner and its guard throughout the night on the chance—which he regarded as a slim one—that some opportunity might present itself. He could hardly believe his ears when the report had been brought to him that the knight had abandoned his post. Seizing his lance and accompanied by two of his servants, the marquis had rushed to the mound, slain the beast that guarded the banner, and stolen the banner.

That this mischief would have grave reverberations throughout the camp he was fully confident; and now, the following morning, while Berengaria and her female companions were pleading with the king, Conrad was seeking some further opportunity to create mischief. He had come to the Scottish camp on the offhand chance that he might find something useful in Sir Kenneth's hut.

Having seen the knight's servant leave, Conrad entered the hut without hesitation. He was startled, therefore, to find a gypsy girl there, crying as she wrapped her clothes in a bundle.

She turned at the sound of his entrance and, frightened by his noble appearance, gasped and dropped her bundle.

"Who are you?" the marquis demanded, trying to fit this new discovery into the scheme of things.

"Elaine," she said in a choked voice.

"Elaine, hmmm." He looked about the shabby interior of the hut. "You were the Scot's woman, I'll wager."

She nodded her head; regardless of what Kenneth had considered her, that was how she had regarded herself: she was his woman.

She was heartbroken and a little resentful that he had refused to flee with her when there was still time. Now, according to the camp gossip, he was going to die, and what was she to do? There was nothing she could do but take herself back to the other camp and the haphazard existence she thought she had at last escaped.

Oh, she knew the Scot didn't love her, but he liked her well enough, especially in bed, and in time he'd have gotten used to having her around. It could have been such a satisfactory arrangement, if only he hadn't been so foolish and stubborn.

Men! What did they know of life? To them it was all honor and greatness, tourneys to fight in and crusades to march in and always some means to earn a little gold or some food, always adventure and glory and conquest. They never had to struggle to keep a lord and master happy; they didn't have to concern themselves with always looking pretty and being pleasing. They didn't know about waiting alone, never knowing; weaving and knitting and cooking and keeping a brave smile on your face. They didn't know what it was to be the plaything or the victim of every randy male who came along, and when they had robbed you of the only thing of value you had they went their own way and took for a wife a maiden who hadn't yet been robbed of hers. And a girl was left to fight and steal and beg and make the most of what she had left, which was only a pretty face and a desirable figure.

And they called men brave!

Conrad had been thinking fast, and while he didn't yet see how this could work to his advantage, he thought it as well to stir up as much mischief in all quarters as he could.

"I suppose you've heard they're going to kill your knight," he said with brutal directness. This brought a fresh bout of sobbing and howling from the wench.

"Unless," he said in an insinuating voice, "someone can intervene."

"But how?" she cried, forgetting to be awed by his splendid appearance. "I'm only a gypsy girl, what could I do, unless—" Her sobs dwindled off and she looked at him with renewed interest. "Unless, my lord, you could do something."

"Not I," he said, brushing aside the suggestion with a gesture. "But perhaps you could. There is one ambassador who might be able to intervene—I speak of Her Majesty, the Queen of England, Richard's wife and, so everyone says, the love of his life."

Elaine ran to him and dropped on her knees before him. "Oh, speak to her, noble sir," she begged.

"A woman knows better how to reach a woman's heart," he said. "Get up, wench. Let me lead you now to the royal pavilion, and do your begging before her."

Elaine was struck with fresh terror at the thought of facing the English queen, who was known to have a temper and a mischievous outlook. But when she considered the desperateness of her plight she let the marquis pull her to her feet and guide her from the hut.

"But will the queen see me?" she asked, indicating her ragged dress; it was not the best of her two robes, but she hadn't expected to do anything more than return to the other camp, where her best dress was wrapped and put away.

"She will," Conrad said, catching sight of a procession through the camp, "if you run fast enough. There, there's the queen now."

He pointed; Berengaria and her women had just fled Richard's tent at his stern command and were on their way back to the queen's pavilion, attended by her men-at-arms.

"Run, wench, prostrate yourself before her and beg for your

lover's life," Conrad said.

Elaine hesitated and would have let the opportunity go by but Conrad gave her a shove and said, "Go, she is kind, she will listen to a woman's pleas."

Encouraged by his insistence, Elaine ran forward and threw herself directly into the path of the queen. The startled Berengaria, fairly beside herself already, screamed and drew up short. The men-at-arms would have dragged Elaine away but the hapless maid, convinced that her only hope lay in the queen's favor, flung herself headlong in the dirt and clung to the queen's skirts.

"Most Noble Majesty," she cried, "mercy, I beg you, have mercy on a poor gypsy girl."

By now Berengaria, seeing that her assailant was only a helpless and rather filthy girl, had recovered a semblance of poise and said, rather stiffly, "What do you want from me, gypsy?"

"They've arrested my lover," Elaine said, the queen's attitude encouraging her. "I beg you to intercede with the king on his behalf."

For a moment Berengaria was at a loss; she had heard no gossip about anyone being arrested other than the Scot, although perhaps a gypsy wouldn't be mentioned. Then, suddenly a thought occurred to her and her look of puzzlement was replaced by the glimmerings of a smile.

"Who is your lover, pray tell?" she asked sweetly.

"The Scottish knight, Sir Kenneth," Elaine said, sure now that the queen meant to help her. The strange nobleman who had since disappeared had been right after all, and this wasn't half difficult, talking to royalty. Why, the queen might almost have been just anybody.

Joan was standing directly beside the queen and at these last words her body stiffened and her face went white, then crimson.

"You must be mistaken," she said, aware that the eyes of all the ladies had turned toward her and not with sympathy.

"Mistaken? Would I be mistaken about who my lover is?" Elaine demanded, wondering who the lady was who wanted to argue with her. "I live in his hut, in the Scottish camp. See, you can see it right along there, that's his pennon outside, with the hawk on it. They arrested him for something—I don't know— leaving his post, I think they said. But you can help him, Your English Majesty."

"I'm afraid you're mistaken, my dear," Berengaria said, not without a certain note of cheer in her voice. "There's nothing I can do. I've already been to see the king on this very matter and he's refused my pleas."

Elaine looked so crestfallen at this remark that Berengaria, who was not without kindness, added, "I am sorry."

"It's all right, my lady," Elaine murmured. She scrambled to her feet and in a moment she was gone, running along the path through the tents.

CHAPTER NINETEEN

Who's there?—Approach—'tis kindly done—
My learned physician and a friend.
                                    —Sir Eustace Grey

When the ladies had gone, Richard looked after them ruefully. "I'll swear—" he started to say.

"Do not swear," a voice said, and in a moment Sheerkohf had entered the chamber.

"Ah, learned physician," Richard greeted him in a friendlier tone than he had been using. "I hope you've come to ask for some reward for your services."

"Noble king," Sheerkohf said, making a low bow, "when we talked before of your recovery I told you that you owed it not to me but to the Divine Intelligence whose agent I am. I believe that you owe a life, and I would like to ask for one now in return."

"And I'll wager I know which one you want," Richard said. "Is it this Scottish knight?"

"Even so," Sheerkohf replied.

"Heaven above," Richard exclaimed, throwing up his hands and beginning to pace back and forth. "I knew what you wanted as soon as you came in. Here am I, a king and a warrior, who condemns justly one man to death, and the honor of my land, my house, my very queen, is involved, and everyone wants to stop me. My wife, my cousin, a holy man, my doctor, all want to run my affairs for me. Why, I'm fighting an entire army. Whom do you have in the wings to argue with me next?"

At this the king laughed aloud; Richard's temper was of too violent a nature to last for long, and his mood had already begun to change.

Sheerkohf looked on in silence. These mercurial changes in mood and the open display of feeling were foreign to the Eastern mind. But when he saw that Richard was calmer, he spoke again.

"May I understand from your laughter that you have granted this man his life?"

"Take a thousand lives instead as your reward from me. I'll give you a warrant to release that many of your countrymen to you. This man's life can't be worth anything to you and its end is already written."

"The end is already written to all our lives," Sheerkohf said. "But the Great Giver of Life is merciful and does not claim them untimely."

"I am sworn to dispense justice," Richard said.

"You are sworn also to dispense mercy."

"This is overly insolent," Richard said sternly. "I took you for my doctor, not my counselor."

Sheerkohf suddenly laid aside his humble posture and himself assumed a more haughty manner. "So," he said, "this is how the famed prince of England repays one who benefits him? Then I will tell you this, mighty king: that I will denounce you as thankless and ungenerous to every court of Europe and Asia, to Christian and Saracen alike, to knights and their ladies, wherever stories are told. Even the lands who haven't heard of you will hear of your shame!"

"You dare to threaten me, infidel," Richard cried, coming up to him in anger. "Are you tired of living?"

"Strike," Sheerkohf commanded him, baring his breast to the king. "Your own actions will paint you more despicable than my words could ever do."

Richard turned from him in a fury and again paced the tent for a moment, his arms folded over his chest.

"Thankless?" Richard muttered. "Ungenerous? You might as well call me an infidel and a coward. Very well, Sheerkohf, you've chosen your reward. I'd rather you had asked me for all my jewels, but I can't refuse what you ask. Take this Scot. He's yours, your servant, your slave, your what-you-will. I'll have him delivered to you. I ask only one thing, that his voice never fall on my ears again."

"I understand, mighty king," Sheerkohf said, once again assuming his humble attitude, "and to understand is to obey."

"Good," Richard said, writing a warrant on paper for the provost. "Is there anything else I can do for you?"

"It would pleasure me to touch the hand of so great a king," Sheerkohf said, "so that if your humble servant should ever again need to ask a favor of the king of England he may do so freely."

"You've got my hand on that," Richard said, as graciously as if they had never quarreled. "But I hope next time you'll ask something that doesn't go quite so against my grain."

"May your days be multiplied and free from grief," Sheerkohf said, and having accepted Richard's hand, he withdrew from the tent with another deep bow.

Richard looked after him with the air of a man only half-pleased with what had transpired. But he had given his word and the Scot would live. Perhaps it was not such a bad thing at that; there were few enough brave men in the world, that was God's truth.

He was alone only a few minutes before William, the Archbishop of Tyre, was ushered into the tent. When they had exchanged greetings, the archbishop said, "I am here on behalf of the Council of Princes. They have been assembled at the order of Philip of France, to seek what atonement they can make to you on behalf of your honor and your sullied flag."

"And what can they do?" Richard asked scornfully.

"For one, they're willing to replace the English banner on the mound and to condemn the criminal who stole it. Moreover, they will announce a reward to anyone who denounces the villain and will see that he suffers the punishments of the damned for his act."

"And what about Leopold? He started all this, and for all I know he may be the thief."

"Austria has agreed to clear himself by submitting to ordeal."

"And will he agree to trial by combat?"

"This is prohibited by his oath, as it is by yours," the archbishop said, "and the Council of Princes—"

"Will not fight the Saracens," Richard interrupted, "nor anyone else. But enough, I submit, there's nothing to be gained from the archduke and I let him go. But I will have him perjure himself. I insist on the ordeal. Let him grasp the red-hot globe of iron and you'll hear his clumsy fingers hiss as liars' fingers do. Or let him try to swallow the consecrated bread—he'll choke to death on it, mark my words."

"So be it," the prelate said. "And now, my noble friend, I am to ask you to accompany me to the council, so these matters can be resolved and so that we may explain the military and political business that has occurred while you were ill."

Richard fixed a stern eye on the churchman. "And is the purport of this discussion to be a truce with the Saracens?"

The archbishop averted his eyes briefly, then raised them to meet Richard's. "It is. It is our belief that there is no further hope of gaining back the Holy Sepulcher."

"On what intelligence, unknown to me, do you base this belief?" Richard asked. Although the announcement was a disappointment to him it was no surprise.

The archbishop explained briefly that Saladin, according to their reports, was now assembling all the force of his hundreds of tribes; even were the Christian host united in their purpose, they would be vastly outnumbered.

"And the European monarchs are far from united," the prelate said. "Many have become disgusted with the various motives of the others. Many have abandoned the crusade already and others do so each week. And lastly Philip of France has declared his intentions of returning to Europe. The earl of Champagne, who leads one of Philip's largest contingents, is doing the same, and it can hardly be surprising that Leopold of Austria is following suit."

"I hadn't realized my stock had fallen so low," Richard said sadly. "Will no one remain?"

"You'll be left with your own armies and whatever volunteers may join themselves to you—and with the perhaps doubtful aid of Conrad of Montserrat and the Knights Templar."

Richard was too much a military man not to see the grimness of the situation and now, having given vent earlier to his temper, he sat calmly and gloomily listening to the archbishop's arguments, that it was impossible to carry on the crusade without his allies. He did not even interrupt when William hinted that Richard's temper had been one factor in discouraging the princes.

"I admit my guilt, reverend father," Richard said with a gloomy smile. "But isn't this penance hard for my frailties of temper! For one or two outbursts I should see before me the glory to God, lost. But no, it shall not be. By Saint George I will carry the Cross to Jerusalem."

"The Cross can be carried to Jerusalem," the archbishop said, "without shedding any more blood."

"You speak of compromise?"

"There is glory enough in having compelled Saladin to restore the Holy Sepulcher and open the Holy Land to pilgrims. And there is even talk that he might bestow on Richard the title of King Guardian of Jerusalem; that would assure the future safety of Christians in the Holy Land."

Richard was surprised and impressed by this report. "I, the King Guardian?" he said. "But that is victory in itself, is it not? And Saladin? What would be his position here?"

"Joint sovereign," the prelate explained. "And sworn ally. And your relative, if that is agreed upon—by marriage, that is."

"Ah, yes," Richard said. "The Lady Joan, my cousin, married to an infidel."

"The pope's consent must be arranged first. And the holy

hermit from Engaddi, who is famed in Rome, has agreed to act as emissary to the pope."

"There have been similar alliances in Spain, didn't you say? And all Christendom would benefit from a union between myself and Saladin, would it not?"

"Don't forget the possibility that in time Saladin might be converted to Christianity. A woman's faith and beauty may do what the armies of Christendom have not been able to do. Moreover, the hermit from Engaddi has read your stars. They say that Lady Joan will marry a strong enemy of yours and thus cement peace."

"That surely is Saladin," Richard agreed.

"And they say that he will be Christian—so you see, his conversion is almost certain."

"There was a time," Richard said thoughtfully, "that had someone suggested a marriage like this to me I would have struck him dead with a blow of my ax, but now I feel differently. I've seen that Saladin is brave, just and generous. He has more love and honor in him than most of the knights of this crusade. Why should I not seek brotherhood with such a man?"

He roused himself and stood, saying, "But come, I'll make one attempt to keep this army together. If I fail, we'll make other decisions, archbishop. Let us go to the council. You complain that Richard is haughty and proud? Now you'll see him as humble as the lowly broom plant from which his name comes."

CHAPTER TWENTY

Must we then sheathe our still-victorious sword;
Turn back our forward step, which ever trode
O'er foemen's necks the onward path of glory;
Unclasp the mail, which with a solemn vow,
In God's own house, we hung upon our shoulders;
—The Crusade, a Tragedy

The council met in a vast tent outside of which carefully selected guards kept everyone at a distance, so that the debates, which were sometimes loud and heated, should not be over-heard.

The various princes of the crusade now waited inside the tent for Richard to appear with the archbishop, and even this brief delay was used by his enemies against Richard; they cited it as proof of his pride and his superior attitude. Everyone tried to bolster his bad opinion of Richard by finding some insult they had suffered from him; this was not because they really hated Richard, but rather because they recognized his greater valor and because each felt he was letting Richard down personally in abandoning the crusade that meant so much to him and which they too had sworn to pursue; and perhaps they felt an instinctive reverence for this man, so impetuous, so stormy and yet so noble.

It had been discussed and agreed by all present that when Richard appeared they would put him in his place by giving him a cool welcome.

But then he appeared; he had been ill, as they all knew, in danger of dying, and so he was pale. But his form was still so noble, his countenance so princely, that they all forgot their decision. They saw that eye which was described in song as the bright star of battle and they remembered his many heroic feats, their inspiration and their envy.

All of this rushed upon them and to a man they rose, cheering, "God save the Lionheart! Long live Richard of England!"

Richard's manner was as open, as warm, as a summer day. He thanked each of the princes and congratulated himself on his good fortune at again being among them.

"I would like to say some brief words," he announced, "on a subject that is admittedly unworthy—myself. Will you permit me?"

The princes took their seats again and a deep silence fell over them.

"We are here on behalf of the Church," Richard began, "and it is right that from time to time we confess our faults. Noble brothers, I hereby confess my chief fault—I am a soldier. My sword is ever faster than my tongue, and my tongue too used to the rough language of war."

There was a murmur and some good-natured agreement among the princes. Richard smiled as if to make light of these weaknesses of his.

"But I ask you humbly, fellow princes, would you forsake the redemption of Palestine for the sake of Richard's hasty words and poor actions? You would give up eternal salvation and earthly reward alike, because my character is stubborn and my manners unpolished? Let me say this to you—if Richard of England has wronged any of you personally, I will make amends now by word and action. Royal friend of France, have I offended you? If so, I humbly beg forgiveness."

"You have no amends to make to me," Philip said, offering Richard his hand. "Whatever decision I make regarding the crusade is due to matters concerning my kingdom, and not from any hard feelings."

Richard walked up to the archduke; there was an expectant silence throughout the chamber.

"My brother of Austria," he said, and Leopold instinctively rose from his seat, "you feel you have a right to be angry with England, and England feels angry with Austria. Very well, let us exchange forgiveness now so that the peace of this noble crusade may remain intact. We are partners in the most glorious enterprise earthly prince has ever known, under the most important banner of all; it would be foolish for us to battle over earthly banners. If Leopold has my flag, let him restore it now and Richard will willingly apologize for his hasty temper in insulting the flag of Austria."

Leopold did not answer but stood with a sullen expression, his eyes on the floor. He was embarrassed and not unaware that Richard, alleged to be no man of words, had in a brief speech put himself in the best light and Leopold in the role of scoundrel.

The earl of Champagne ended the awkward silence by pointing out that the archduke had sworn by a holy oath that he had no knowledge, direct or indirect, regarding the insult to England's banner.

"Then we have done the noble duke a great wrong," Richard said, "and do now beg his pardon. I offer my hand in peace. But what's this—Austria refuses a friendly hand as he did an angry one? We're to be neither his friend in peace nor his opponent in war? Well, very well. We'll regard his scorn as our punishment for whatever we've done against him and I'll regard the quarrel as settled anyway."

He turned from Leopold with an air of dignity that did much to impress the other princes while Leopold looked after him like a truant schoolboy who has just been excused by his schoolmaster.

"Prince Marquis of Montserrat," Richard said, his gaze sweeping the assembly, "noble Earl, Grand Master—all of you princes—I am here as if in the confessional. Bring your charges against me; Richard will make them right."

Conrad stood and said smoothly, "I don't know what charges we could bring against Richard unless it were that he wins all the fame we might have hoped for."

Richard acknowledged the compliment graciously and turned to the Grand Master of the Templars, who had risen.

"Since Richard asks the truth he must not be angry or surprised when he hears it," Giles Amaury said, "and I speak what is, I know, in the heart of everyone here. We all praise the courage and the honor of the king of England, and admire his achievements. But is it fair that Richard should at all times maintain superiority over us all? We are independent princes, yet we are made to submit, like vassals, what we would otherwise grant from courtesy. Richard snatches all, as if by right, and so degrades us in our own eyes and in the eyes of our soldiers, and takes all the luster from our command, which indeed he sometimes even exercises."

Those who observed him saw that Richard colored highly while he listened to these remarks, and some expected an outburst of that temper which was as famous as Richard's bravery. A murmur of agreement went up from the princes when the Grand Master was finished.

Richard was no fool, however, and with a strong effort he swallowed his anger and remained silent until he had mentally finished a paternoster, as the archbishop had once suggested. When he did speak it was as calmly as before.

"Is that how it seems to you?" he said. "It is true I have a natural temper and a considerable zeal for the crusade, so that I may sometimes have issued commands when I thought there was no time to hold council. But these are casual offenses, certainly unplanned, happening in the heat of battle, and I would not have thought they would embitter the hearts of my friends and allies in a holy crusade, and make them abandon the Cross when the end was in sight. For my humble offenses, turn back from the open way to Jerusalem which now lies before us? Can't the small services I have performed outweigh my foolish errors? It's true I pressed the men in an attack, but it's also true I was always the last to retreat. Yes, I put up my banner—the banner of England—over conquered fields, but this was all the reward I sought, while I left others to divide the spoils. I may have given my name to a conquered city, but I made no attempt to rule it, leaving that to others. I admit I am headstrong in urging bold actions, but grant me that I never spared my own blood or that of my men. And yes, in the heat of battle I've assumed command over some of your soldiers, but in such times I've treated them as my own, and my own money has paid for their medicines and provisions, my own doctors cared for them, my own soldiers and I defended those who were wounded, even those who retreated."

There was an embarrassed silence after this speech, for no one could deny the truth of what he said, and in the light of his remarks their complaints had begun to seem petty.

"But it is as well that everyone has forgotten these things which I remember," Richard went on. "I haven't come to beg your obligations to me, but to turn to the future. I give you a solemn oath, gentlemen, that never again will you find the pride, the anger, or the ambition of Richard to be a stumbling block in the path toward the Holy City. No, I would not survive the knowledge that my frailties had been the cause of ending this crusade. I would sooner cut off my right hand, and I'll do so now if you ask it, to prove my sincerity. If you so wish, I will relinquish even the command of my own troops and take up a lance to serve under anyone you name, as the humblest knight serves—yes, I'll even serve under Austria. Or, if it's simply that you're all tired of this crusade, then leave, but leave with me some ten or fifteen thousand of your troops and I give you my oath, when we've taken Jerusalem I'll put not my name on the gates, but the names of those who leave their troops."

Again, when Richard paused, there was a silence. His rough eloquence and fiery enthusiasm had their effect. He had the rapt attention of everyone present and the more honorable of the princes had blushed to think what petty considerations had moved them before when here was a man sincere in the vow they all had taken. Someone cheered and another voice cried, "All hail Richard."

In a moment everyone was shouting and the tent shivered with such roars as "Lead us to Jerusalem, Lionheart!" and "Long live King Richard!" and "We will follow!"

So hearty was the shouting that it was heard beyond the tent, even beyond the ring of sentinels who guarded it and like a brushfire the cries began to sweep through the camp of soldiers dispirited like their leaders and sunk in gloom. The sight of Richard restored to health had begun to change the spirit of the camp and now from all quarters could be heard cries of "Zion! Zion! To war! Death to the infidels! The will of God!"

The sound of the cheering and uproar outside only added to the enthusiasm within the pavilion, so that for some minutes a glorious pandemonium reigned. Even those who did not share the feeling felt called upon to give the impression they did. No one spoke now of retreat, but only of the proud advance upon the Holy City and the means by which this could be accomplished. In a short time the council broke up, the princes apparently all in enthusiastic accord.

But all that Richard's eloquence and zeal had been able to do was to rekindle the fires that had burned in their breasts at the outset of the crusade. And once they had returned to their own camps and begun to think with less passion, most of the princes quickly saw that nothing had really changed. They were still hopelessly outnumbered; they were still pitifully short on supplies with no apparent way of getting them; their plight was in fact as desperate as it had been before Richard so stirred them.

Enthusiasm died in some breasts; it had never existed in others. The Grand Master and Conrad of Montserrat withdrew together from the pavilion, out of spirits and displeased with the day's events.

"You're a fool," the Grand Master said when they were out of earshot. "You made a net out of spiders' webs and expected it to hold a lion. Did you think those fickle fools would stand up to Richard? All he has to do is speak, and his breath stirs their purpose like straws before a wind."

"But when the wind has passed the straws settle to earth again," Conrad said.

"And even if this discord flares up again and the armies withdraw, it'll all be wasted. I've learned from the archbishop that Richard is not opposed to this plan to marry his cousin to the sultan. He'll end up the king of Jerusalem anyway."

"Whoever would have guessed that he would agree to marry his blood to a heathen?"

"Your fine-spun methods have greatly underestimated Richard. I'll rely on them no more, but will try my own way. Are you still in with me?"

"It's a desperate method," Conrad said, "to speak of murdering a king. It would solve our problems, of course, and yet—"

"Yet," the Grand Master said scornfully. "Yet and but are fools' words. Wise men don't hesitate, nor do they retreat. They make up their minds and they carry out their decisions. Are you with me?"

"Yes," Conrad said. "How will you do it?"

"We'll find a way," was the answer. "There are men who can be hired for any job. There's a suitable assassin available, if we only find him and pay the right price."

CHAPTER TWENTY-ONE

Rugged the Breast that Beauty cannot tame.
—Sonnet in Praise of Delia

It was not quite noon when the queen and her ladies were surprised by a visit from Sir Thomas, requesting the presence of the queen's attendant, Lady Clorise, before the king.

"My lady, what am I to say?" the trembling woman asked. "He'll kill us all."

"No, don't be afraid, madam," de Multon said with a smile. "The Scottish knight's life has been spared. The king will hardly be less merciful to a lady."

"Think of some clever story," Berengaria said.

"No," Joan said. "Tell the story as it really happened, or I will tell it for you."

"With your humble permission, Your Majesty," Sir Thomas said, "the Lady Joan gives good advice. King Richard is pleased to believe what Her Majesty tells him but I doubt he would put as much faith in the Lady Clorise. I would advise telling the truth."

"They're right," Clorise agreed. "Even if I could think of a plausible story, I doubt I'd have the courage to tell it."

The lady was conducted to the king, and at his questioning gave a complete and honest account of the previous night's incidents. She absolved Lady Joan of any blame and put the blame where it belonged, on the queen's shoulders, knowing full well that Berengaria would be the most quickly forgiven by Richard.

The fact was, as she knew, Richard was a fond—even a foolishly fond—husband and now that his rage had passed he was not likely to condemn what he could forgive.

When she had been dismissed, Clorise hurried back to the queen with his message that the queen should expect a visit from him.

"I'm convinced he means to show just enough severity to make you repent," she confided, "and then he'll grant everybody a gracious pardon."

"So that's the way it lies, does it?" Berengaria replied, greatly relieved. "Well, that being the case, we'll know how to deal with it. Many a one comes for wool, as the old saying goes, and goes back clipped."

By the time Richard arrived he found his queen in her most ravishing dress, awaiting him with a confidence he hadn't expected to find. He had expected to come as a monarch, rebuke her and her ladies, receive their humble submission and then graciously make pardons. Instead he found a household in defiance.

Berengaria was well aware of her charms and knew that, when Richard was not in a temper, she had considerable influence over him. Far from listening to his scoldings, she defended her actions as a harmless joke. She denied with many a pretty gesture that it had been her intention to shame the knight; indeed, she had never intended for him to be introduced into her tent, nor kept from his post more than a minute or two. For this she put all the blame on the unfortunate dwarf, who trembled in silence behind her and dared not disagree.

Having thus acquitted herself, Berengaria then proceeded to berate her husband for his cruelty in refusing her a simple boon, the life of the poor knight.

"If you really loved me," she cried, breaking into sobs, "you would have granted my request at once, gladly, happy to relieve my heart of its burden of guilt in the matter. But no, you would sooner make me unhappy for life, drive me to a cloister. The image of that slaughtered victim would have haunted me forever, and all because of the cruelty of a man who, while pretending to love me, would sooner make me miserable than miss a chance for revenge."

This lecture was delivered with so many tears and such gestures and poses as to convey the idea that the queen's pride did not enter into it, only her hurt feelings at finding that she meant less to her husband than she had believed.

Richard was at a loss to deal with these complaints. It was impossible to argue with Berengaria in such a state, and he could hardly exercise his kingly authority over anyone so beautiful and so grief-stricken. This mighty king was thus reduced to alternately pleading with her to stop her tears and gently trying to chide her for thinking he did not love her greatly. He even pointed out that she need not fear Sir Kenneth's ghost, as he had been spared and given to the Saracen physician who would certainly keep him alive a long time.

At this the queen gave a pitiful shriek and burst into fresh tears. "There, it proves it: you would give to a Saracen—a heathen—the favor I begged from you on bended knee."

At this point Richard's patience began to wear a bit thin, as he was not accustomed to begging from anyone, and he said sharply, "Berengaria, I owed the man my life. I could not with honor refuse him his payment."

Seeing that she'd gotten all she could out of the scene without driving her husband into a mood, Berengaria stopped her tears at once and, sniffling, made to patch things up. "Beloved," she said in a still-choked voice, "you should have brought the leech to me that the queen of England might have honored him who saved not only the light of chivalry and the honor of England, but also the whole joy of poor Berengaria's life."

The result of all this was that king and queen alike agreed that the blame rested with Ectabanus and the dwarf, Berengaria by this time bored with his humor, was lightly whipped and sent off as a gift to Saladin.

Having made up with his wife, Richard still had to see his cousin. The truth was he was rather indifferent about this interview; although his cousin was also beautiful and highly thought of by the king, she was neither his mistress nor his wife, and he was less afraid of her reproaches than of those of Berengaria, despite the fact that Joan had suffered the real injury.

Joan was in her own apartments. She was one who did not like her feelings to be public and she was at the present so unhappy regarding Sir Kenneth that she had felt the need to withdraw from the other women and take such solace as she could find in solitude.

Her feelings since the singular confrontation with the gypsy girl, Elaine, had varied from heart-rending grief to the most violent anger. She thought of the knight and was glad he was in slavery. She wished it could have been worse, even the death Richard had threatened him with. She wanted to hurt him as he had hurt her, because her hatred was really love.

But when she had thought these odious thoughts and acted them out to the very point of completion in her mind, she at once regretted them and, flinging herself upon her bed, gave vent to her feelings in a fit of hopeless sobbing.

But again she would think of his lips on hers—so strong, so demanding—and she would imagine them kissing the lips of the gypsy girl, and her grief would turn to loathing. She loathed not only the Scot, but everything about her existence here in this awful place. The desert that had once charmed her with its mysterious and harsh beauty was now unbearable to contemplate. She hated the queen and despised the king. She longed to be back in England, back on her father's estate.

She thought of the home in which she had grown up. It was far removed from London and the intrigues of court life, which she hated. She had loved to mount at daybreak and ride into the woods; she thought with a passionate longing of those cool, shaded glens, the luxuriant green, the forest smells, the calls of the lark and the finch. They were unspoiled, those green forests of home, and she could ride all morning without seeing another person. She felt that if she were to meet anyone it would not be a man, but some forest creature—half man and half myth. She might hear a rustle in a thicket and turn her head quickly, half expecting to see a little faun riding on the back of a centaur— but they always vanished before she could spy them.

A woman interrupted her reverie to tell her that King Richard was outside and wished to see her. Even in her grief Joan could not keep a king waiting and, taking only a moment to compose herself somewhat, she asked that he be shown in. She rose as he came in and made him a low curtsy.

"Be seated, cousin, be seated," Richard said; he was accustomed to being familiar with her, and especially now did not care to stand on ceremony.

Joan seated herself as he commanded and sat in utter silence waiting for him to speak. Richard sat beside her a bit stiffly. He could not help noticing the coolness of his reception, and it was with a sense of embarrassment that he was at last forced to open the conversation.

"You are angry with me, cousin," he said, "and rightly so, to some extent. Appearances caused me to suspect you of conduct that in a more reasonable moment I know would be alien to you. But I am only human too, and while men abide in this dark valley of life they will confuse the shadow with the substance. Can you not forgive your somewhat headstrong cousin?"

"I can forgive my cousin," she said, "but the king is another matter."

"Oh, come now, this is too somber," he said, trying to chaff her. "By now you've heard that the knight didn't die after all, so why all this gloom?"

"Perhaps I'm mourning for the departed honor of the name Plantagenet," she replied as coolly as before.

"You are privileged, cousin," he said with a frown. "And I have treated you harshly, so you have a right to speak a bit harshly with me, but at least tell me in what way the honor has departed our name."

"A Plantagenet," she said, for the first time facing him directly, "should have given his pardon for a crime or punished it. If you had killed the knight, it would have had at least a show of justice. It ill becomes you to give a free man—a Christian and a brave knight—into slavery to an infidel."

"An absent lover is not as bad as a dead one, no matter what you may think now," Richard said, irked because he could not help but see the truth of her remarks. "You mourn your distant love but be patient; in good time there will be others wooing you."

Joan blushed deeply and said, "Enough—you have sullied my name enough—not to mention your own."

"Come, Joan," Richard said, "you aren't thinking of what you say. Your anger or your grief for your lover makes you unfair to your cousin who, notwithstanding your sullen mood, still values your high opinion."

"You have no right to call the knight my lover," she said sharply.

"Oh, well, I know you haven't bedded him—at least I feel it. But I'm not unfamiliar with the ways of love. It starts with distant adoration and mutual and silent respect—but then opportunities occur, the two become more familiar and—well, why am I wasting my breath, since you seem to know everything already."

Joan was all the more disturbed because Richard's description so closely matched the progress of the relationship between herself and Sir Kenneth.

"I gladly listen to my cousin's advice when he is not unfair," she said.

Richard, tired of this interview, said, more sharply than he intended, "A king does not advise, fair coz, he commands."

"A sultan commands," Joan corrected him. "But that is because a sultan has slaves, not subjects."

Richard sighed and rose. "Perhaps you'll learn to think more highly of sultans. Considering how highly you've thought of Scots, that shouldn't be so difficult. I wager this Saladin is a better man than any of Scotland including the Lion, William himself. It may be better for you, Joan, to live with a true Saracen than a false Scot."

"Never," she cried, leaping to her feet. "Not even if King Richard himself should embrace the false religion. You have asked me before about this alliance, and I tell you it will not be."

"Well, I'll give you the last word," Richard said, preparing to leave. "Think of me what you will, I will still consider you my near and dear relative."

He went out, leaving Joan even more agitated than she had been before, for now she not only grieved for her knight but looking ahead, feared Richard's further ambitions regarding her marriage to Saladin.

CHAPTER TWENTY-TWO

That I for poor auld Scotland's sake,
Some usefu' plan or beuk could make,
Or sing a sang at least.
  —To the Guidwife of Wauchope-House

Only the day before a free man, Kenneth found himself now a slave and banished from the ranks of crusaders. He was brought by the provost officer to the tent of his new master, Sheerkohf. He was stunned, as if he had just fallen from a great height and found himself able to drag himself from the spot, but not yet able to judge his injuries.

Left by the officer, he threw himself down upon a couch and groaned heavily, burying his face in his hands. Sheerkohf, busy giving his servants instructions for their departure, heard him and paused to kneel beside him.

"My friend," he said gently, "be of good comfort, for although your king has given you to me as a slave, I have taken you as a brother."

Kenneth tried to thank him but his heart was too full of grief and all that he made was an indistinguishable sound; after a moment Sheerkohf left him and went back to work.

They rose about three the following morning, as Sheerkohf had explained that he wished to do as much traveling as possible before daybreak.

Kenneth had declined the food offered him the night before and had scarcely slept at all, finding wakefulness preferable to the shaming dreams that had accompanied sleep.

Outside the camels were kneeling in the moonlight, all loaded but the last, who would bear the tent in which they had slept. A number of horses were saddled and waiting. They mounted. The tent they had just left was struck and loaded upon the last camel.

"Allah be our guide," Sheerkohf intoned; at once the caravan was in motion.

They were challenged by the sentinels as they traveled through the camp but Richard had sent them an escort and their progress was unhindered save for a few curses thrown at them by overzealous crusaders. At last they were beyond the camp. A small party of horsemen rode in front as a vanguard, and another small group in the rear. Others rode along at the side, where the ground permitted, to guard their flanks.

As they came over a rise Kenneth looked back upon the moonlit camp. He was banished, not only from those gently waving banners, but from honor and liberty as well.

His horse stumbled though and he had to give his attention to the animal. In his bitterness he said to Sheerkohf, "I would thank you more for my horse if she stumbled and caused me to break my neck."

"You speak foolishly," Sheerkohf said with good-natured frankness; but he did not pursue the conversation and Kenneth was glad to let it lapse.

After a time Kenneth's attention was attracted to the low whine of a dog, carried in a wicker cage. He recognized the voice of his faithful Krouba and knew that the dog had scented his presence and was begging his aid in escaping a confinement he was little used to.

"Poor Krouba," Kenneth said in a low voice, "you call for the sympathy and help of one who's more in slavery than you are." He didn't answer the dog's low pleadings in any way, thinking that to do so would only make a subsequent parting all the more difficult.

So they rode through the hours of the night and into the dim, hazy dawn. But when the first rim of the sun was visible above the distant horizon the journey of the caravan was interrupted by a call from Sheerkohf that rang across the desert.

"To prayer, to prayer," he shouted. "God is most great. God is most great. There is no God but Allah. Mohammed is the apostle of Allah. To prayer, to prayer."

In a twinkling the men had each cast themselves from their mounts and knelt facing towards Mecca while each one fervently commended himself to the care of God and the Prophet and begged forgiveness for his sins.

Even Kenneth, who had always reacted with distaste towards these acts of idolatry, was forced to respect the sincerity of their zeal and was moved by it to render his own prayers to Heaven while wondering how he had come to be praying with heathens. His prayers at least comforted him and strengthened him in his resolve to submit to whatever destiny God had chosen for him.

By evening of that day they were in land not unfamiliar to the Scot. The unfriendly waters of the Dead Sea, the mountains arising on one side and a glimmer of green from a distant oasis made him realize they were near the Diamond of the Desert, the oasis where he had first met Sheerkohf. When he had traveled this way before it had taken longer, but Sheerkohf knew the land better and they traveled more swiftly on their unarmored Arabian horses.

In a short while they reached the fountain and Sheerkohf invited him to dismount and take his rest. They only unbridled their horses. The mounted slaves would arrive soon and do the rest.

"In the meantime, let us eat and drink," the physician said, spreading some food on the grass. "And be of good cheer, my friend; fortune rises as easily as she falls."

Kenneth was not ungrateful for his friend's kindness and he tried to eat, but suddenly the memory of his last visit came over him like a dark cloud. Then he had been the ambassador of princes, an honored and honorable knight, a combatant on equal terms with this same man.

A groan escaped him and putting aside his food he threw

himself on the ground. In a moment Sheerkohf was beside him, feeling his pulse.

"You've exhausted yourself with worrying, with neither eating nor sleeping. You need rest. Here, drink this."

From his little traveling chest he produced a silver vial and mixed a few drops of its contents in a cup with some water from the fountain.

Obediently Kenneth drank the potion and, at Sheerkohf's further orders, wrapped himself in an Arab cloak and lay down in the shade of a palm.

Sleep came, but first came a period of lifting spirits, as if the burdens that oppressed his soul were dissolving, floating upward from his shoulders. He now saw all that had happened to him as if it were upon a stage, and while he could recognize the horror, the agony, the shame, they did not touch him with the same personal unhappiness.

His tranquilized thoughts turned to the future and he saw that hope yet lay before him, that the future still glittered with happy hues. There waited still freedom, success, glory—even love.

After a time these happy dreams faded, like the fading colors of sunset, and at last Kenneth slept soundly.

* * * * * * *

When he woke he found himself in such a different setting that for a moment he wondered if he were still dreaming. He lay not on the ground, wrapped in a cloak, but on a couch of considerable luxury, dressed in a gown of silk, in a silken tent. Everything about him was luxurious and expensive, suitable for a prince. A bath stood nearby, steaming with a scent. A dish of flavored snow stood on a table by the bed, and was welcome, as he had awakened with a thirst.

Having bathed and dried himself he looked for his own clothes but couldn't find them. In their place someone had provided a Saracen gown of rich cloth, complete with a saber and a dagger.

It was a costume suitable to an emir, and the Scot was at a loss to explain to himself why he should be treated so royally.

It was while he was pondering this question that Sheerkohf came into the tent. "May I visit with you?" he asked.

"The master doesn't need the slave's permission for anything," Kenneth said.

"I come not as a master but as a friend," Sheerkohf said; he had exchanged his more humble outfit for a princely costume with jeweled turban and silver ornaments. "Do those clothes seem unworthy to you? I can have them exchanged."

"Yes, exchange them, Sheerkohf; give me the clothes of a slave," Kenneth said.

"I have told you I am not your master; you are not my slave."

"Then I thank you for this undeserved kindness."

"Do not say undeserved," Sheerkohf said. "Did you not accompany me to the Nazarene camp, thus giving me your protection? Without it I might never have seen the most beautiful sight these eyes have ever enjoyed."

"What do you mean?" Kenneth asked. "What did you see that was so remarkable?"

"What was so remarkable? Why, you saw her too; it was you who rescued her from those treacherous Arabs in the desert. What tenderness in her lovely blue eyes, what gold in her hair. By the Prophet's beard, never was there a houri who could stir a man's blood like that one."

"Sir, you speak of the king's cousin," Kenneth said, blushing, "and a lady of noble birth."

"Ah, I forget you Christians like to put your women on pedestals, to be worshiped and respected rather than loved as a man loves a real woman. I warrant for all her nobility if she met a real lover she would be grateful to be treated like a woman instead of a goddess."

"Sheerkohf, you are both friend and master, but I will still demand that you treat the Lady Joan with respect."

"Respect?" Sheerkohf laughed, his white teeth in striking contrast to his dark skin. "I will respect her enough when she is the wife of Saladin."

Kenneth, who had seated himself on his couch, now sprang to his feet. "Do not insult that lady by linking her name with that of the infidel sultan!" he cried.

"Ha! Insult her?" Sheerkohf replied hotly, his hand going to his sword. The sheen of sweat on his brow made it gleam like copper and the muscles in his cheeks worked as he tried to suppress his anger. He looked like a furious tiger, his green eyes flashing.

But Kenneth had faced the lion without fear and he was not likely to be intimidated by the tiger. He said with a sigh, "Sheerkohf, if I were truly free I would repeat that charge and back it up with my sword."

Sheerkohf removed his hand from his sword, but although he regained his composure it was obvious he was still offended.

"By Allah," he said, "a man doesn't value his life very highly to speak like that to me. But your hands are tied, as you put it, and for the present I'll not untie them. You and I have tried one another's strength before this, and someday we may meet again in fair battle. But for the present we are friends, and I had come to you to ask your help rather than your insults."

"You're right; we are friends," Kenneth said, offering the other man his hand. "I spoke hotly."

"And I think I know why," Sheerkohf said; when Kenneth made an exasperated gesture, he silenced him. "No, let me say this. I think you are in love with this lady."

"I did love her," Kenneth said.

"You love her no more?"

"I am no longer worthy to love her. Please, let us not talk of this, it pains me."

"But let us continue it only a minute longer so that I can better understand—if you were restored to your former good honor, would there be any hope for this love?"

"Love needs hope to exist," Kenneth said, "even a love as distant as mine."

"Then, if you could find the thief who stole the English

banner, your reputation would be restored, would it not?"

"It would, surely."

"Then I think I can tell you how to do this, if you will follow my instructions to the letter."

"I know that you are wise and generous," Kenneth said. "Give me your instructions; so long as they don't contradict my loyalty and my Christian faith, I'll obey."

"There is a condition attached to this, though," Sheerkohf said, holding up a warning hand. "If I send you back to the Christian camp—"

"—Where my life is forfeit," Kenneth interrupted.

"Trust me to deal with that. But if I send you there, you must carry a letter from Saladin to the cousin of the English king, the lady whose name is as difficult for my Eastern tongue as her beauty is wonderful to my eyes."

Kenneth hesitated for a moment and Sheerkohf asked, "Are you afraid to undertake this mission?"

"Not if I knew the outcome were certain death," Kenneth said. "I'm only considering whether it goes against my honor to carry a letter from the sultan."

"By all that I consider holy," Sheerkohf said, "I give you my word the letter is written with all respect and honor. The sultan would no more offend her than the nightingale offend the rose bower."

"Then I'll carry it faithfully," Kenneth said. "But you understand, beyond this simple act, he cannot expect me to mediate or press his suit."

"Saladin is noble and wise. He would not spur a horse to an impossible jump. Come with me to my tent; we'll arrange these things."

CHAPTER TWENTY-THREE

Or ever the Knightly years were gone
With the old world to the grave,
I was a King in Babylon
And you were a Christian Slave.
                                    —Echoes

It was several days since Sheerkohf and Kenneth had left the Christian camp. King Richard was inside his pavilion enjoying an unusual coolness of weather, welcome after the heat they had endured in the desert since their arrival.

At the moment the king was alone, all his attendants preparing for renewed hostilities when the truce was ended.

Richard sat listening to the busy hum from the camp, music to his ears after so long a period of inactivity. There was a clatter from the forges and from the armorers. Soldiers' voices called loudly and cheerfully to one another. As he drank in these sounds Richard entertained himself with visions of their forthcoming victory.

While he was thus occupied an attendant came to tell him that a messenger had arrived from Saladin.

"Bring him in at once and with all due honor," Richard said, rising.

In a moment the attendant was back, leading a Saracen messenger and a companion. Richard's smile of welcome faded as he recognized the companion as Sir Kenneth. The Scottish knight led a noble deerhound on a leash of twisted silk and gold.

"What does this mean?" Richard demanded angrily, cutting off the messenger's words of greeting. "Is this some sort of joke? Why has this man—of all men—been brought to my tent again?"

"Mighty king," the messenger said, prostrating himself and beginning his message again, "Saladin, King of Kings, sends you greetings. We are informed by your messages that you wish war instead of peace and consider you blind in this regard, but we shall soon convince you of your error, with the help of Allah. We do thank you for your gift of the dwarf, and in return we send you this noble deerhound whom we deem fit to be your hunting companion. We have also sent his trainer, who knows better than any other how to handle this animal, and who will also act as a servant to you. We are aware that this man is not unknown to you and that your last commands were that his voice should never fall upon your ear again; therefore we have sworn him to an oath of silence and having thus met your requirements, trust you will see to his welfare as he is well regarded by us."

Having recited the message, the messenger handed Richard the scroll on which it was written and on which the signature and the seal of Saladin had been affixed.

Richard, having restrained himself to listen to this report, now turned a stern gaze upon the Scottish knight, who had remained standing while the explanation was given, his eyes cast down upon the ground.

"Was this your idea, sir knight?" the king demanded.

Kenneth shook his head and kept his eyes down.

Richard, who had expected to trick him into breaking his silence, regarded him for a long moment. He felt there was some trick to this, something more than Saladin's scroll told him. The sultan was neither foolish nor mischievous, and since he obviously knew the full story of this knight's disgrace he would certainly not have sent him here without some purpose beyond acting as a groom to a hound.

"It is a noble hound," he said aloud, admiring the animal. He remembered de Multon's description of this same beast, which had after all not been exaggerated, and he remembered that it was this beast who had come close to death in defending the English banner—an act of faith that would better have become his master.

"Well, stay then," he said, "but remember your oath, and we shall see how to use you best when we have had some time to consider it. As for you," he addressed the messenger, "return to your sultan and give him our thanks for this gift. Tell him that when we have had an opportunity to better appreciate it we will know how to better show our gratitude."

Bowing again, the messenger withdrew, leaving the king alone with the man whose life he had a few days earlier ordered ended. He observed that the knight, haughty to a fault before, had adopted a humble attitude befitting his new station in life, and the king could not but see that this must have taken great effort on the part of so proud a man, especially a Scot.

Kenneth waited now as if awaiting commands from his new master. Richard said, "You'll commence your duties soon enough. For now rest yourself and see to the needs of your hound."

Kenneth went obediently to a corner of the tent and seated himself with the dog. An attendant came in, bringing Richard a packet of letters from England, which the king began to read. From time to time he looked over at the man seated in the corner, as if by staring at him he could see what the wily sultan had in mind.

Sir Thomas returned from his mission and entered the royal tent; he had greeted his king when he discovered the Scottish knight in the corner, eyes downcast.

"What?" he said, dumbfounded. "That man here and kneeling in the corner like your serving man?"

"Do not quarrel with me on this," the king said. "He came to me with the dog, as a gift from Saladin, which now more than ever I have reasons for accepting."

"Had we replaced the banner on the mound," Sir Thomas said sarcastically, "perhaps we could entrust another one to him."

The king scowled at this reminder that his banner had not yet been returned, nor the culprit caught. "You speak angrily," he said. "And yet, if this Scot could find that thief for us, I would consider his honor well restored."

At that the knight leapt to his feet and came closer to the king, gesticulating as if there were some message he wanted to get across.

"What!" the king said, surprised. "Would you undertake to find the culprit for me?" Kenneth nodded his head quickly in agreement. "This may be the sultan's purpose in sending him here against my pleasure," Richard said excitedly.

"And it may be a trick of some sort," Sir Thomas said doubtfully. "If this man could not name the culprit when he was here in the camp, how has he learned his identity while he was gone?"

"Be quiet," Richard said. "Do not hope to stop a Plantagenet when he is seeking to restore his honor. Scot, can you write? Put your intentions on paper."

Kenneth went to the table nearby and taking pen and paper began to write quickly. When he had finished he brought the note to the king, who read it aloud:

"Were your servant placed where the holy knights must pass before him, he is convinced that if the guilty man is among them, he will be pointed out."

"By the saints!" Richard exclaimed. "This is too good to pass up. Tomorrow all the troops are going to parade, and to make up for the insult to our banner, they have promised to pass before the mound where a new banner will be placed and to salute the banner. The traitor will have to be among them or his absence would be a suspicion. Scot, you'll stand with me there and if you can detect the villain, believe me, I'll know how to reward him and you."

"My lord," Sir Thomas said, "take care what you arrange. Remember that the peace of our Holy League has only been restored after some difficulty. Upon the suspicions of a proven traitor, will you open those wounds again? Tomorrow those men have agreed to parade before our banner as a gesture of unanimity, and now you mean to use that parade to revive those old quarrels. Isn't this a breach of the promise you made to the council?"

"Silence!" Richard commanded him. "You go too far in questioning me. I never promised that I would fail to do whatever I could to find the culprit in this crime. I would have sooner renounced my kingdom. I promised, if Austria stepped forward like a man and admitted the crime, that I would forgive him."

"And what if this Scot plays tricks with you?" de Multon asked, unintimidated by the king's command.

"I'll know whether he's playing tricks or not. And you, Scot, do what you've promised, and name your own reward—but look, he's writing again."

The gist of this new note was that the king's servant had been entrusted with a letter, from Saladin to the Lady Joan, and begged the opportunity to deliver it.

"This may still be a trick," Sir Thomas said, reading the message when Richard had handed it to him.

"There are mysteries surrounding this," Richard said.

"Perhaps this land of mystery has cast some spell on me."

"As for you," he said, turning back to the mute Scot, "you will see the Lady Joan and deliver your message, but let me give you warning: do not suddenly regain your voice in her presence. If the sight of this lovely lady should loosen your tongue, beware not to speak a word, or it will be your last. So be wise and be still."

Having spoken so sternly, he laid a hand on Kenneth's shoulder and prevented him from kneeling as he would have done.

"On your honor, which I think you still have as a knight, do remain silent, for now at least."

Kenneth raised his eyes for the first time and looked directly at the king. There was a grateful look in his eyes for this reference to his honor, and he nodded his head in quick agreement, putting a hand over his heart.

A messenger was sent requesting a private audience with

Lady Joan and when she sent back her permission the king sent Kenneth in the company of an attendant.

"This is the same king who only a few days before condemned me to die," Kenneth thought as he followed the attendant through the camp. "But I can't see that he holds any real animosity towards me now. He's given me a noble chance to redeem myself."

They arrived at the queen's pavilion where the guards let them in and escorted them to a private chamber. Here the attendant left Kenneth and he was once again alone in a canvas room of the queen's pavilion.

He waited only a moment before one of Lady Joan's servants came and signaled him to follow. He was led to a separate tent and in a moment more ushered into Joan's presence; the maid withdrew.

Kenneth threw himself on one knee, his eyes cast down, arms folded, as if expecting his doom. His inmost soul was humiliated at thus showing himself before the lady he loved, and yet this was the errand he had promised to do for Sheerkohf and if it paid for his chance to redeem his honor then it was worth the effort on his part.

Twice before he had been alone with this lovely creature and each time she had been clad—or unclad—in a scandalous manner. Yet he thought she looked even lovelier now in full dress—she wore a bliaut that fit close to her slim hips and then flared out freely; it was laced at the sides and cut low at the neck to reveal her undertunic. She wore a jeweled belt, passed twice around her tiny waist and knotted in front. Her wimple and veil and the barbette that she wore tied under her chin and pinned together over her head made a frame for the oval of her face and seemed to render those features even more expressive. In her hand she held a lamp which seemed to shed an unusual brightness throughout the chamber.

She had come toward him when she stopped and her eyes grew wide. She held the lamp toward him for a moment and then set it aside.

"It is you, then?" she said in a voice that was calm, yet sad. "Sir Kenneth, the Falcon, playing the role of a humble slave."

Hearing these words from her an answer rushed to Kenneth's lips; but he suddenly remembered his promise and Richard's warning, and instead he only sighed.

"Speak without fear to Joan Plantagenet," she said, misjudging the sad sigh. "She will know how to help the knight who served and honored her in the past. What—you still won't speak? Is it shame that makes you mute, or fear? You have nothing to be ashamed of, let those who offended you be ashamed. And as for fear, I thought it was unknown to you."

Kenneth was in an agony at being thus forced to remain silent throughout this interview. He put a finger to his lips, as if that gesture might explain everything.

Far from understanding, Joan was angry at this posture which seemed to be in some way a criticism of herself.

"Are you a mute slave in fact as well as appearance?" she asked. "I didn't bargain for this. Perhaps you scorn me for the response I've given to your attentions in the past. Hold no unworthy thoughts of me for that, they were moments of high excitement and I did not know of your lady love, the gypsy girl. But—oh!"

She gave a gasp and her hand went to her mouth. "But is it possible...did they actually deprive you of your speech?"

He shook his head firmly and for a moment she looked relieved. Then, piqued again, she said, "Well, whether it's a spell or just obstinacy on your part I don't know and you apparently don't mean to explain, so I'll question you no further. Do whatever you came for. I can be mute also."

Despairing, Kenneth presented the letter to her. Although it was wrapped in silk and cloth of gold she took it carelessly, and again her eyes went to his handsome face.

"Not even a single word of explanation?" she asked in a low voice filled with sadness.

He shook his head and she turned from him in anger. "Go, then," she said, "I've said enough—too much in fact—to a man who won't waste a word on me. If it's because I've wronged you, believe me I have been punished enough, merely in knowing it was I who brought you to shame. And now in this meeting I've forgotten my station and lowered myself, in your eyes and in my own."

She put a hand over her eyes and fought back the tears that threatened to flow. Kenneth rose and would have approached her but she waved him away.

"Don't touch me!" she cried. "Your soul has adapted itself quickly to your new station in life. Anyone but a mute slave would have given me at least a word of thanks, a word to help me bear my own shame and unhappiness. Why do you stay here? Go please."

Kenneth's tortured eyes went to the letter in her hand, which until now she had forgotten. She glanced at it and in a voice of contempt said, "Oh, I forgot this. The dutiful slave waits for an answer, I suppose."

She tore it open, her eyes going to the signature. "What, a letter from the sultan?" She read it quickly and when she had finished she gave a bitter laugh.

"This is beyond belief," she said. "This is a transformation worthy of a wizard. One day you are a Christian knight, said to be the bravest in the crusade. You profess undying love for me and live only to serve me and the Cross. And the next you are a willing slave to a heathen sultan, the dust-kissing slave who bears the infidel's proposals to the very lady you swore to love—but what's the good of talking to you. Tell your master— if you get your tongue back—how I treated his proposal."

She threw the letter to the floor and, placing her dainty foot on it, trod it into the ground.

"Say to him that this is how Joan Plantagenet feels toward all unchristened pagans."

So torn was the Scot by the scorn and hatred in her eyes that, heedless of his tattered pride, he again fell to his knees before her and touched the hem of her garment.

"Did you hear me?" she cried. "Tell your sultan, your master, that I despise his proposal as much as I despise a worthless scoundrel who turns his back on both religion and chivalry—and on God and his lady too."

With that she tore her dress from his grasp and ran from the room, leaving him alone. After a moment the attendant who had brought him here appeared and signaled for him to come. Kenneth was stunned and drained by the scene he had just endured and now he staggered from the pavilion, making his way unhappily back to the tent of King Richard.

CHAPTER TWENTY-FOUR

Thyself shalt see the act;
For, as thou urgest justice, be assur'd
Thou shalt have justice, more than thou desir'st.
                                    —The Merchant of Venice

On the following morning Richard sat on horseback on the now-famous mound in the center of camp. On one side of him was Sir Thomas, on the other his natural brother William, Earl of Salisbury. On his feet beyond Sir Thomas was Kenneth, the dog Krouba at his side, while further back was the pavilion that had been built for the ladies, toward whom Richard smiled from time to time.

The armies of the various princes had gathered under the banners of their leaders and began a long procession around the mound. As each contingent came by, their leaders came a step or two up the hill and gave a courteous salute to Richard "as a sign of their regard and friendship, not of subjection."

Despite the various causes that had diminished their numbers, the file of warriors was a long one and gave an impression of a mighty host. The various knights felt freshly inspired by this demonstrable proof of their united power and sat more erect in their saddles than they had done in a long time. The trumpeters sounded their horns more shrilly and the horses, after their long and beneficial rest, trod the ground proudly.

It was an assemblage to stir the heart of any military man, and even the most doubting among the princes began to feel that perhaps Richard was not altogether wrong in his ambitions to push on. On and on the troops came, banners waving, sunlight glancing off of spear and armor, plumes dancing proudly.

Richard wore a morion on his head, topped by a crown, which left his rugged face exposed to view. With a cool but regal eye he observed the ranks as they passed before him and returned the greetings of the leaders.

Some of the men passing looked a little surprised at the sight of Sir Kenneth upon the mound, in however servile a stance, but none of them interrupted the formalities to question his presence.

When Philip of France approached at the head of his troops Richard descended the mound to meet him and the two met in the middle with brotherly greetings. The sight of Europe's two greatest monarchs greeting each other with such friendliness brought a thunderous acclaim from the crowd. Yet for all this display of warmth, Richard was suspicious of Philip and displeased that Philip was considering withdrawing from the crusade, while Philip still thought Richard should be left to fight the crusade alone.

When the knights and squires of the Templars approached, Richard cast a quick glance over his shoulder at Sir Kenneth, who stood motionless with no expression on his handsome face. As yet he had given no indication as to how he intended to uncover the culprit.

The Templars were burned to Asiatic darkness by the desert sun, but their horses and appointments were finer than any of those of Europe. The Grand Master gave Richard his blessing as a priest, rather than saluting him as the other military leaders had done.

The archduke of Austria approached accompanied as usual by court jesters and buffoons, his soldiers trailing behind. Again Richard glanced toward the Scot, who still was motionless.

"I think your boasted success is the stuff dreams are made of, my friend," Richard thought with growing scorn.

Leopold approached with the sullen look, mixed with fear, of a delinquent schoolboy, and made a reluctant obeisance.

The troops of the marquis of Montserrat were the next to pass before the King. These men too were better outfitted than those of Europe, spending greater sums of money on armor and steeds. Conrad himself rode before this small army of men, dressed so richly that he seemed to be ablaze with gold and silver. He wore a tall, milk-white plume and as he drew near the ladies in their platform noticed and remarked that it was fastened with a clasp of diamonds.

Conrad had always made it his policy to openly court Richard's favor, so that when he approached Richard came down a step or two to meet him, saying with a smile, "Lord marquis, now that I see them assembled I must confess you have more of an army than England has here."

Conrad smiled in return and was about to make reply when something extraordinary occurred. Krouba barked savagely and sprang forward. Kenneth let go the leash and the beast charged at the marquis, leaping upon his horse and throwing the marquis from his saddle to the ground. In an instant Krouba was at the throat of the fallen man, who rolled helplessly in the sand while the horse, terrified, neighed and charged through the camp, kicking up a veritable dust storm.

"Your dog has pulled down his quarry," the king said to Kenneth with a satisfied if bitter smile. "Pull him off before he kills him."

With some difficulty Kenneth got the dog away from Conrad and restrained him by tying his leash to the new banner standard on the mound. Krouba struggled against the leash, highly excited, until Kenneth was at last able to calm him with a few repeated and stern commands.

Meanwhile the followers of the marquis, seeing their leader thrown to the ground, began to cry, "Seize the Scot and his dog! Tear them to pieces!"

The voice of Richard boomed over all the others, silencing them. "Anyone who touches that hound dies a thousand deaths. He has only done his duty as God has given him wisdom, and I wish I'd thought to use it before. Conrad, Marquis of Montserrat, stand forward as a traitor. I charge you with treason."

Several of the princes had come up by this time and Conrad, struggling with anger and embarrassment, said, "What does this mean? What am I charged with? Why do you treat me like this—is this the new concord England promised us lately?"

The Grand Master of the Templars, the first of the leaders to reach Conrad's side, said, "Are the princes of the crusade to be made into rodents for Richard so that he can send his hounds after them?"

"There must be some mistake," Philip said, riding up.

"A trick of the enemy," the archbishop suggested. "String the Scot up and the dog with him."

"If you love your own lives," Richard cried, "don't lay a hand on them. Conrad, stand forth and deny if you can the charge this animal has brought against you."

"I never touched England's banner," Conrad said passionately.

"Ha! Your words betray you," Richard said. "I didn't mention the banner. Your guilty conscience supplied that charge."

"You arouse the whole camp for this," Conrad said scornfully, having regained his shattered composure. "On the word of a dog you accuse Conrad, Marquis of Montserrat, a prince and a comrade, of a crime some serf probably committed to get the gold thread."

By this time the turmoil around them had become great and Philip of France said in a low voice, "My brothers, your followers will soon be at one another's throats. In the name of Heaven let's disperse our troops and meet in the council in an hour."

"Very well, we'll bow to the wisdom of France," Richard said, "although I'd rather have this out now."

The various leaders separated at the head of their troops, bugles and trumpets sounding on all sides to call the various stragglers, and in a short time each group had returned to its quarters. But while violence had been prevented for the moment the incident had fired the passions of the knights. Those from other countries, who had just this morning hailed Richard, now were confirmed in their resentment of his pride and haughtiness while the English again felt that the honor of England was in question.

In an hour the princes assembled in the council. Conrad had changed his dirtied clothes and with them had shed his earlier confusion. Now he was dressed royally and had put on his customary suave manner. He arrived in the company of several princes who had made a show of supporting him, including the Grand Master and Leopold of Austria.

Richard entered the council dressed in the same clothes as before, as if he had just alighted from horseback. He gave a brief and scornful glance at the leaders who had gathered beside Conrad.

"Conrad of Montserrat," he said loudly, without waiting for anyone to begin the discussion, "I charge you with having stolen the English banner and at the same time wounding the faithful dog who defended it."

Conrad rose boldly and replied, "I vow myself innocent of those crimes despite the charges of man or beast, king or dog."

"Royal brother," Philip said, "this is a serious charge you bring. Your evidence seems to be that of the hound, but surely the word of a prince is worth more than the barking of a cur?"

"Noble prince," Richard replied, "we both know that the same God who gave us the hound for a companion gave him a nature incapable of deceit. He'll remember always either a friend or an enemy. He is intelligent, more so than some men, but incapable of lying. A knight may be bribed, a witness may be false, but you cannot make a dog attack his friend and you cannot disguise his enemy from him. Dress Conrad in whatever clothes you like, change his appearance in any way, hide him in an army of men, and I'll bet my royal crown the dog will know him and treat him exactly as he did today. This is not the first time an animal has given evidence against a man; even inanimate objects are used to convict men."

"True," Philip said, "but we can hardly condemn Conrad to a trial by combat with a dog."

"That was far from my mind," Richard said. "It would be beneath my honor to risk the dog's life in a fight with such a traitor. But here is my own glove. I charge Conrad with these crimes and challenge him to trial by combat. Surely a king is at least the equal of a marquis."

So saying, Richard threw his glove down in the middle of the assembly. Conrad made no move to pick it up and after a moment's pause, Philip said, "A king is too much of a match for a marquis, good brother. Richard, this combat cannot be permitted."

The earl of Salisbury stepped forward and retrieved Richard's glove. "I would not have my royal brother risk his life, which is England's valuable property," he said. "Here, brother, take back your glove and let mine lie in its place. Surely I'm a fair match for this jackal."

"Noble friends," Conrad said, addressing the entire assembly, "I'll not accept Richard's challenge. He has been a friend to me and he is our chosen leader. Perhaps his conscience can let him make such a challenge, but mine wouldn't let me accept it. But as for his bastard brother, the earl of Salisbury, I'll meet him or any other who dares to make this same charge. I'll defend my name in the lists and prove any accuser a liar."

"The marquis speaks wisely and with temperance," the archbishop said. "Having heard him swear, perhaps this quarrel could be ended if Richard would withdraw his charges."

"Never," Richard said firmly. "I've called Conrad a thief who at night stole England's banner and wounded the dog who guarded it; moreover in pretending to be a friend, he has been a traitor to my trust in him. My charges stand, and all I ask is that a day be appointed for the combat. If Conrad declines to meet me, I'll find someone to appear in my place. And as for you, brother," he said, addressing the earl, "this is my quarrel. While I appreciate your interest, let me settle it."

"Since there seems no alternative," Philip said, "I will name the fifth day from now as the day for the trial, according to knightly custom; Richard of England to be represented by his champion and Conrad of Montserrat to appear in person as defendant. But I confess, brothers, I don't know where this trial can be held without arousing the soldiers to warfare with one another. We need some neutral ground."

"Let me appeal to Saladin," Richard said. "He is a heathen, but he has been noble and shown good faith before this."

"Let it be so," Philip agreed. "But I myself will communicate with the sultan. In the meantime let us disperse and I charge you all as Christians and knights not to let this unhappy business result in brawling in the camp. It has been referred to God's judgment, and let us pray that He will give victory in accordance with the truth and His will be done."

Those who left the pavilion were of many different minds on the matter, some admitting that Richard was just in issuing the challenge, others criticizing him.

The Grand Master came up to Conrad, saying, "You'll meet this challenge?"

"Surely," the marquis said. "I'll admit I'd have been reluctant to meet Richard's iron arm, but from his bastard brother down, there's no one I'm afraid to meet in the lists."

"This dog has done more to dissolve the league of princes than any of our schemes," the Grand Master said. "Philip looks like a pleased man; no doubt this gives him the excuse he's wanted to bow out of the crusade. Henry of Champagne is smiling too, and the archduke thinks you're going to avenge his own quarrel for him."

Leopold walked up to them just then, smiling. "We were saying," Conrad remarked, "that this quarrel may loosen the bonds of our crusade."

"I wish this crusade were ended," Leopold said, "and I were safe at home—I say that in strictest confidence, you understand."

"Ironic, isn't it," the Grand Master said, "that it should be Richard to bring the crusade to an end, he who is most interested in seeing it through."

"I don't think Richard can be classified as wise," Leopold said. "And as for his warfare, it's my personal opinion that if the marquis had met him in combat, Richard might have been the loser. True, he wields a mighty ax, but he's not as good with the lance. I myself wouldn't have been afraid to meet him in combat if my oath hadn't forbidden it."

CHAPTER TWENTY-FIVE

We heard the Techir—so these Arabs call
Their shout of onset, when, with loud acclaim,
They challenge Heaven to give them victory.
                                   —The Siege of Damascus

The following morning Richard received a message from Philip of France, announcing his decision to return to France and the needs of his kingdom. Richard called upon the French king and pleaded, but in vain, and when he returned to his own pavilion he was little surprised to receive similar messages from the Austrian archduke and several other princes.

All hope of success in the crusade was now lost to Richard, and he shed bitter tears of disappointment. Nor was his mood helped by another interview with Lady Joan in which he again urged her to consider Saladin's proposal, which she again rejected.

The king's mood was so dark that Sir Thomas gave a prayer of thanks when an ambassador arrived from Saladin, who had cheerfully agreed to provide a site for the upcoming trial and a safeguard for those traveling to watch it. Richard turned his attention to the details of the lists, and for a time his spirits lifted.

Saladin had proposed an oasis called the Diamond of the Desert, roughly halfway between his camp and that of the Christians. It was negotiated that Conrad and his supporters, the Grand Master and the Austrian archduke, should appear there on the fixed day with one hundred armed men and no more. Richard of England, with his brother the earl of Salisbury, would appear with the same number, while Saladin would appear with five hundred followers, these being considered by the council as the equal of two hundred knights. The Christians must come without armor and armed only with their swords, and any who wished to come merely to watch must come completely unarmed. Saladin would make the preparations for the trial and provide accommodations for the visitors. He expressed himself eager to meet the English monarch in person and under friendly circumstances.

On the day before the combat, each of the two groups set out from the Christian camp, each group taking a different route to avoid any quarrels along the way.

In fact, Richard didn't feel like quarreling with anyone. The mere prospect of a bloody combat in the lists had greatly lifted his spirits and he rode toward it in a merry mood. Only being in the combat himself could have pleased him more, except that in his present expansive frame of mind he was half inclined to forgive Conrad if it hadn't deprived him of the sport.

Dressed richly and lightly armed, as agreed with Saladin, Richard rode alongside the queen's litter, as gay as a bridegroom. The queen's ladies who had wanted to see the combat rode pillion as before, when they had been on pilgrimage.

Joan had been of two minds regarding the journey, wishing to refuse and so forego actually meeting this sultan who sued for her hand, and at the same time eager to see the combat and eager for the diversion in their rather monotonous routine. In the end her curiosity and her youthful craving for adventure had brought her along.

Riding along not far behind the queen, Joan listened to the cheery conversation with which Richard attempted to allay Berengaria's fears. The queen was not altogether happy with this journey; she couldn't forget that they had been ambushed before and she didn't have Richard's faith in this heathen sultan. She wouldn't have been surprised had a band of Arab cavalry appeared at any moment to pounce upon her.

Her fears were not lessened when, towards the end of their journey, they spotted a single Arab on horseback atop a ridge in the distance. As soon as he had seen them, the horseman darted off out of sight.

"One of Saladin's outposts, probably," Richard said. He called to the knights to ring themselves around the ladies and in this compact formation they rode on.

Soon they could hear the noise of cymbals and horns, and while many of those present still felt some fear there was a great deal of curiosity too.

Sir Thomas, riding beside the king, said, "My lord, perhaps I should ride ahead and see what's waiting for us. From all the noise there are either more than five hundred men, or every one of them is a musician."

"No," Richard said sternly. "It would show distrust, and it's too late now to prevent such a surprise if that's what they intend, which I doubt."

In a short while they came over a hill of sand and at last came in sight of their destination, the oasis called the Diamond of the Desert.

To their surprise the oasis, until now a mere patch of trees and grass in the desert, was a vast encampment. There were large pavilions of gay colors, scarlet and blue and gold, and the tent poles were decorated with silken flags. Their ornaments glittered even at this distance.

But what most concerned Sir Thomas was the vast number of ordinary white tents, of the kind used by the Arabs; enough, he thought, to house many times the five hundred warriors Saladin was supposed to have with him.

A vast host of Arabs and Kurds were assembling before the tents, each leading his horse, while at the same time a group of musicians continued their clamor.

Suddenly a shrill cry rose over the music and as one man the host sprang to their saddles. At another yell they began to advance toward the Christians, raising a great cloud of dust that all but obliterated the encampment from view.

They came at a full gallop, dispersing themselves so that they approached Richard's small band from all sides until the Christians were surrounded and nearly choked by clouds of dust, through which they saw the wild faces of the Arabs, brandishing their lances and shouting wildly. Those in the rear shot volleys of arrows over the heads of the Christians.

An arrow hit Berengaria's litter and at once a look of fury crossed Richard's face. "Now, by Saint George, this is treachery," he said.

"Richard," Joan cried, "take care what you do. Those arrows are headless."

Richard leaned from his saddle and seized an arrow that had fallen. Joan was right and he gave a sigh of relief.

"Wench, you are sensible," he said with a smile. "Do not be alarmed, Englishmen, the arrows are headless and now I see that their spears do not have their steel points. It's their wild welcome, although I do think they'd enjoy seeing us frightened. Advance slowly and steadily."

They continued forward, accompanied by the wild Arabs with their cries, while the archers shot their arrows over them, coming as close as they could without actually hitting anyone.

When they had nearly reached the camp another shrill cry was heard; at once the Arab horsemen wheeled off and formed a long column which took up the rear behind Richard's party. And now through the clouds of dust that had been raised another party rode out to meet them; unlike the wild Arabs this group was completely armed, both offensively and defensively, and they might well have served as a bodyguard to the proudest princes of Europe. Their helmets and hauberks were made of steel rings that shone like silver; their tunics were of the brightest colors, some even of cloth of gold. Their turbans were plumed and jeweled, as were the hilts and scabbards of their swords.

This band of warriors advanced to the Christians and when they had reached them parted to right and left so that the

Christians rode between their ranks, Richard in the lead.

It was obvious that Saladin himself was approaching. In a moment, surrounded by his domestic officers and a number of black slaves, he appeared, with the manner of one born to be king. He wore a snow-white costume of turban, vest and wide trousers, the only ornament a crimson sash. At a glance he might have looked plainly dressed but a closer look revealed the diamond, known by the poets as the Sea of Light, in his turban. On his finger he wore another diamond worth nearly as much as the crown jewels of England, and the sapphire that gleamed in the hilt of his dagger was worth not much less. In addition he wore a sort of veil attached to his turban and partially concealing his features, and he rode a milk-white Arabian stallion which pranced so proudly that it was clear he knew he carried a king.

The two renowned rulers needed no introduction. They halted and dismounted and while everyone watched in silence they embraced as brothers.

"The English lion is welcome," Saladin said. "I hope he is not alarmed by these men. Except for my slaves, they are the privileged nobles, the chiefs of my tribes. Each could claim right to be present today, and none would miss the opportunity to see Richard, whose name is used to frighten children and horses into obedience."

"All of these are nobles?" Richard said, looking about with surprise at the wild men who had greeted them.

"Even the humblest," Saladin said. "But though they are more than I offered to send, they come under the treaty, unarmed except for their swords."

"Noble sultan, I've brought some champions too," Richard said, indicating the ladies. "But I'm afraid they are armed— pretty faces are weapons, I think you'll agree."

Saladin turned toward the ladies and made a low obeisance. To Richard he said, "Your last letter dashed my fondest hopes regarding one of those fair warriors. But come, let me escort you to the pavilion your servant has prepared for you. My chief slave will see to the princesses. The officers of my household will look after your men and I myself will be royal Richard's servant."

Saladin led them into the camp, to the chief pavilion there, a splendid dwelling that had been prepared for Richard and furnished with every luxury. De Multon, who was in personal attendance on Richard, helped him to remove his cape and Richard stood before his host in close dress.

"But how is it, brother," Richard said, "you've had time now to see my face at close range but yours is still hidden from me?"

"You're right," Saladin said and with a gesture he removed the veil, smiling as he did so.

Richard gave a gasp of surprise; the man standing before him was none other than Sheerkohf, the physician who had cured him of his fever.

"You?" he said. "The leech?"

"Even so," Saladin said.

"And it was you who helped the Scottish knight and saved him from death, and then sent him back to me."

"I wanted to heal his illness too, but I knew that his honor had been sorely wounded and unless the bleeding was stopped his life would not last long."

"And I'll wager he's the champion you've picked to represent me tomorrow," Richard said.

"He is, and full of high hopes," Saladin said. "I've furnished weapons and horse, but it's his courage and skill that will tell."

"And he knows who you are?"

"Yes, I had to confess in order to send him to you," Saladin said, not a little pleased at the success of his disguise.

"And he hasn't yet confessed where his love lies?"

"I know where it lies—in the same quarter as my own desires," Saladin said. "But his affections were placed there before mine and are likely to survive them. If this kinswoman of yours loves him better than me, who is to blame her for choosing such a knight?"

"But his rank is too low to mix with the blood of Plantagenets," Richard said.

"In the East we rate a brave camel driver more fit to kiss a queen than a bad prince. But with your leave, royal friend, I must go from you and welcome the Austrian archduke and the marquis of Montserrat, who are approaching."

With that the sultan left to greet his new guests. In a short time the slaves had served a royal banquet to each of the visiting princes, each in his own pavilion, and no effort had been spared to make the meal a memorable one. Even wine, forbidden to the Saracens, was served in great quantities.

Richard had barely finished when a messenger came in to say that the knight who was to do battle the following day requested permission to pay duty to the godfather of the quarrel.

"Tell him," Richard said, "that I will see him when he atones for his fault on the mound of England by his victory at the Diamond of the Desert."

About an hour later Richard wrapped a cloak around himself and walked through the encampment in the direction of the queen's pavilion. When he arrived there he found the tent guarded by a number of slaves, who lowered their pikes and cast their eyes down as the king approached.

When Richard had greeted his wife, whose anxieties had all been put to rest by the opulence of their host's hospitality, he asked to speak to Joan aside, where he informed her who the knight was who would be fighting in his behalf.

"What's more," he added, "I've decided if he wins to give him full forgiveness and restore him to full knighthood. I tell you all this in the hope that you and I will be enemies no more and I may be readmitted to your good graces, as he is to mine."

"My lord," Joan said in a happier voice than she had used for some days, "no one can remain unhappy with King Richard when he shows himself as he truly is, noble and generous." She gave him her hand and he kissed it.

"Your knight has not yet won his battle," Richard cautioned her. "Conrad is considered an excellent fighter. What if he should win tomorrow and the Scot lose?"

"Impossible," Joan said. "I saw Conrad tremble and blush

when you accused him. No, this trial is an appeal to God's justice and Conrad must lose. I myself would not be afraid to meet him in such a cause."

"By God, wench, I think you would too," Richard said, chuckling. "And probably beat him. There was never a truer Plantagenet than you, Joan."

They exchanged affectionate smiles, for they were very fond of one another. Then Richard grew more serious and said, "Only remember your station, and his. Let's speak frankly, Joan, as friend to friend. What if this knight does win tomorrow? What will he be to you?"

"To me?" Joan blushed at this question but spoke as firmly as before. "He will be an honored knight, of course, one whom Queen Berengaria herself might grace with a smile, a word of congratulation. The lowest knight may devote himself to the service of a queen, but his reward is in winning in her name, no more."

Richard sighed and said, "Maidens always talk like that. But when a lover presses his suit, well...we shall see."

He took her hand and they rejoined the others, where a minstrel was entertaining the queen and her ladies.

CHAPTER TWENTY-SIX

Heard ye the din of battle bray,
Lance to lance, and horse to horse?
                                        —Gray

Because of the desert heat, it had been decided to hold the combat one hour after sunrise. Kenneth himself had supervised the construction of the lists, which enclosed a space of hard-packed sand one hundred and twenty yards long by forty wide, ranging north to south so that neither combatant would have the advantage of the rising sun.

Saladin's royal gallery was built on the west side, while directly opposite was a gallery for the queen and her ladies, constructed so that they could see without being seen. The sponsors of the match were to remain on horseback, to avoid quarrels over rank. At one end of the lists were the followers of Richard and at the other end those of Conrad, while the rest of the enclosure was filled with spectators.

By the time appointed for the trial, an even larger number of Saracens than the day before had appeared around the lists and Sir Thomas pointed out that today their lances were no longer pointless.

"Oh, I trust the sultan," Richard said impatiently. "But if you're afraid you have my permission to flee now."

When the timbrels sounded to announce the approach of the queen and her ladies, all of the Saracens prostrated themselves as they had for morning prayer, in order to permit the ladies to reach their gallery unseen. They were escorted by fifty guards from Saladin's seraglio with naked sabers and orders to cut to pieces any Saracen—prince or slave—who ventured to gaze upon the ladies. Berengaria, who enjoyed being seen quite as much as seeing, was not overly fond of this Oriental super- stition, as she termed it, but when they were secured in their gallery she found she must be content with things as they were.

It was the duty of the sponsors of the two champions to see that the men were properly armed and ready for combat. The archduke, who had spent the greater part of the night enjoying Saladin's hospitality, overslept, so that the Grand Master, abste- mious as always, approached Conrad's tent alone in the morning. He would have entered straightaway had not the attendants, to his surprise, refused him.

"Why, what is the meaning of this, knaves?" he demanded angrily. "You surely know me."

"Indeed we do, most reverend Grand Master," the squire replied. "But the marquis is about to make his confession and even you may not intrude."

"Confession," Giles Amaury exclaimed with some alarm, "to whom is he confessing? Fool, get out of my way."

Pushing the servant aside, he entered the tent. He found the marquis kneeling before a priest in the act of making his confes- sion.

"What does this mean, Marquis?" he demanded hotly. "Get up, for Heaven's sake. Or, if you've something more to confess than you've already confessed to me, then here I am."

"I've confessed too much to you," Conrad said. "Begone, friend, and let me open my conscience to this holy man."

"Is he holier than I?" the Grand Master asked. "Priest, begone! The marquis will confess to me this morning or to no one, because I'm not leaving his side."

With an anxious look at the marquis, who nodded mutely, the priest left.

"Now," the Grand Master said, "if we must go through with this...I know the frailties of your heart already, so we can omit the details and go straight to the absolution. It hardly matters how many spots of dirt we wash from your hands."

"It's blasphemous for a man like you to speak of pardoning another's sins."

"Nonsense, the absolution of a wicked priest is as good as that of a saint; you know that. Shall we get on with it?"

"No, better to die without confession than to make a mockery of the act," Conrad said.

"Come, come, my noble friend, screw up your courage; don't speak of dying. An hour from now you'll be standing victorious."

"Or confessing in my bloody helmet."

"As good a confession as any," Giles said with a shrug.

"The omens are all bad," Conrad said. "To be discovered by a dog...the reappearance of this Scot, who should be dead...no good can come of this."

"Bah, I've seen you tilt lance against better men. Think of yourself as in a tournament. Come, out there, you squires, your master must be armed."

The servants entered and began to arm their master; Conrad suffered their efforts in gloomy contemplation and in time even the Grand Master began to feel dispirited.

"This coward," he thought, "will let his faintness—which he no doubt calls conscience—lose the day for him. It would be better for me if the Scot strikes him dead on the spot. If he's wounded and seeks to confess...our sins are too joined together; he might be confessing mine along with his."

At last the hour arrived, the trumpets were sounded, and the champions rode into the lists in full armor; their visors were open and both men made a handsome appearance, although it was noted by some that the Scot wore an air of manly confidence while Conrad seemed ominously despondent.

An altar had been erected at one side, and several priests, including the archbishop, waited there. Each knight was brought in turn, escorted by his sponsors. There he dismounted and, kneeling, swore to the justice of his cause and prayed that success would be given according to the truth of what he swore. He swore also that he came to fight in knightly armor and used no spells or charms to aid him.

Kenneth made his vows in a firm and manly voice, his manner cheerful and confident. When he was finished he glanced briefly toward the gallery and nodded his head, and all the women there knew to whom he was dedicating his victory. Then, despite the weight of the armor he wore, he sprang to his saddle and rode, in a succession of caracoles, to his place at the eastern end of the lists.

Conrad looked bold enough as he presented himself at the altar but his voice grew faint as he swore and his lips trembled. As he prepared to mount his horse, Giles Amaury approached him and, making a pretense of adjusting his bridle, whispered, "Fool, control yourself and fight well, because I swear to you if you escape him you won't escape me."

This whispered warning only intensified Conrad's confusion so that he stumbled as he attempted to mount and though he quickly recovered himself the incident was duly noted by those who watched for omens.

The priests issued a solemn prayer that the one who was in the right would win with the aid of God; then they departed from the lists. Richard's trumpeters rang a flourish and a herald proclaimed, "Here stands Sir Kenneth of Scotland, a good knight and champion in the cause of the royal King Richard of England, who accuses Conrad, Marquis of Montserrat, of treason and dishonor to the flag and the King of England."

When Kenneth's name was announced the followers of Richard, many of whom had not known the identity of the champion until now, gave forth a loud cheer that nearly drowned out Conrad's reply in which he asserted his innocence and offered to do battle in proof of it.

The esquires approached and delivered shield and lance to each man, helping him hang the shield around his neck so that his hands were free to manage the horse and direct the lance. Their visors were closed.

Kenneth's shield displayed the falcon, while Conrad's bore an emblem of a rocky mountain, representing Montserrat. Each man tested the weight of his lance before laying it to rest.

Everyone else now retired to the barriers and the two knights faced each other with lances ready, their forms so completely enclosed that they looked like statues.

There was a suspenseful silence—not a sound to be heard but the snorting and pawing of the horses, who seemed impatient to charge. Men held their breath. All eyes were glued on the knights.

This lasted perhaps a minute; then Saladin gave the signal. A hundred instruments created a clamor that rose violently on the air. Each of the knights spurred his horse and slacked the reins. The two horses broke into full gallop, racing down the lists toward one another.

The combatants met in the middle with a crash like the breaking of a thunderbolt. For a split second the end was in question—then no more.

Conrad had proven himself an experienced jouster. He had struck Kenneth squarely in the middle of his shield, so true and so powerfully that his lance had shattered into splinters from its tip up to the very gauntlet. Kenneth's horse stumbled two or three yards and half fell to his haunches before Kenneth brought him back to his feet.

For the marquis of Montserrat there was no such recovery. The Scot's lance had gone through his shield, through linked mail and undertunics and hauberk, and deep into his chest. He fell from the saddle to the ground.

Kenneth drew his sword before he realized that his opponent was helpless and the fight over. The sponsors, the heralds, even Saladin, crowded around the wounded man.

"Conrad of Montserrat, do you now avow your guilt?" Kenneth demanded, approaching on foot.

Conrad's visor had been opened and he gazed wildly up at the sky. "Why do you ask?" he said hoarsely. "God has decided. I am guilty, but there are others at hand more guilty than I. Let me have a confessor, for my soul's sake."

He fainted as he made this last request.

Saladin said, "The traitor should be dragged by his heels through the lists."

"Perhaps, but I pray you, use your healing arts on him," Richard said, "at least to give him time enough for a confession. Don't kill the soul with the body. A half hour of time may allow him to enter Paradise."

"Your wish will be obeyed," Saladin said. "My slaves will carry him to my tent."

The Grand Master, who had stood by in silent gloom, stepped forward and blocked the approach of the slaves. "No," he said, "the Austrian archduke and I are this man's sponsors and we will not permit a Christian prince to be delivered to the Saracens for poisoning. He will be assigned to our care."

"In other words you refuse to let his life be saved," Richard said.

"Not at all," the Grand Master replied. "If the sultan uses lawful medicines, he can attend the patient in my own tent."

"Do so, please," Richard said to the sultan. "Never mind this lack of graciousness; consider it a request of a royal brother. And now, there are more glorious matters to be attended. Sound the trumpets, you heralds, shout, you knights, shout the glory of England's champion."

At once a great uproar arose, drums, clarions, trumpets, and cymbals making a brazen clamor and the Englishmen present raising a great cry. The Arabs too joined in the shouting, for Richard was an object of great admiration and respect to them.

When a relative silence had fallen Richard addressed the Scottish knight. "Sir Kenneth," he said, "you have redeemed yourself. Come with me to the pavilion of the ladies, who know how to reward such deeds of chivalry. And you, noble sultan, will accompany us."

"I must prepare my medicines," Saladin said, bowing graciously, "if I am to attend the wounded man."

"Well, then, you'll give us an opportunity, before we leave, to repay your hospitality," Richard said.

"If you will humble yourself to sit in the black tent of a chief of Kurdistan, we will have a feast together at noon," Saladin said.

The invitation was accepted and further given to such noble princes as might attend such a royal feast. Saladin meanwhile went to his own tent to prepare what he needed to help the wounded marquis.

"Come, Sir Scot," Richard said. "To the pavilion! Let me lead you in triumph."

* * * * * * *

In the Grand Master's tent, where he had been carried, Conrad lay in a fitful stupor. Gradually he returned to consciousness and became dimly aware of his surroundings. He was just recalling how he had come to be here, in such pain, when he heard a sound and looked in that direction. The Grand Master entered and carefully secured the covering of the tent.

Conrad started; in a tone of alarm he cried, "Why have you come to disturb me?"

"I've come to hear your confession," the Templar said, "and to absolve you."

"My friend," Conrad said, his voice weakening, "I beg you, do not break a wounded reed."

"Your sins are too close to my own, Conrad," the Grand Master said. With one swift blow he thrust his dagger into the heart of his former ally. Conrad made a little gurgling sound in his throat, and died.

Giles Amaury removed the dagger and carefully wiped it clean before replacing it in its sheath. Then, with a last contemptuous look at the dead man, he left the tent.

Saladin, attended by warriors and slaves, was just approaching.

"It's too late for your art," the Grand Master said, looking sorrowful. "He has died of his wounds."

CHAPTER TWENTY-SEVEN

It is the end that crowns us, not the fight.
—The End

As the hour of noon approached, Saladin awaited his guests in a tent that was not much different from the shelter of the common Arab, except for its size; but inside he had prepared a banquet after the lavish manner of the East, heaped on tables set upon rich carpets; the guests sat or reclined if they wished on silken cushions.

Here the sultan received the various princes who had come to dine with him, bowing to each one as they entered. Richard arrived last, accompanied by his ladies and Sir Kenneth. The champion knight was saluted by all present and Saladin proposed a toast to him. A huge goblet of sherbet was handed from man to man.

When Archduke Leopold had drunk from it greedily, as his carousing of the night before had left him with a frightful thirst, he handed it next to the Grand Master, who likewise raised it to his lips; but before Giles Amaury's lips could touch the goblet Saladin had put a hand on his arm to prevent his drinking.

"If you drink that," the Saracen said, "I will be bound to honor you by the rules of hospitality, and I would not be bound to such a traitor as you."

There was a confused murmur of voices and the Grand Master rose angrily to his feet. Richard too rose at once and for a change he was the one who urged peace.

"These are serious charges, noble friend," he said. "I made similar ones myself and we've seen the outcome of it today. But on what do you base your remarks? Believe me, if they are true, I myself am willing to be your champion, as this knight was mine."

"I will give you evidence enough," Saladin said, "that this man and his friend, the marquis of Montserrat, plotted against you and against your holy crusade. I can show you the letters each of them wrote me, plotting to betray you and your allies. They have negotiated secretly with the Turks as well, and they plotted at your death, Richard; to that end they arranged to have us attacked today by Maronites, as the terms of our meeting limited each of us to a few warriors and they thought we would be vulnerable. That is why I have more men here than agreed, and why they are fully armed. And there is more—this very day he has murdered the man who was his accomplice in these schemes."

"What, Conrad murdered!" Richard said. "We thought he died of his wounds."

"He died of one wound, inflicted by a dagger," Saladin said. "Examine his body yourself if you wish, as I did when this snake had left his tent."

"Traitor!" Richard said, turning upon the Templar. "Infamous villain! Prepare for combat, I myself will teach you how God and Richard deal with such wickedness."

Having offered his challenge Richard turned his back and would have strode from the tent; but the Grand Master, seeing his schemes brought to an end, drew the dagger with which only a short time before he had murdered his friend, and tried to bury it in Richard's back.

His dagger was not half so fast though as the sultan's scimitar. The latter could hardly be seen moving, it was so swift, and in an instant the head of the Grand Master had fallen to the floor while the body remained standing for a second or two as if it had not yet accepted the reality of what had happened. Then it too fell, blood staining the ground.

"Noble friend, you've again saved my life," Richard said, staring in awe at the weapon and the arm that had moved with such incredible swiftness. "Name your reward and you shall have it."

"The friendship of Richard of England is all the reward I wish," Saladin said, "and I think I already have that. But let my slaves remove this villain, that we may resume our interrupted banquet."

The body was removed and all the stains swiftly obliterated; in a few moments the entire company was able to sit down to their feast, albeit with somewhat dulled appetites.

Richard's spirits, however, were far from dampened, for there was nothing he liked better than a bit of excitement, and this day so far had left him in a glorious mood.

"Princes," he said, addressing the company, "it is foolish to break up such a gathering as this without making some plans for the future. Saladin, what do you say to the two of us, before this fair company, settling once and for all the question of who shall rule Palestine. The lists are ready outside and I'll gladly lay down my gauntlet on behalf of Christianity, to meet in the lists such a champion as yourself. Are you willing to do mortal battle for Jerusalem?"

A deep silence fell upon the company, all eyes turning toward the sultan. For a moment he sat in thoughtful silence and it was easy to see that this suggestion tempted him.

"It is true," he said finally, "that if I were to fall in death to your sword, I couldn't ask for a better means to pass to Paradise. But Allah has already given the true followers Jerusalem, which I hold securely. It would be an offense to Him to gamble it away for my own vanity."

Richard sighed and turned to Kenneth. "You have had all the fortune, it seems. Is it true, Saladin, that you honored this knight with combat?"

"We met in the desert," Saladin admitted, "and had a go at one another for half an hour, as warriors are likely to do. But while the issue was not decisive, I would say that the Scot can take the most pride in the event."

"No, no," Kenneth said, laughing, "I recall it otherwise."

"I'd have given the rest of my life for such a half hour," Richard said. "But you may as well know, Sultan, that it was no ordinary knight you fought with."

"Not ordinary, certainly," Saladin agreed.

"Nor ordinarily born," Richard said. "Enough of your games, knight; kneel before me, by my good sword. Sultan, princes, my queen, and ladies, this man has knelt before you as an unknown knight and as a slave, and today as a champion. But he rises a man distinguished by birth and fortune. David, Earl of Huntingdon, Prince Royal of Scotland, arise and take your rightful place among these princes."

There was a general outburst of surprise and Joan, who had been holding a goblet, dropped it with a clatter.

"Yes, my friends," Richard said, beaming upon the embarrassed knight and the astonished assemblage, "it is the truth. You all know that Scotland originally planned to send a contingent of knights on this crusade, but for reasons best known to Scotland the troops were not sent. This youth thought it unjust that his arm should be held back from this holy cause and against his father's orders he joined us at Sicily with a handful of personal followers, where his ranks were increased by the various other Scots who joined us and who did not know the true rank of their leader. Those few who did know died except for one old servant who was recently set free and whom I tracked down and questioned. Otherwise this secret might have died with him. Prince, why did you not inform me of your noble rank?"

"My pride would not have let me mention my title only to save my life," Kenneth said, "and I had taken a vow to keep my rank secret until this crusade was successfully carried out. I only mentioned it under the seal of confession, to the hermit."

"And that was why he was so anxious to have me stay the sentence," Richard said.

"But how did you guess the secret?" Berengaria cried.

"A letter came from England and I learned that the King of

Scotland had seized three of our nobles; he claimed that his heir was in our camp, in our power, and that he was holding these three men as hostages for his safe return. That gave me the first suspicion and when Sir Thomas had tracked down this knight's old servant he learned the truth from him. I should add that de Multon did this on his own initiative."

"Only because my heart is softer than a Plantagenet's," Sir Thomas said.

"What, your heart soft, you old scoundrel!" Richard exclaimed. "Why, it is we Plantagenets who have soft hearts and deep feelings, isn't that true, Joan?"

He turned to his cousin, who blushed furiously.

"Give me your hand, cousin," Richard said, "and you, prince of Scotland, give me yours."

"But my lord," Joan said, "I thought that my hand was promised to the sultan as a means of converting him to Christianity."

"That's the hermit's fault too," Richard said. "With his star gazing, he saw that you were going to be married to an important enemy of mine, and he saw that your husband would be Christian, which he is."

"Do not think, noble friend," Saladin said to the Scottish prince, "that the prince of Scotland is more welcome to Saladin than Kenneth, the Scottish knight."

For a moment Prince David of Scotland was mute in the presence of Lady Joan, as he had been in the past with her. But then he had been an obscure and nameless adventurer and now he no longer was. In the time that followed, he found the words he needed to express his love for the English princess, and she for him.

* * * * * * *

Outside among the tents in which the English visitors had made themselves at home, Elaine stood in the shade, weeping.

Having heard that her lover had been sent to the desert, she had persuaded a fat, jolly cook in the king's kitchen to bring her along as his daughter on this journey to the Diamond of the Desert. Once here, it had been an easy enough matter to lose herself in the crowds. She had searched and searched yesterday for Kenneth, and had finally slept hidden behind an Arab tent.

She had had no real interest in the trial by combat, but as that was where everyone else was, she had gone to watch too, and to watch for the Scottish knight.

Imagine her excitement at discovering that the English champion was none other than her own Scot; and when he won...for a moment it had seemed things couldn't be better.

But of course, his victory hadn't brought him back to her arms, as she had foolishly hoped for a few minutes; it had only sent him to the arms of that high and mighty English lady.

Even then, she had hoped...he was still only a lowly knight, and she was a princess, so they said...too far above him for anything to happen.

But now...one of the princes had left the banquet; he had told his servant, who quickly told his friends, and the whole camp was buzzing with this new bit of gossip: The Scottish knight wasn't just a knight after all; he was a royal prince of Scotland, and he was going to marry the English princess, and everyone thought it was just like a fairy tale.

"Isn't it romantic," the plump maiden who had told her sighed. She looked quite astonished when Elaine burst into tears and fled.

Now what was she to do? She was in the desert, miles from anywhere. She hadn't gotten her knight back, and she certainly couldn't return to camp with the cook she'd run away from. The mere thought of her plight brought a fresh torrent of tears.

"What, tears, on a festive day like this?" a baritone voice said.

She hadn't heard anyone walk up and she turned about startled, to see a knight standing nearby. He was tall and sturdily built, with a thick reddish beard and merry eyes.

"And what could such a pretty maiden have to cry about anyway?" he added, smiling at her.

It had been so long since anyone had really talked nicely to her and despite her tears she couldn't help smiling a little.

"Ah, that's better," he said, nodding his approval. But his eyes twinkled merrily as he said, "But if my words are enough to stop your tears, I wonder what my kiss would do?"

She sniffed and stopped crying altogether. What nice eyes he had, and so friendly. There was something about him that reminded her of her first lover in a way, probably it was that red beard, just like his.

"You think I kiss every knight that comes along the path?" she asked him with a saucy expression.

Far from taking offense, he only laughed and came closer, and she couldn't help smiling again as he took her into his arms and brought his mouth down to hers.

My, but he was handsome, though.

ABOUT THE AUTHOR

VICTOR J. BANIS is the critically acclaimed author ("...a master storyteller"—*Publishers Weekly*) of more than 200 published novels and numerous shorter works in a career spanning nearly a half century. A longtime Californian, he lives and writes now in West Virginia's beautiful Blue Ridge region.

www.ingramcontent.com/pod-product-compliance
Lightning Source LLC
Chambersburg PA
CBHW050415260626
47156CB00003B/1020